NIGHT SHIFT

SHADOW BOUND CHRONICLES
BOOK 2

A.L. SCARBOROUGH

For my Family

This book is a work of fiction. All of the characters, organizations, and events portrayed in this novel are either products of the author's imagination or are used fictitiously. Sometimes both.

Copyright © 2024 by Alicia Scarborough

Cover by Alicia Scarborough

Cover copyright © Alicia Scarborough

A.L. Scarborough supports the right to free expression and the value of copyright. The purpose of copyright is to encourage writers and artists to produce creative works that enrich our culture.

The distribution of this book without permission is theft of the author's intellectual property. If you would like permission to use material from the book (other than for review purposes), please contact alicia@aliciascarborough.com. Thank you for your support of the author's rights.

Version 1.00, July 2024

eBook ISBN: 978-1-963727-04-3

Print ISBN: 978-1-963727-05-0

CHAPTER ONE

DUSK

OUR 1978 VOLKSWAGEN Super Beetle veered around the corner as the sun sunk down below the horizon. Both feet slamming on the brake and clutch, the car came to a screeching halt right before the wall of the living dead.

Mary and I both exclaimed in long drawn-out vowels, "Oh, hell, no."

The zombies closest to us turned their ugly mugs our way and lifted their forearms in classic undead fashion and groaned. "Brains."

"Blondie, move over. I've got the wheel, you start shooting," Mary said while she pushed me out of the driver's seat. Well, honestly, she and I scrambled over each other as zombies surrounded the vehicle and rocked us. I plunked my keister in the passenger bucket seat of the slug bug and snatched my cursed camera, which I bought from a local pawnshop, off the floor.

Mary revved the engine of the slug bug and rammed her into gear. The bug screamed and jerked forward, but did not stall. The wall of zombies hindered progress, so Mary backed up the car and tried again. Meanwhile, I caressed the case of my camera and asked, "Hey, Seth. You there?"

Seth was the djinn I had bound to my camera six weeks ago after the calvary from Wings of Virtue showed up and saved my butt from becoming a zombie due to a deal gone south. I could hold conversations with him while he inhabited the camera, as long as I held the camera, or my skin was in contact with parts of the camera.

"Yes, Sarah. I'm always here. When would I not be? Not like you let me out long enough for me to go anywhere."

"Geez, you were just out, and watching shows, I might add. When was the last time you took a nap, mister grumpy pants?"

"I'm a demon. I have no need of sleep or other stupid, time-wasting crap you humans require to live."

"Sure, sure." I absently waved his snark off. "Say, do you think you can help us out with these zombies?"

"No."

Mary piped in as she slammed the car forward, making a dent in the undead foes who blocked our paths. "He gonna help?"

I shook my head and frowned. "He doesn't feel like it."

In frustration, Mary reversed, went back into first, followed by second and third gear in a split second. Guts splattered onto the windshield as she cursed. "Dammit Seth. We could use a miracle about right now."

"Tell Mary I could care less."

Ugh. I hated being the go-between in these conversations. Like playing telephone all the dang time.

"He said he couldn't care less."

Hordes of zombie bodies moved out of the way while the slug bug picked up speed. Also, it didn't hurt, the car had a plow attached in the front to help in these types of situations. Mary shifted gears again and spun a donut in greasy smears of zombie goo on the asphalt.

She whipped her head at the camera and said, "I will change the Netflix password if you do not help us, Seth."

"Ooooh, I'm shaking in my boots. Still don't care. You interrupted my shows for this escapade."

I shook the camera. "Dammit, you little shit. Get out here and help."

"Nope. Think I'll go take a nap now."

"But you said you don't need sleep." My fingers tightened around the body of the camera. "Were you lying?"

"Even if I don't need sleep doesn't mean I won't do such activities anyways. Besides, a nap sounds far more important than granting wishes or doing the equivalent of janitorial magic clean up. I hope you will have resolved the issue by the time I wake up. Good luck."

My connection to Seth promptly went blank, like he hung up the phone or cut the cord. This wasn't the only time he had pulled this stunt and, quite frankly, it was annoying. I reached out and popped open the glove box, snatching one of several film canisters.

Mary's lips grimaced. "The little twerp ain't helping, is he?"

"Correct," I said and opened the back of the camera to insert the thirty-five millimeter film. This camera was not like others, nor was the archaic device even digital. A digital camera would have been far better than this monstrosity, mainly because people didn't sell thirty-five-millimeter film anymore. So finding the ammo this camera needed was getting difficult.

Mary continued to bash and run over the undead minions of the supernatural boss, Avarice. She had escaped the last encounter back in the cavern while I was being zombified, and we hadn't seen her since until today.

I nodded at Mary, who returned the nod while I unbuckled my belt, slid the moonroof of the slug bug back, and stood up in my passenger seat, camera in hand. Seth or no Seth, I was going to take these bastards down. Though if Seth were to help, all I needed to do was wish these expired squishy bags of meat away like nothing happened.

However, Seth was being rather persnickety today because we interrupted his binge watching for *Real Housewives* and was in no mood to help. And if Mary changed the password on the Netflix account, he would more than likely get even more moody because he couldn't watch his shows. Never thought a djinn would enjoy reality shows full of drama and staged acting.

The zombies noticed I had moved beyond the steel shield and revealed my upper half above the moonroof. I had to brace my feet on the seat while Mary took wicked turns to smear more undead guts onto the pavement. I took pictures of the zombies in front and watched their decayed forms crumple to the ground.

Mary called out, "Yea-haw. Now this is what I'm talking about. Hold on, Blondie."

I braced myself as Mary did another three sixty turn in the slug bug and ran over more bodies of the expired kind. I continued to snap pics left and right, reloading after every twenty-fourth shot, while the camera grew hot in my hands.

The camera was getting to the point I would not be able to hold on anymore until it cooled off. So, I sat back down and closed the moonroof. The horde of zombies did not appear to be thinning at all. We really needed Seth right about now.

The walkie-talkie on the dash crackled to life with Ivan's Russian accented voice.

"Mary. Sarah. Where are you?"

I snatched the comm and answered back, "We're in the midst of undead soup. You?"

"Crew and I are stranded in library. We have kids here and zombies are about to break down the door. Are you close?"

One look at Mary told me we were nowhere near the library. I replied, "We're not, but I'm sure Mary can cut a path to you."

"Seth not helping?"

"No," I replied. "He's pissed we interrupted his binge watching."

Ivan chuckled. His black and silver peppered beard with an endearing smile came to mind. I wish I knew what he knew about our djinn, but he told me I needed to figure things out on my own. Good thing Ivan forgave me for stealing his beloved truck, Betsy, back when we first met. I thought he'd hold a grudge, but he was a man of God and forgiving, unless withholding information about djinns was his form of payback, could it? Naw. Though, if you asked me, my form of discovering things as we went was kind of dangerous, because sooner or later, I'd mess up royally.

Mary said, "We're coming Ivan. With or without the little ungrateful djinn's help. You keep those kids safe."

"We will, and Godspeed, Mary," Ivan replied.

I tried again to talk sense into the djinn. "Seth, there are children involved. Surely you can postpone your nap until you save them."

"I'm trying to sleep."

Again, he disconnected me. Silence rang between us as I held the camera in my hands. I chewed the side of my cheek and considered the repercussions of chucking the camera out the window and if I'd survive its destruction or if the camera could even be destroyed.

"Shit." Mary spat. "I can't see anything past this zombie mosh pit. Blondie, go up and tell me where to go so I don't hit a building or a pole."

"But—"

"Do it," she growled. "Kids' lives are at stake."

My fingers found the handle to the moonroof and slid the top back open. I stood back up on the passenger seat while Mary continued to drive through the forest of undead bodies. The zombies continued to take swipes at me as we whizzed on through the streets.

The horde seemed to be thinning, but not by much. Mary yanked on my pants legs and said, "You can sit down now. I can see… kinda."

Greasy grimy zombie guts smeared across the windshield of

the slug bug, but at least we were through the thick of the living dead. A glance in the rearview mirror showed the horde was following us.

A chilling thought sent icicles down my spine, and I shuddered. What if the number of zombies weren't truly thinning? What if they were sinking into the ground to spring a surprise attack? All the zombies from the supernatural mafia didn't normally travel above ground. Instead, they traveled underground, because it was faster, and boundaries did not extend below the earth.

The library came into view and no zombies were in sight. A worrisome feeling gnawed at the pit of my stomach and refused to let go. Mary drifted in front of the library doors and got out. I looped the strap of my camera round my neck and followed her up to the front.

She pounded on the door and yelled, "Ivan! We're here."

I glanced around, sweat slicking my hands and dribbling down my back. My heart pounded in my chest while Mary continued to pound on the door. Only Ivan came to greet us, and the worrying feeling continued to thrash around in my belly.

He slammed the door shut and put the weight of his body up against the door. Ivan exhaled and said, "The zombies are gone. They were here at the doors and the next moment they left."

The kids were nowhere to be seen, nor was Ivan's team. I asked, "Ivan, where are the kids?"

"They're downstairs, in the basement. Why?"

Screams erupted from the doors leading down, and gunshots followed by loud moans. The three of us rushed to the stairs, our feet going as fast as they could, and we hustled down to the basement. Ivan smashed through the door, and we followed, hot on his heels only to stop in our tracks.

The children cowered in the corner away from the hole in the basement wall where the undead were funneling in. Two of the team members were down and being devoured by the zombies. The children screamed while the living dead advanced to their location.

I shook the camera and shouted at Seth, "We. Need. Your. Help. Now."

CHAPTER TWO

A GOLDEN MIST seeped from the lens of my camera and pooled on the floor at my feet. The wispy vapors rose and formed a seven-year-old boy with a dark complexion and dark hair with a tinge of blonde. His eyes shone a bright amber with molten gold.

The young man, oblivious to the zombies in the room, crossed his arms and faced me. He looked me up and down with a frown on his face and said, "This better be good. I was in the middle of a nap."

"Seth," I yelled. "Cut the crap and help us with these squishy meat suits, who are trying to kill all of us."

He sidestepped one which tried to chomp down on his shoulder and watched the decomposing attacker fall to the floor with a splat. "You know as well as I do I cannot do anything until you make a wish… or grant me more freedom to act without wishes."

Mary whacked a zombie away from me with a baseball bat she found somewhere while I rubbed a hand over my face. I swear this djinn was the reason I had high blood pressure.

"We've been over this." I front-kicked a zombie away. "Giving you the ability to act without direction is bad juju in my book."

"Then make a wish," he replied in a matter-of-fact tone.

"Fine, but remember I tried earlier, and you said you were 'busy'." I donkey kicked a zombie behind me. My fighting skills had gotten way better since I crashed out on Mary's couch for the past few weeks. Ivan insisted I join their self-defense classes every Monday, Wednesday, and Friday night. He wouldn't take no for an answer because it allowed him more opportunities to try to get me to become an official member of the Wings of Virtue organization. Hard pass. Sure, I was a temporary member right now, but only to pacify him. It didn't bother me if I screwed up and got kicked out. Which would be fine with me. I had enough of the supernatural. I just wanted out of all this and to become a regular plain Jane again.

Ivan yelled, charged past me, and bum rushed more zombies funneling out through the hole. Seth merely stood there and watched with one eyebrow quirked up. Another team member guarded the children who attended the library's special read-a-long day before the zombies attacked. He held an impromptu bat made of a table leg to beat the zombies away.

The children cried scared tears and wailed loud enough to hurt my ears. It wasn't just one kid, the whole lot were trying out for resident banshee. I leaned toward Seth and said, "I wish for these zombies to stop attacking us."

"Done," he said while he snapped his fingers. At least he changed from the *I Dream of Jeannie* method of wish granting to something with more speed.

A poof of smoke erupted in the middle of the small room, followed by hacking. The clouds dissipated and revealed Avarice in all her glory, still in her fabulous white custom-tailored suit, bent over coughing out a lung. She wiped her hand across her mouth, stood up, and flashed her new dollar bill green eyes at the room, mostly in my direction. Zombies shambled around her, focused on their desired targets.

"Seth," I hissed. "I didn't mean for you to bring *her* here."

He batted a zombie with snapping teeth and replied, "You wanted to stop the zombies? Avarice can and will stop these zombies. They are, after all, her minions."

"I wanted you to poof them away. Not bring more trouble here."

"Hey, djinns have the right to interpret a nonspecific wish whatever way they choose. Not my fault you were specific. Besides, djinns do have limits, you know."

Limits? Since when did djinns have limits? From what I remember, they're all powerful and only bound by their masters' wishes.

Avarice smirked, primped her hair, and said, "You are quite right, djinn, calling me to dispose of my horde, but what do you offer in return?"

"How about a wish?" He returned her smirk.

"Seth," I shouted, grabbing his shoulders and shaking him, all while dodging incoming zombies. "Are you nuts?"

"From you, djinn?" Avarice dropped her head back in a

haughty laugh, hand on her chest. "No, I don't think it would be wise of me to accept a wish from you. Your kind has a tendency to twist things around. No, I do not want your wish."

I turned to her, dodging another feeble attack from her zombie minion, and asked, "What do you want?"

"Vincent. I want him back. There are several debts I need him to collect for me." She surveyed me with her eyes, a long slender brow rising upwards. "And your camera."

"No, on both counts." My foot snapped outwards, kicking the thighs out from under another zombie. Children continued to wail in the background. "How about a wish?"

"What makes you think I won't wish for those things anyways? I would ask if you were stupid, but I already know you are." Avarice peeled her lips away, revealing the sharp nonhuman teeth. "Fine. Give me Vincent and I will call my minions off."

Mary decapitated a zombie with a table leg and called out, "Oh, hell, no, lady. The dude is going nowhere, if I have any say so."

"So, be it," Avarice said, turned toward the hole in the wall, readying herself to leave. "Unless you can either free my employee, hand over the camera, or pay me, I will leave you here to deal with my minions. They are rather hungry since I have not let them eat in weeks."

"But there's children here." I gestured at the kids huddled behind the Wings of Virtue team members, who were fending off the various hungry zombies. "Avarice, have a heart."

Since when do you care about others"? Stop using the children as a shield Sarah."

"I'm not. Unlike the cold-hearted bitch you are, I've actually learned to care."

"So, you say." She sniffed. "I've stated my terms. I leave you to decide what is more important, keeping one lowly demon behind bars or the children's very lives."

Seth sucked in a hiss. "Ohh, wicked. She has you over a barrel."

"Seth," I admonished him. "Who's side are you on?"

"Mine," he replied and rolled his eyes. "Obviously."

Ivan shattered a zombie's skull like a gored pumpkin. The slushy insides splattered onto the walls and surrounding areas. The children squealed. He called out, "We agree."

Avarice stopped, her mouth held in an 'o' shape. "Oh?"

The zombies paused when she lifted her right hand up. Their undead form was held in stasis, glowing eyes dimming as though their powers ran low like a toy with batteries almost drained. Everyone on the Wings of Virtue crew let out a breath but kept in place in case the zombies became animated again.

Ivan wiped the zombie guts from his salt-and-peppered beard and shook the remains from his hands. He made eye contact with Avarice and said, "For the children, we'll let Vincent go."

CHAPTER
THREE

"EXCELLENT." Avarice clapped her hands together, a burble of laughter escaping her haughty lips. The zombies' bodies stayed frozen while their heads turned toward her, awaiting her command. Seeing a zombie turn their head one hundred and eighty degrees was unnerving and gruesome.

"Now, Avarice," Ivan said, cold steel laid deep within his words.

Her lips pulled forward into a pout and she said, "You're no fun."

Avarice lifted her hands into the air and snapped her fingers. Every single zombie in the room, outside the tunnel and elsewhere, came back to life and sunk into the ground. With the zombie threat addressed, Avarice sashayed over to Ivan, caressed, and patted his cheek.

"My part is done. And will you keep your end of the bargain?" She smirked.

Ivan moved her hand away from his face and replied, "Yes. I will call and tell my people to release Vincent."

Avarice pushed herself upwards on her toes, allowing her to plant a long, lingering kiss on his cheek. Ivan stepped away from her, held up his phone, and said, "Stop. I will not be able to call if you continue to distract me with your seductive ways."

"Mmmm," Avarice purred, tapping an index finger on the bottom of her chin. Her green eyes trained on Ivan while he called headquarters.

Children continued to sniffle and cry in the background. Mary and crew did their best to settle the children's fears of what they had witnessed. Several promises of hot chocolate and pizza were made to distract the sniffling mob. Ivan paced the small room, stepping over the rubble and fallen expired beef jerky.

A heated discussion was in play, for he kept his voice low, his face strained, and teeth clenched. Heck, if I was the person on the other end, I would not want to release the sex demon, either.

But a deal was a deal. Avarice would summon the zombies once more if we did not hand over her minion. An idea crossed my mind, and I turned to Seth.

He backed away with his hands held high. "Sarah, I do not like the look in your eyes. Whatever crazy idea you've got rattling about in your noggin, you can discard such things."

"You haven't even heard me out." I pouted.

"Obviously, a wish." He darted his golden fiery eyes over at Avarice.

She whipped her head around and hissed. "Sarah, if you make any wish to stop the release of my Vincent, there will be hell to pay."

"Once Vincent is released, I'll just wish Vincent away," I said with a smile, propping a hand on my hip. "I have the power of a djinn at my disposal."

"You're playing with fire, you fool." Avarice frowned. "Each wish you make might be your last."

I waggled the camera in my other hand. "I highly doubt you'll be able to make good on your threat."

Avarice's eyes went wide, her mouth fell open, a small squeak escaped her lips. A moment later, she batted her eyes and rushed over, trying to seize the camera from my hands.

"Not possible," she squawked. "No."

"Very much possible." I pulled the camera away, the smile still plastered on my face. "Unlimited wishes with no consequences."

Seth interjected, "Uh, about that..."

I ignored him, moving forward in Avarice's direction, and poked her in the chest. "The way I see things, my friends and I have the upper hand."

Avarice batted my hand away. She got back in my space, teeth bared, and said, "You forget your djinn brought me here. I recall him saying something about limits? Or do you feel that he is all powerful and if so, why don't you wish me, my minions, and Vincent to go away permanently?"

"Maybe I will." I smirked. "Seth, I wish for you to make Avarice, Vincent, and her minions go away. Make them go poof."

Seth tugged on my shirt. "Sarah."

I held up a finger to Avarice, turned to Seth, bent down, and asked, "What?"

"Can we talk? Privately?" he said and motioned for us to go upstairs.

"Just spit it out," I said, the high of knowing we had the upper hand here buzzing through me. With my unlimited and powerful wishes, I could keep sleaze bags like Vincent behind bars, no matter how many deals we made with Avarice. We were unstoppable.

"I can't keep on granting wishes all day long. There's a limit to my powers," he blurted out.

Like a splash of cold water, the high left me as blood drained away. Chills wracked my body, and I shuddered. Our ace-in-the-hole, Seth, had limits?

I immediately spluttered, "Since when?"

He cocked an eyebrow upwards. "Since you bound me to you and the camera, dumb-dumb."

Avarice's frown turned upwards into a smile, like a cat who ate the canary. Her green eyes sparkled, and said, "Well, well, well."

Oops.

"I think the tables have turned," Avarice cooed. "Your djinn does not possess unlimited powers, like you assumed. No, he has limits, which he said earlier, if you cared to even listen, and why he summoned me, you fool. And why he could not make my minions disappear. I believe you owe me more for the disposal of them."

I swallowed the lump in my throat and tried to pass off a laugh. The laugh came out false and unconvincing, while I tussled Seth's hair and said, "He's just kidding. That's Seth, always kidding around. Of course, he doesn't have any limits, do you, Seth?"

He stared at me with his fiery golden eyes, brows furrowed down, lips in a neutral state. "I do have limits."

"Ah-ha-ha-ha." I laughed. "Right. Sure you do, bud, but you never told us about these limits until now. So, you're kidding, right? Right?"

"No." His serious gaze bore deep into me, plunging my hope deep into icy waters. "We've never pushed them until now."

Crap.

"How? How have we used up all of your powers? I highly doubt refilling bowls of cereal would be a drain on your magical resources."

"No, it wouldn't, but..." he counted on his fingers, "doing all of your household chores, lawn care, and keeping your electronic devices charged would. Your careless wishes are what have maxed out my resources."

I paled. Seth was right. We did all those things, but he never told me he had limitations. Limitations we now had to face, in front of my old boss. A cool trickle of sweat trailed down my spine.

Avarice's knowing smile grew wider. She absolutely purred when she spoke. "I can only assume our bargain stands? My Vincent will be freed, and not wished away. Oh, and I will be needing the rest of your debt paid, Sarah."

I did a double take. "W-w-what?"

"You heard me." She flashed her unnatural, nonhuman, sharp teeth. "Your debt, from your previous gambling losses, still stands. Glenda, your dear deceased mother-in-law's, funds went to her darling son, Walter, your ex-husband and he refuses to pay what is owed."

Double crap. My skin color was so pale right now glue companies were paying me for infringement rights. I rolled my head to Seth and squeaked out, "Can you do something about any of this?"

"Not today." He huffed, walked away from me, scratching his chin. "I really should follow what other djinns do and put a daily limit on wishes. Three seems about right."

"Seth," I said, to snap his attention back to me. "Are you saying your powers are done for today?"

"Short of granting a refill on a bowl of cereal? Then yeah. Totally done."

I laid a forearm across my face and groaned. Not good. So not good. Avarice now knew we had limits. Why the hell did I not talk to him in private? Augh.

Ivan walked over to us, shoving his cellphone in his rear pocket, a grimace on full display. His brows furrowed forward, making his eyes darker than needed. He stopped in the middle of us all and asked, "What did I miss?"

Avarice took this moment to gloat. "Not much. Just your dear honorary member divulging your weaknesses right in front of moi. Oh, and she still owes me money."

Ivan ran his fingers through his short-cropped beard. "Hmm. How much?"

"Oh, a piddly sum," she cooed.

His voice deepened with a heavy edge and asked, "Avarice, how much?"

"Three million." Avarice shifted her weight and stood straight.

Shock stole the air from my lungs, and I tried to suck in air but ended up hacking instead. I coughed. "Wait, I only owed you half a million. How'd my debt jump up to three mil?"

Avarice's smile held with smug satisfaction. "Interest, my dear. You should really read the fine print. I would recommend paying the debt before things get out of hand."

Mary whistled right at me. "Dang Blondie. I'd call three mil way out of hand. We don't got that kind of money laying around or we'd help you… well, we'd loan you the money."

"Oh, dear." Avarice placed a hand to her cheek, eyes widened in mock surprise. "Well, you could give me the camera and we can call the debt paid in full."

"Never." All four of us, Ivan, Seth, Mary and I, said in unison.

"Very well." Avarice took two steps over to Ivan, trailed a finger on his chest, and let her fingers linger there. "And you, big guy, have you released my Vincent?"

"Yes," Ivan said, his jaw muscle tensed. "Your minion is freed."

"Good," Avarice said, glancing over at me. "Sarah, if I were you, I'd find some way to repay the debt you owe me. Don't wait too long, the zombification process calls your name."

With as much fanfare as Avarice had when she arrived on scene, she used little to none on her exit. One moment she was there, the next, with a snap of her fingers, she disappeared.

CHAPTER FOUR

WE ALL CONTINUED to gaze upon the spot Avarice stood. No one in the room said anything. Of course, children whined in the backdrop asking when they'd be going home or see their mommies or daddies.

No matter how frigging hard I tried to get away from the Supernatural Underground Mafia, also known as S.U.M., they found ways to hook their claws into my flesh and drag me back down with them. A shuddering breath escaped my lips, and I sank to the floor. My legs were too tired and jelly-like to continue holding me up.

The little bits I'd been piecing together were being washed away, like a sandcastle when the tide came in. Crap. My hands reached out, seeking reassurance, while I continued to stare at the cement floor, spattered with zombie guts. A small hand met mine, and I pulled them closer.

"Don't yank my arm off, Sarah," Seth complained.

Between each labored breath, for I was wheezing, barely able to inhale normal breaths, I asked, "Please tell me you can magically pull in this kind of cash."

"And where do you think the money is going to come from?" he said, sharp thorns barbed each word.

"I don't care." I breathed, held the breath for five seconds, and released. "Just give me the money."

Seth sunk down to my level on the floor. He sat on his haunches, glared at me with his fiery golden eyes, and exhaled a reply: "No."

"No?"

"No." His stern look pinned me in my place. "You forget, often, I'm a djinn. My magic has a tendency to twist things. If I were to magically give you the money, you need to pay off the debt. The money would probably come from a nearby bank."

"Oh." My brows went downward and met in the middle. "Stolen money. Not good."

"Wow, your hamster is on point tonight. Didn't have to think hard on that one," Seth snarked back with a devious smirk.

"Shut up." I shoved him, and he laughed.

Ivan called out to the room, "Crew and children, let us go upstairs and start getting things back to normal. Mary, will you supervise?"

She replied, "Sure thing, Ivan."

Her kick-ass zombie stomping heels clacked on the cement, while she clapped her hands and shouted, "All right, everyone, upstairs, let's go. Children grab an adult and have them lead you back up. Crew, partner up with a child. Make sure they get what they need and let's see if we can get in touch with their parents so everyone can sleep under their own roof tonight. Let's go."

A bevy of footsteps echoed in the small room, children squeaked and shouted, each person partnering up, and the crowd cleared out from downstairs.

Only Ivan, Seth, and I remained. Ivan cleared his throat and said, "Sarah, we can still pay your debt and we can work out a fair payment plan with Wings of Virtue. You only need to ask."

"But Mary said you did not have the funds," I replied, tears blurring my view of the floor. "I don't want to put Wings of Virtue in any kind of trouble."

"No, we help those who are in need. And you…you, my friend, are in need." His heavy hand patted the top of my head.

I swallowed the lump of guilt lodged in my throat and gave in. With a shuddered breath, I glanced up and asked, "Will you lend me the money?"

"Of course," he replied. "Least we can do."

CHAPTER
FIVE

IVAN TALKED TO MICHAEL, the archangel, head and owner of the nonprofit Wings of Virtue, to grant me the money to pay off my debt. He agreed. Though there were strings attached. This wasn't a loan. Michael wanted me gone.

After the short month I had spent with the crew, after the whole zombification fall out happened, and my ex-husband didn't want me back, Michael knew how much trouble followed me around. Instead of exposing his crew to the potential threat I posed, he wanted me to resign my temporary membership and leave town.

Being the stubborn person I was, I refused to leave town, but I left the nonprofit. Only Ivan was privy to why I was truly leaving while Mary was kept in the dark because they knew she wouldn't keep quiet about the whole deal. She would have told others and brought on a mini civil war within the organization. Or she would have pestered Michael until the end of days because of his decision. You did not want to be on Mary's bad side. And here, yours truly, was about to be on her bad side once more.

I sat on the couch I had inhabited for the past month, with the camera around my neck, and looked at Mary with pleading eyes, ready to tell her the by-the-script excuse Michael gave me to feed her. She stood there, with her imposing aura, arms crossed, wearing tight black leather and bad-ass sunglasses with a grumpy pout.

"You're dead to me, Blondie," Mary growled. "Wings of Virtue paid your debt and here you're abandoning us. I wish I left your ass back in the zombie chambers. You're one ungrateful idiot who doesn't know she had things good, real good."

"Sorry." I covered my face in my hands, peeking out between my fingers. "I just can't keep on exposing all of you to the dangers. Or continue exposing the supernatural to regulars. You've seen how trouble follows me and I don't want you to get hurt. Or them."

"Yeah, sure," she sneered. "Why didn't ya leave those few weeks ago? Oh, wait, you still had a debt to pay and were trying to figure out how to sucker us into paying your financial woes for you. You think we're fools?"

"No," I cried, unable to look her in the eyes and ducked my head. "I never thought—"

"Of course you did." She grabbed one of the plastic totes, stomped over to the door, opened it, and threw the tote outside. "Well, Blondie, I'm done. Just go."

She stomped back and grabbed another tote. I leapt to my feet and got in her way. "Please Mary, I'd stay if I could but you've seen how my troubles continue to cause problems for Wings of Virtue. You have to understand."

"Oh, I understand." Mary hefted the tote to one hip. "I understand completely. You're nothing but a gold-digging twit. Well, I'm not going to have you living under my roof if this is the case. Find another idiot to leech off of."

She pushed me aside, stomped to the door, and tossed the bin outside, spraying clothes all over the soggy lawn.

"Mary—" I said, my bottom lip quivering. This was not how I wanted things to end with her. I wish I could tell her, but Michael only wanted Ivan, me, and him to know. Okay, Seth too, but he was threatened with a smiting if he breathed a word to Mary. Michael wanted Mary in the dark because he knew she would have caused the Wings of Virtue to become divided due to her vocal opposition to such unfairness. Though I suspected he did not want her to know for the reason, he would never have any peace from Mary.

Mary pointed to the opened door. "I've had enough of your bullshit and lies. I'm done, Blondie, I'm done. Now, leave."

I held up my hands in a placating manner, side stepped around her and out the door. She continued to stare me down before she went back into the room and threw another plastic bin outside. The contents exploded on impact. Satisfied, she slammed the door; the locks clicking into place. Thunder boomed overhead, just before the bottom dropped out. I let out a shuddered breath. "That went better than I thought. At least she didn't shoot me."

CHAPTER SIX

TWO MONTHS LATER

THERE WERE times at a job you seriously wanted to reach out and throttle the person who was annoying the ever-loving piss out of you. But you couldn't because they were the customer, and you would get fired and possibly get charged with assault and battery. And yet, the person who continued to press on your last frayed nerve. Made the consequences not seem so bad. You could give yourself the satisfaction of eliminating one more asshole from the face of the earth.

After the whole debacle with Wings of Virtue, with Vincent being freed and them paying off my huge debt, kind of left the organization with a huge financial burden. Michael booted me from the nonprofit because I was a magnet for trouble and apparently a stressor for Wings of Virtue's wallet. And so, yours truly was left with no job, no place to go, and no money. No, I never did get the job at the advertising agency, the one I did the video interview for, before Mary hauled me and Seth off to go fight a zombie horde. Instead, I swallowed my pride and applied to work at several places, which ended with me being fired due to me giving asshole customers what's due to them. My most recent employment was at the local cafe called 'The Coffee Bean.'

Not a bad place. No, The Coffee Bean (TCB), was not the same cafe I met with my mother-in-law. TBC was an entirely different cafe the locals liked way more and wasn't so overhyped, like the big coffee franchises.

Though, there will be, as with all retail and food, jerks will come in and demand that you bend to their every whim because they were brought up to compete for the title of ultimate entitled dick.

A prime example was this woman, in her early thirties, slightly pudgy, frazzled hair, standing there and shaking her coffee cup in my face. She continued to shake the almost empty cup and exclaimed, "I ordered an iced latte with whipped cream and caramel drizzle. This is a hot latte with chocolate drizzle. I want a refund."

Putting on my most pleasant customer service grimace, my hackles continued to rise as I faked being nice, and replied, "I'm sorry for the mix-up, ma'am. I can get you another drink if you'd like."

"No, I want a refund." She slammed the cup down on the counter. Nothing sloshed out since the drink was mostly gone. The label on the cup revealed she had grabbed someone else's drink and not hers.

I took the cup and turned the paper container around to show the label and was about to point this out when a slender guy in his early forties, a delicious dimple in his left cheek, walked up and pointed to his drink.

"Sorry, miss," he said. "But I think I was served the wrong drink."

"Let me guess. You received an iced latte with caramel drizzle, right?"

He bobbed his head, his brown hair shifting into his eyes, and smiled.

The woman at the counter seethed and shoved him away with force. "I was here first. Get in line, asshole."

"Ma'am." I pressed my lips together, pinched my brow instead of throwing a punch and said, "I can't believe I'm about to say this, but keep your hands to yourself."

"You can't tell me what to do," she replied. "I'm the customer and the customer is always right."

Massaging between my eyes, fighting the urge to give this woman a well-deserved whooping, I said, "Yes, ma'am, the customer is always right, but customers don't go around hitting people either."

"I didn't hit him." She set her jaw forward. Her hand slapped the counter while she said, "Refund, now. Stop, stalling."

The guy cleared his throat and glanced over at me. "Um, I'd like to take you up on the replacement drink."

"Didn't I tell you to get back in line? I was here first." She shoved the man again and turned back to me. "Don't just stand there, you idiot. Refund. Now."

Again, with the insults about my intelligence. Only a select few would I allow such slights about my IQ, but this woman was not among them. I looked up to the ceiling, held my breath for a moment, the urge to do physical harm rising, and exhaled.

The entire time I reminded myself I was behind on rent, and I had no place to go. If I acted on my impulse right now, then I'd be homeless. Well, not really. Ivan still said his sofa was always open if I needed a place to crash, but I couldn't put the gang in a dangerous situation again. Trouble followed me and they were too good of an organization to put them through the wringer again. Not to mention, Michael would have kittens if he found me lurking on Wings of Virtue's premises.

The lady's hands wrapped themselves around my TCB apron and yanked me forward. This bitch was looking for a fight. Her face mere inches from mine, breath rancid like ripe cheese left out in the hot sun all day, as she sneered, "Look, blondie, you're going to go over to the cash register and issue me my refund or I'm going to give you a really bad time."

Right about now, would have been great to have Seth around. But no, he was locked up with my camera in the back room in the employee lockers. I couldn't exactly shout for his help, since I needed to have physical contact with the camera to let him out.

So, instead, I reached over until I felt the slick cool round sugar dispenser, no longer denying myself the urge to do harm, and smashed the canister over the woman's head. The glass shattered everywhere along with the sugar while the woman screeched like bloody murder had happened. Everyone in the cafe turned eyes our way and my first response was to say, "Oops."

Unfortunately, the manager happened to come in for her shift at this exact moment. She came in screaming, "What the hell, Sarah?"

Never was she there when this ass of a customer harassed me and other customers. The manager, her face a dark shade of red and crumpled, dark eyes darted my way, hustled behind the counter and grabbed several white towels and soaked one in water. She ran to the pain in the ass customer and began fawning over the waste of air.

"I'm so, so, so, sorry. Please, don't sue." The manager winced as she applied the soaked towel to the back of the customer's head where she was bleeding.

Whoops.

The woman jerked away from the manager but snagged the towels and kept them compressed on the back of her head. She pointed at me and shrieked, "Fire that bitch! She's the one who did this to me."

My manager's lips were compressed into a thin line. She knew I needed this job, and I was actually pretty good. Sure, there were incidents along the way, but they were usually with good cause. The crazy customer yelled again, "Fire her or I'll sue you and everyone who works here."

Caught between a rock and a hard place. The number one reason why I never wanted to be a manager is because of these types of situations. The manager's hands curled into fists, her face still the dark shade of red, stomped over to me.

Ultimate butterflies had taken flight in my belly and threatened to bring a storm of serious heartburn very soon. I swallowed and waited.

She held out her hand, "Your apron and nametag, now, Sarah,

I can't give you any more chances and besides, this is the third time. You're fired."

With dramatic flair, I removed the name tag and slapped the plastic on the counter, took off the apron, balled the fabric up and threw it at my manager. All the while, the sorry excuse for a human being sat there with a smile, which I so wanted to wipe away with a well-placed punch.

On my way to the back of the shop to get my things, and totally not being immature, I made sure to bump the crappy customer's shoulder. She whined and pointed at me again. "She did that on purpose. I want to press charges."

The guy from earlier spoke up. "Lady, if you're going to press charges on the ex-employee, then I'd like to press charges too… on you."

I swear I'd never seen a better imitation of a fish out of water. The woman opened and closed her mouth several times while the man stepped in her way to block her view of me. I nodded at him, mouthed a 'Thank you,' and ducked into the back room.

Shouts continued, but I didn't care anymore. I concentrated on the combination lock and dialed the correct code. The locker clicked and unlocked. As long as I didn't end up behind bars; I was good with how today turned out even if I was fired.

I bent down to grab my purse and the camera. As soon as my hands touched the case, Seth laid into me.

"You got fired, again?" he said. *"What's the count up to now?"*

"Doesn't matter," I said under my breath. No one knew my camera was special. The supernatural had to be kept under wraps around the norms, else there would be consequences. Consequences, I didn't want to end up footing the bill for.

"Doesn't matter? Doesn't matter?" he intoned. *"You know full well what will happen if you're behind on rent. If the landlord learns you no longer have a job, again, I might add... he'll chuck you out onto the street."*

"I know," I said and rubbed my temples. "I know. Just let me go home and lick my wounds. I'll get a new job tomorrow. Even if I have to work fast-food. Certainly, better than nothing."

"Sure, sure." He was quiet for a moment. *"You know you haven't wished for anything lately. I could get you your job back."*

"No. I'm not going to depend on wishes to make things better. This is my mess. I'll deal with the aftermath."

"Fine."

I hefted the camera strap around my neck and exited through the back so I wouldn't have to deal with the wicked witch in the front. Just as the door closed, I heard someone call out.

"Hey," they said.

I turned to look and saw the guy from earlier. He walked straight up and waited for me to descend the small staircase to the back parking lot. I waved.

"Hi and thanks for earlier."

He held his hands in his pockets and replied, "You're welcome. I couldn't let the woman completely ruin your day."

"Much appreciated."

He pulled out one hand and held it out to me. "Nathan."

I grabbed his hand and shook. "Sarah."

"Do you need a ride home?" he asked.

"Well, to be fair, I was going to call a ride service..." I replied and twirled my hair.

"No, I insist." He turned and pointed at his fancy high-end

electric car. "Figure I could give you some sort of highlight in your day, right?"

Get in a car with a complete stranger? Sure, what could happen? Not like those other ride services didn't have the same risks about complete strangers. But then again, those apps had details of when you hailed the person who picked you up, and where. Whereas, with Nathan, I had no clue as to who he truly was and for all I knew; he was some sort of serial killer.

Meh. You only lived once. I bobbed my head and answered, "Sounds like fun."

CHAPTER
SEVEN

NATHAN, to find out, was a newbie in town. And he had a delectable hint of a British accent which turned my insides into jelly upon hearing such verbal linguistics. He had settled into the more upscale apartments about a week ago because of his job at the new law firm who had just opened their doors.

The previous firm, a front for the Supernatural Underground Mafia, was *'mysteriously'* blown up because the mafia decided to cut ties to this small town because of Wings of Virtue putting a hamper in their business. I was one-hundred percent okay with one less facade for the supernatural mafia to hide behind.

The hum of the electric vehicle was almost too quiet. You had to listen hard before you would recognize the resonating energy which powered the car. Though, the luxurious leather seats were nothing to sneeze at with their fresh scent of new car. I leaned into the headrest and inhaled. Ah, yeah.

"Like the car?" Nathan asked.

"Mmm, yeah. Love the fresh scent of new car. There's nothing like it."

"Ah." He bobbed his head. "I hear ya. Though, I prefer fresh linen. Gives me the comforting feel of outside wrapped up with childhood nostalgia."

"Ohh, you're right. Totally forgot about fresh linen. That's one of the better ones, too."

"Wipe your chin," Seth snarked through the camera. *"You're practically drooling."*

"Shush," I said under my breath.

Nathan lifted his chin. "Hmm?"

"Oh, nothing." I batted my hand playfully at him and held up my camera with a nervous laugh. "I have a tendency to talk to my camera when I get nervous... you can kind of call my camera here an emotional support camera."

The corner of his lips quirked upwards while he kept his delicious brown eyes trained on the road. "I see."

"Awkward," Seth said. I tried to ignore him.

Silence hung between Nathan and me while he traveled down the streets to the less than stellar parts of town. His smile faded as we went deeper, and his eyes grew wide. By the time he pulled up to my apartment complex, his mouth hung open.

"Well," I said, gathering my purse from the floorboard of the car, glancing between him and the apartment. "This is where I get off. Thanks for the ride."

As I went to open the door, his hand reached out and grabbed mine. "Please tell me you're joking."

"I'm not. This is where I live," I said and gently removed my hand.

"Sarah." He paused. "I do not feel safe leaving you here in this dangerous area. I won't be able to sleep at all if I didn't know if you were safe or not."

Oh? Was this his ploy to get my phone number? Mmm. He was cute.

"Just give him your number or I'll never hear the end of your whining about not getting his number." Seth's voice carried more edge than necessary.

Looking into Nathan's brown puppy dog eyes melted my heart even more. I most certainly could not let this man have sleepless nights because he was worried about my wellbeing. So, I did the right thing and pulled out a receipt from my purse and wrote my number on the back of the slip of paper and handed the paper to him.

"Here's my number. You can call me later to check up on me if it will let you sleep better." I smiled.

He took the receipt with gentle hands, held the paper close to his heart, and smiled as well. "Thank you. You have no idea how much this means to me. I will be giving you a ring in an hour or so to check up on you, alright?"

"Yeah, sure. I look forward to your call," I said and opened the door. The sounds around the area blasted us and made me realize the excellent soundproofing in Nathan's car. I turned around, closed the door, and waved. He waited until I walked up the sidewalk and climbed the ancient, rusted staircase, which shook with each step.

I watched his silver car leave the apartment's trash strewn parking lot and dodge kids who had no common-sense about getting out of the way of moving vehicles. The entire time, my heart skipped an extra pitter-pat. He was such a cutie, especially with those chocolate brown eyes. And his genuine concern over my wellbeing was a huge plus in my book.

Walter was never that way with me. He kept me sheltered the entire time I was with him and found reasons for me to skip the necessary training for members of the supernatural mafia. If I had to compare the two, they were completely different, night and day.

"*Already comparing them? Seriously? The guy gives you a ride home and you're ready to jump his bones because he allegedly is concerned for your wellbeing? Good lord, you are so not bright,*" Seth said, again in an edgy tone. Was he jealous?

"*I'm not jealous. I only wish you had more than those two brain cells to realize the dude could be setting you up.*"

That was like a splash of cold water. Two months ago, my mother-in-law stabbed me in the back to get her son back, and I almost turned into an expired bag of meat kept on a short leash… aka zombie minion.

After two flights of stairs on the rickety metal stairwell, my thighs were burning, and I was literally puffing to catch my breath. I crawled onto the landing when my legs gave out only two stairs away from my end goal. Whoever said late thirties was the new twenties was lying out of their ass.

I laid there, wheezing and gasping for air, before I noticed the pink slip on the door. Tired legs and shortness of breath forgotten, I leapt to my feet and snatched the paper off the heavy metal door and read the note.

"Aw, come on," I shouted and crumpled the paper. "Evicted? How can I be evicted? He said I had two more weeks."

"That was two weeks ago," Seth reminded me.

My hand slammed against the metal door, and the pain radiated down through my limbs.

"Son of a biscuit," I shouted and shook my injured hand. "Damn, damn, damn."

The neighbor across from me opened his door. He looked me up and down before he said in a whisper, "Can you tone things down? I just got the baby to sleep, and I don't need her waking up again."

Oops. I winced and replied, "Sorry."

He nodded and said, "Yeah, me too. I'm gonna miss ya. Most other tenants didn't care much for me and my family, but you did. So, I'm sorry to see you go. I wish you the best of luck, Sarah."

"Thanks," I said and waved him off. He closed his door with barely any sound. Great neighbor. He and his family were proof people lived in all sorts of areas and they were not inherently bad. Sometimes life wasn't fair.

I un-crumpled the note and reread the words written upon the sheet of paper. All my stuff was being taken, too. I'm not sure if what my landlord did was legal, but this landlord followed through on their threats, legal or not. Well, crap on a stick. Today was just getting better and better, not.

Reaching into my purse, I pulled out my cellphone and dialed the one person I knew who could help me out. Desperate times called for desperate measures.

CHAPTER EIGHT

"THIS IS IVAN," Ivan answered with a cheer. Apparently, he must have been having a good day or something. Too bad I was about to yank the rug right out from under his feet. In the background was the loud chatter of people and music blaring over speakers. Several people came up and wished him a happy birthday. Oops. I swallowed. Hard.

"Hey Ivan." I replied in the same cheery voice and absently tucked a stray hair behind my ear. "Long time, no hear? Right?"

Ivan was silent for a moment. I could literally hear the smile get wiped from his face as his brows furrowed down into a serious expression. He said, "Sarah?"

"Yup, the one and only."

Ivan sounded like he walked away from the party to get to a quieter space before he talked again. He spoke into the phone in a low whisper, "You know Michael will not like you calling. You've been banned, remember? What happened?"

I raked my fingers through my hair and said, "I've run into a bit of bad luck, and I don't have any more spare sofas to sleep on."

"You're not gambling again, are you?" His voice took on a fatherly tone. "Because I cannot help you if you're gambling again."

"No, no, no, no."

"Good."

More awkward silence. Ivan was waiting for me to confess why I was calling him for help. Especially since Michael forbade my interaction with the organization two months ago. I did not have any viable options else I would not be calling him. There was nowhere safe I could rest my eyes without fear of Avarice's zombie minions popping up out of the ground and dragging me down to my untimely death. Well, multiple deaths until the camera used up all of my life-force because I didn't recharge the dang thing.

"Ivan, can I come stay with you?" I begged. "Please?"

Someone came up on Ivan and asked in a loud voice, "Ivan, who in the hell are you talking to?"

"A person who needs help," he said.

"On your birthday?" she said. "Tell them you'll help them tomorrow."

"Mary, you know we don't operate that way," Ivan replied in a patronizing tone. "We help those who are in need no matter where their moral compasses point. Our job is to help them and guide them back to the path of light."

"For real?" Mary said and asked, "Who is this person in desperate need? They cannot wait until tomorrow to be rescued?"

"Sarah," he said.

"Oh, hell, no," she said in long drawn out vowels before the sounds of a struggle of who handled the phone ensued. Ivan cried out while the phone relayed air whooshing by the speaker before the phone landed with a hard thud.

Dirt crunched nearby before the phone was picked up. Mary took on a singsong honey toned voice when she said, "Remember Blondie, you left us. It's your shit pile. You deal with your crap. So, fuck off."

The call ended. I heard Ivan call out to Mary for her rude behavior as she pressed the end call button on the phone. I stared at the dark screen of my phone for a good five minutes when the screen lit up with an unknown number. The person on the other end could be Avarice or some other minion. Or worse, Vincent. Ever since his release, I've never felt safe with the sex demon back out on the prowl. He and I still had some unfinished business, or as he called our relationship, a debt I owed him.

My body was wracked with shivers just thinking of the slimy worm's touch. Granted, he was a looker, but his approach with his targets was why I didn't want to be in the same room with him. I scanned the stairwell for any weird-looking shadows and answered the call.

"Hello?"

"Sarah?" Nathan said with warm undertones. "I know I said I'd call you an hour after I dropped you off, but my subconscious wouldn't let me wait. I hope that's alright with you."

"No, Nathan. I'm not upset at all. Thank you for calling."

He let out a breath he was holding. "Thank goodness and

thank you. I was worried sick. Something kept on nagging me to turn around. Kind of like a guardian angel whispering in my ear to double check on you."

"You don't say." I cocked my head to one side. Searching for his iconic silver car, I asked, "Are you coming back?"

"Do you need me to?"

"Um, I kind of need a ride to another friend's house. I was going to call a ride service, but since you just called, I figured I could ask you."

"You don't need to ask me twice. Consider your shining knight in armor on his way."

I grinned. "Thanks Nathan."

"Anytime," he replied with a small chuckle.

"So, how long do you think you'll be?"

"Oh, about fifteen minutes. You can meet me in the lot. Please don't go before or, I'd worry about you getting mugged, kidnapped, or worse."

"I'll wait up on the stairwell for you and come down when I see your car. Sound good?"

"Yes," he replied, then added, "Okay. I'll see you soon, Sarah. Bye."

The call ended, and I couldn't wipe the goofy grin off my face. Just talking to Nathan helped wash away the negative vibes I'd been feeling. Sure, today was a total crap day because of my job and getting evicted. But at least I met Nathan. He was a ray of sunshine on this very cloudy, craptastic day.

"You know, he could still be a serial killer or setting you up."

Even if the demon denied such feelings, I still sensed a tinge of jealousy. I was certain his sour mood got worse ever since I accepted the ride from the British hunk.

"Not jealous," Seth argued. *"Just cautious since you're being a pea brain."*

"Whatever, Seth, whatever," I said and rolled my eyes. Ladies and gentlemen, I give you tonight's wet blanket and party pooper extraordinaire. Seth was certainly trying to douse the little bit of happiness I was feeling tonight.

"Fine. Don't expect me to help if the guy turns out to be one of the supernatural mafia's stooges or he outright goes all Jeffery Dahmer on you."

Wow, dark much, Seth? Supernatural mafia I totally got, but mentioning one of the more heinous serial killers? Ick. I one-hundred percent needed to cut him off of the true crime podcasts.

"I haven't had access to those in four weeks when you didn't pay your subscription, numbskull."

"Woah, Seth. Can you go easy on my IQ for once? Why don't you take a nap or something, Mr. Cranky-pants?"

"Demons don't sleep, moron."

"Ugh, just stop talking to me for the rest of the night, okay? I don't want to deal with your negative attitude during my ride with Nathan."

"You're not going to go sleep at his place, are you?"

"What? No. That'd be stupid. I might not be bright, as you all seem to think I'm not, but I'm not that dumb."

"Right. Let me out."

"Uh, what?"

"Let me out. I'll be able to watch your back if you let me out. Beside

it'll be harder for the serial killer to take you if you have another witness."

"That's ridiculous." I snorted. "Won't the guy just kill you, too?"

"*A normal person, yes. But you forget, I am a demon, after all. I can't protect you if I'm stuck in this blasted camera.*" He let out a huff. "*So, let me out.*"

Seth had a point. He was a demon, and he seemed to, naturally, act as my bodyguard when he was out of the camera. Might be something to do with our bond, which made him overprotective.

"And how am I supposed to explain your presences to Nathan?"

"*Lie or something. Just let me out.*"

Ass. Negative, pushy, asshole. But negative, pushy, asshole with a point. Those with nefarious ulterior motives will have a harder time pulling a fast one on me if Seth was watching my back. I gripped the case of the camera and caressed the lens. "Seth, I give you permission to come out of the camera to watch my back and to cast any magic, depending on the situation."

"*Excellent.*" The golden mist seeped out the lens of the camera and pooled on the metal landing. Slowly the mist grew taller and into the form of a seven-year-old boy with dark hair and gold highlights. His amber eyes shone with fiery molten gold.

Seth stretched his arms above his head, sending an array of crackles and pops as he arched backwards. He was pretty flexible, but again he was a demon. And at this moment, very opaque. He cracked his neck and plunked down on the ground opposite of me with crossed legs. A smirk plastered on his impish face.

"So, when's lover boy going to show up?" he asked, knowing full well when Nathan said he would be here.

"Fifteen minutes or so. Why?"

"Gives us enough time to raid your apartment. Let you grab the essentials you might need later on."

My mouth dropped open. "Seth, I can't. You know I've sworn off that type of stuff. Anything of the bad girl vibe, like breaking into dwellings, gambling or of that nature, will ping the supernatural mafia and all sorts of cronies will come down on us. So, no."

"You're not the one doing the wrong. I am."

"But you're under my command."

"True, though you could say you forgot your keys and needed me to act as a locksmith for you."

"Seriously? You think the supernatural mafia is going to let us get by on technicality? You know that's bullshit."

"Fine. Though I will point out there are several boxes of 35mm film canisters in there, you will not be able to replace if you do not get them now. Think of how hard you worked to hunt down the current supply? And you know for a fact the camera needs them to function. We've tried running with a blank canister, which didn't work."

Crap. Seth was right. Those boxes of 35mm were expensive and hard to get ahold of and would be stupid of me to let my landlord keep possession of them. I glanced at the door and back at Seth. There was no choice, and since we'd be in the apartment, it wouldn't hurt to grab a few of my other things before we hustled out of here.

"Do it," I said.

Seth clapped his hands and rubbed them together while he giggled. With him around, there was no way I could walk the straight and narrow. Instead, we meandered in the gray area. Which was good enough, to be honest. As long as we didn't summon any zombie minions, I was fine with our little heist.

The djinn jumped to his feet and was at the door in two strides. He made a flourish with his hands and touched the deadbolt of the door before we heard the audible click of the lock disengaging. Seth grabbed the doorknob, turned the knob, and pushed the door open. He bowed and said, "Ladies, first."

CHAPTER
NINE

NATHAN WAS KIND ENOUGH to help Seth and me move my boxes down to his car and stuff as much as we could into his vehicle. He, of course, offered for me to stay at his place once he found out I was evicted. But I gave him a hard pass, mainly on the grounds I hardly knew him, and I already had another place lined up. He was also pretty peeved at the fact the landlord was taking ownership of my stuff within the apartment.

I could still see his jaw tense and the muscles twitch as he continued clenching his teeth while he drove us to Ivan's place. Yes, even though Mary told me to go away, I was still going to show up on his doorstep. Ivan can't turn someone away when they appear on his doorstep. Besides, he knew the truth, and the bonus part was Mary wasn't his boss.

"Are you sure you don't want me to help you get the rest of your stuff back?" Nathan asked.

I caught Seth's narrowed eyes as he shook his head at me.

"No, I'm sure. Thanks though. Seth and I got most of the essentials. The stuff can be replaced… so I think I'm good." I replied.

"So, Seth, is your…"

"Uhhh," I said and rubbed the back of my neck, wracking my brain for a plausible excuse. Seth merely arched his eyebrow my way. The corners of his lips quirked upward.

The wheel creaked under Nathan's hands when he tightened his grip. "Never mind, you don't have to answer…"

Nathan put the car in gear and drove. Silence held, awkward silence, until he cleared his throat and said, "Well, the landlord of yours is doing some shady shit. I'd hate to see other people run into the same issue like you've just dealt with. I might go after them myself to save others the headache."

"Suit yourself." I hooked my hands on my knees and leaned forward. His car might be fancy, but the vehicle was not one you felt the road under you. Instead, there was no sense of movement, which made me a bit antsy.

Seth leaned between the two front seats and whined, "Are we there yet?"

I shoved him back. "Put your seatbelt on."

"Spoilsport," he shot back, flounced into the back seat, and buckled his seatbelt. "If this tin can didn't have windows, I would not believe you were actually driving us anywhere."

Nathan looked up into the rearview mirror. "Yeah, buddy? It's what I like the most about this car. The ride is so smooth you don't even feel potholes. Some say it magically glides over them."

I snorted. "I used to have an old car which glided over potholes."

"Really?" Nathan said as his voice took on a wondrous quality. "A magical one like *Herbie*?"

"Yeah." I nodded. "Though my car was not a vee-dub bug. She was a nineteen eighty-nine Ford Mustang. Fox body model, but was not the five point o. Instead, she was the pony model."

Nathan whistled. "They don't make those anymore and the Fox bodies are getting fewer and fewer with all those idiots buying up the two point four liters for their bodies and converting them to five point o's."

Seth asked, "What happened to yours?"

"Pawned the car," I said and frowned. Unsettling butterflies swirled around in my stomach while I blinked back tears. "Needed the money and, like the fool I was, I sold her to get quick cash. Wish I never did."

"Oof." Nathan winced. "Sorry to hear that. Well, if it makes you feel any better, I totaled my first car. All because I was a stupid teenager and didn't learn cars needed to be maintained. Wrapped the vehicle around a tree when I jumped the ditch after the brakes failed to work to slow down around a steep curve. Still don't know how I survived the accident."

"Wow," I said and looked out the window to watch the streetlights pass over us while Nathan turned off onto the exit.

"Guess you could say I had a guardian angel looking out for me that night." He glanced around after he stopped, then turned left.

Seth replied, "Guardian angel? Malarky."

"Oh, you don't believe in guardian angels, eh, sport?"

"No." He scowled. "Most of the time, people get out of near death situations due to a series of events. You're only saying there was a guardian angel who saved your butt that night because you don't want to face the facts."

Nathan shrugged. "Whatever bud. You can choose to not believe, but I do. Ever since, I kept faith."

"A lawyer keeps faith?" I giggled. "That's an oxymoron if I ever heard one."

He gave a mock stare and held his left hand against his chest and said, "I'll have you know there are several lawyers out there who are good Christians."

"Define good," Seth insisted while he leaned his elbows on the center console.

I turned and saw he was not wearing his seatbelt again and gave him an arched eyebrow. He stuck his tongue out at me.

Nathan turned down another street and replied, "Well, good is obviously the opposite of evil. But you have to get into the whole discussion of what is really evil. And plays along with what is the societal norm. What we think is good today might become evil tomorrow."

"Hum." Seth's eyes took on a thoughtful expression. "You may have a point."

"I always do," Nathan said and hooked a thumb at himself. "I am, after all, a lawyer."

The car was approaching the turnoff for the dirt road. I cleared my throat and pointed. "Turn here."

"Here?" He raised his eyebrows.

"Yes, here." I continued to point at the upcoming turn. He turned, and the wheels crunched on the gravel in the road and slid down the hill. The forest canopy encased us on the dark, narrow dirt road. Guess he did not have all terrain tires.

He chewed on the inside of his cheeks while his eyes scanned the road ahead. The lights of the car only offered visibility where they shone on the road. Seth kept quiet and watched.

I could see Nathan's shoulders hunch the further we went down the road. He finally asked, "You're not leading me out to the middle of nowhere to kill me, are you?"

"No," I replied. "That's ridiculous."

Seth added, "If there was anyone who would be doing any killing, I thought you'd do the honors, Mr. Lawyer. After all, you'd know all the legal loopholes to get away with such things."

Nathan slowed the car to a halt and stopped. He rested his hands on the wheel and bounced his eyes between Seth and me. His jaw muscles were visible as he clenched his teeth.

"I'm not a serial killer."

"Aren't you?" Seth argued.

Nathan let out a big sigh and started the car forward again at a snail's pace. His eyes searching for the slightest movement, which was a good idea since deer and coyotes were known to play kamikaze with vehicles going this route.

"So, your friend lives down this road?" he asked.

"Yeah. Not too far now," I said, just as the tree canopy gave way to a big clearing.

Up on the hill sat the second headquarters for Wings of Virtue after the original one was destroyed by the supernatural mafia. The house was a big ranch like style but with a second story in the middle portion. The rest of the house sprawled out into two wings with rooms for those seeking a place to stay while they got back on their feet. Thrills raced through my limbs, making my hands vibrate. Even though it had only been two months, I missed this place.

Lights were on in the living area and lit the front lawn with the two-story tall scenic glass panels. There were several members lounged on the furniture watching the latest heist movie on the seventy-inch tv. My stomach tied itself into knots, for I wasn't expecting many members to be here tonight. I wasn't sure if I could handle them. Mary, yeah, but the whole crew? Nope.

Nathan pulled up to the house and turned off his car. He got out, ran to my side, and opened my door to let me out. How sweet. I glanced over my shoulder just in time to catch the death glare Seth threw Nathan.

Nathan let out a long whistle. "Wow. Your friend must be loaded to afford a place like this..."

"The place isn't all his. In fact, this is an organization for those who fall on hard times. Their policy is not to refuse those in need..." I left the comment hanging and moseyed up to the door and knocked.

Laughter rang out with cheer while the sound system boomed the loud explosions from the high action scenes. I knocked again. Someone heard my knock and stomped over to the door, rumbling about how this idiot should have a damn good reason for ruining movie night, and opened the door.

"Oh, hell, no," Mary said and slammed the door in my face.

My fist pounded on the door, and I shouted, "Mary, I need to talk."

"Blondie, we talked," she yelled back. "You left us. Go away and deal with your own shit pile."

"Did Ivan say that too?"

She didn't answer.

"He didn't, did he?" I asked again. "Go get him."

"No. I ain't letting you drag us back into the shitstorm which is your life. Wings of Virtue don't need your trouble magnet and I sure as hell don't need the added blood pressure spike of dealing with your crap."

More voices came to the door. I recognized one of them and breathed a sigh of relief when his deep basso voice asked, "Sarah?"

"The one and only."

The door opened, and light filtered out of the doorway. Ivan stood there with arms held wide, took a step forward, and gave me a great big hug. He lifted me up off the ground while he continued to hug me and swayed me back and forth. A chuckle emanated from deep within his chest.

"You came back," he said, putting me back down and kissing the top of my head. "You came back. I always knew you would."

"Ivan, this is one bet I wished you'd lost." Mary huffed and walked away.

Nathan came up behind me with Seth in tow. He reached his hand out and Ivan grabbed it. They shook hands while Nathan said, "Nathan Walker. People call me Nate or Nathan. And, err… what's the deal with Mary?"

"No need to worry. She'll come around. I'm Ivan."

"Pleasure to meet you, Ivan."

Seth pushed through and exclaimed, "Ah, entertainment, how I've missed you."

He made a beeline to the couch and plunked down with the other members while they continued to watch the action-packed movie about a heist. Ivan chuckled at Seth's antics. He knew too well about Seth's addiction to streaming TV and premium channels with no commercials. I shrugged because I couldn't refute his love of TV shows and movies.

Ivan clamped a hand down on my shoulder and asked, "Sofa or bed?"

"Do you need to even ask?" I replied. "Bed, please."

CHAPTER
TEN

IVAN HAD a funny idea of what constituted a bed. After everyone had gone home and Nathan left, Ivan showed me to the back spare room, which only had a sofa. No, the sofa was not the kind that pulled out into a bed. Instead, the sofa was one of those you would find on the side of the road and quote unquote rescue.

The fabric stains were beyond removing and had a lingering cat pee smell every time you sat down or moved on the sofa cushions. But still, Ivan had gathered fitted sheets, extra blankets, and pillows to make the sofa more comfortable. Bless his heart.

I didn't know what was worse. The constant creak of the rusty springs deep within the sofa whining about my somewhat pudginess or the fresh whiff of cat whiz with each turn I did. Down the hall, the TV in the main room still played shows. Seth had refused to go back into the camera because he wanted to catch up on what he missed on the various movies and premium channels.

On the floor of the low piled carpeted, meager furnished room was my camera. I reached down to feel its soothing vibrations and to ease my nerves that the camera was still safe beside me. Ever since the time Avarice took the camera from me, I'd been way more protective and stressed if the camera was not in arm's reach.

Let's just say if the camera were to go on a joyride without me, I'd suffer the consequences. First, my body would begin to shut down and not regulate the temperature. My limbs would end up getting serious frost bite. The further the distance the worse the symptoms get, for the camera liked to pull my life-force like a tether. Kind of like, *'Hey stupid, if you don't come find me then I'm going to end you,'* type of thing.

So, I learned. Never lose sight of the camera, keep the camera within arm's reach, and for the love of the almighty, don't lose the frigging camera. And if anyone asked, because believe me they have, I usually told them the camera was my emotional support camera.

My god, the looks I'd get from people after I told them that line. But, hey, at least they had the sense to about face and leave me the hell alone instead of continuing their stupid interrogation as to why I would even bother to take pictures with an outdated camera. It was an art form people. An art form, seriously. Get over it.

Taking pictures with your phone or digital camera made the process of taking pictures too easy and people just snapped pics of the most ridiculous things nowadays. Back then, when you were allotted only twenty-four slides, you thought about your shots before you took them. And mind you, they weren't instantaneous, either. You had to use up the entire roll before you could go get them developed, which could take up to six to eight weeks. Thus, you never knew if you messed up the shot until after you got the film roll developed.

I traced circles around the lens and the case of the camera while staring up at the ceiling. The Sandman, a fictional warden of sleep, was waylaid somewhere, and I suspected it was why I couldn't sleep. And there was the constant creak of the sofa springs accentuated with the poof of ancient, powdered form of feline urine.

Ugh. Gross. I threw the covers off, put on my pants and t-shirt, shucked my tennis shoes on, grabbed the camera off the floor, and hustled out the door. I wandered down the hallway until I found the Wings of Virtue's gym.

The gym was not small by any chance. There were two levels and by the looks of the layout they dug to make the lower level. On the top was your usual run-of-the-mill gym equipment, treadmills, ellipticals, jump rope, and weights. Downstairs was split into three areas, one part was for boxing, another was for martial arts, and the third was walled off for the bath area. Which was where they housed the showers, baths, and saunas.

Down below, I saw Ivan working on the punching bag in the boxing ring. Guess he couldn't sleep either. He paused and waved for me to come down to him. I glided down the staircase and approached him.

"You should be sleeping," Ivan said.

"And yet, I'm not... might be due to the smelly, creaky, cat whizzed sofa someone had me sleep on for the night. Or not." I shrugged.

He chuckled. "Ah, I am sorry. Mary was the one who told me which room to give you."

"Are you pointing fingers?"

"Maybe." He grinned and jerked his head at the boxing gear. "Suit up. Let's see how much rust you've gained since you left."

Not wanting to argue with Ivan, I grabbed the gear off the shelf. After I pulled on the gloves, Ivan grabbed the target pads and guided me over to the ring, and helped me up.

Once inside, he held the targets up and I started hitting them in a slow but steady rhythm.

"Seth told me," Ivan stated in a matter-of-fact tone.

I punched and followed with a double tap with the other hand. "Told you what?"

"That you got fired from your last job."

"Yeah," I said and punched harder. "So?"

"So, makes what, six jobs you've been fired from in two months?" He moved the targets around and I followed with tenacity.

My right hand slammed into the edge of the target. I had to skip to catch myself. "I don't see how this is a problem."

"It's a problem because I know you. How long before you turn to old ways?"

"Never." I frowned and sped up my patterns. "I've sworn off gambling, remember?"

"You know, my job offer still stands," Ivan said.

"No."

"But here, you can find your way back to the path of light."

"Ivan, have you forgotten? Our deal with *your* boss? Me being here is risky enough, but I had nowhere else to go. It was here or a cardboard box."

"Sarah, if Wings of Virtue was not meant to save you, we'd never have met." He sighed and swapped the target for the longer ones. Ones I could practice kicks with. He added, "I refuse to give up, even if Michael disapproves. I answer to Him, and Him alone and not his children. Only He has the last word."

"Sorry, but no." I did a back kick and missed the target. Ivan was quick to avoid getting hit down below. A smug look on his face with a twinkle in his eye was all he gave me.

"Remember, you will always be welcomed back, regardless of Michael."

I tried the back kick again and went slower this time to work on the technique instead of speed. Speed was always built upon what you'd learned, never the first thing to do.

My breath was getting labored, with only thirty minutes of punching and kicking. Though the workout could have been longer. Man, I really was out of shape. Of course, my jeans were telling me two weeks ago when I had to suck in my gut to get the suckers on.

Ivan motioned for us to stop and had me do a few laps around the ring to cool down. Once done, we crawled out of the ring and over to the benches nearby. Between labored breaths, my hand snatched out, sending sweat flying and almost missed the fresh towel thrown at me. My camera sat on the bench, and I picked the camera up in a cradling fashion.

An elated shiver rushed through my entire being as the camera greeted my embrace with what I considered to be a happy emotion. Kind of like a dog with its owner when they'd gone and came back.

Seth told me he suspected the camera to be sentient. I wouldn't doubt the suspicion based on how the camera reacted to my touch. I leaned up against the wall and basked in the warm glow the camera sent through me. Ivan stood there and stroked his beard while he watched my interactions with the camera.

"When was the last time you fed the camera?" he asked.

"Um, I think five days ago," I replied with one eye peeked open. "Why?"

"I've never seen a camera do that." He gestured to all of me. "Powers are different, now."

"We all change." I shrugged a shoulder and stretched my neck.

"Has Seth made updates to the camera?"

"No. He would have told me if he did and I don't think the camera would let him anyways since the camera acts as his vessel."

"Hm, you do have a point."

The area upstairs sounded with footsteps followed by Mary, who called out, "Ivan, you in here?"

"Yes, Mary. Come. Sarah is down here, too."

"Good."

Uh, Mary happy to know where I was? No, this was certainly not good. All kinds of bad juju was making my hair stand on end as I watched her bounce down the stairway. She walked up to us and said, "Morning, Blondie. Did you enjoy Le Hotel a Chat Eau de Whiz?"

"Hardly." I glowered and looked up at the windows in the

upper portions of the gym. The sun was rising, and the sky had the pink tinge with minimal cloud covering. Birds were chirping their morning song.

"Here." She shoved a piece of paper toward me. I took the paper from her, glanced down and back up at her.

"What's this?"

"A potential new job, Blondie."

"Why?"

"Do you enjoy sleeping on a sagging sofa with cat whiz?"

"No, no, you're right. I don't enjoy the gross sofa… but why?"

"Seriously, Blondie, your hamster must be on vacation again. I got you an interview so you can get out of my hair faster."

"That was kind of you, Mary," Ivan said.

She flapped her hand at him, smiled, and said, "It's what I do."

Ivan turned to me. "When is the interview?"

I glanced down at the sheet, my eyes nearly popping out of their sockets. No way I would make the interview in time. I needed a miracle… or a wish.

CHAPTER ELEVEN

THE MAN SAT THERE behind the desk with his hand held over his chest, breathing in deep breaths, mouth agape, his eyes wide, and leaning far back from me. Seth literally dropped us in the chair of his office for the interview. I should have been more specific as to how Seth granted said wish, because he wore a wicked smile and rubbed his hands together while he cackled before he said, "Wish granted."

"Sir?" I got up and went over to help him. He held his fingers up in a crucifix and screamed in a high-pitched voice like a little girl, "Get away from me!"

Seth stayed seated, picking at his cuticles, momentarily biting them before he spat the skin out onto the floor and continued his grotesque habit. I turned to him and motioned at the poor frightened man and said, "You scared him. Now he's probably having a heart attack because of your antics."

"You and I know, Sarah, you were not specific enough with the wish." He bit into another cuticle.

I wrinkled my nose and said, "Will you stop picking at your nails? Besides, when do demons obtain such habits?"

"Bored ones," Seth said and continued to rip the skin away. Blood trickled from parts he tore too deep, which he wiped on his khakis. Classy, real classy Seth.

A clatter happened and I turned back to see the man had fallen onto the floor and was ceasing up. The man had stopped breathing. His gaze stared aimlessly up at the ceiling as his body went limp. Oh, for the love of anything holy. I rolled the rather hefty man the rest of the way onto his back, and I was about to initiate CPR when Seth asked, "Want a do-over?"

D'oh.

"Yes, I would like a do-over," I replied. "I had no idea you could manipulate time."

"Short answer, yes." He flapped his bloodied fingered hand at me. "The actual explanation would fly so far over your head I would have to call air control for clearance."

"Har-de-har-har," I replied and stood back up.

"Well?" he said with an arched eyebrow and leaned on the arm of the chair while resting his cheek on his hand. "Be specific this time."

"Seth, I wish for you to take us back ten minutes before my interview and have us arrive in the waiting room and hide our arrival so we do not cause any commotions or scare people."

He got up from his chair, walked over to me, took my hand in his, snapped his fingers, and said, "As you wish."

Blinding white light flashed and we were both seated in the

waiting room as the light faded away. People in the room blinked their eyes and complained about the sudden flash of light. Better than them to see Seth and me pop out of nowhere. I had no desire to use my last wish of the day for another do-over.

The door to the manager's office opened to let one of the potential candidates leave while the receptionist took notice, shook her head, and glanced down at her clipboard. She called out to the room, "Ms. Sarah Knight?"

"That's me." I bounced out of the chair and up to the front desk. Seth trailed behind me. "I'm Sarah Knight."

The receptionist waved me toward the door as she said, "Good. Mr. Sels is waiting for you."

I walked to door and Seth continued to follow until the receptionist held out her hand to block his way. I stopped and looked over my shoulder. Seth gave the woman a scowl with serious eyes, which promised pain if she didn't let him through.

"Sorry, young man. Why don't you go watch TV while your mom goes on the interview?"

He cut his eyes to me and back to the woman. "You don't have any of the good channels. I hate commercials. Besides, I cannot leave her side."

"Aww," the receptionist said as she held her hands to her chest. "A mama's boy. Aww, how sweet."

I couldn't help but snicker. Seth scowled. "Lady, if there is anything I am not, it is a mama's boy. I am her guardian, so let me through."

The receptionist continued the argument with Seth while I slipped into the office to talk with the manager about the potential job. Their voices raised as I shut the door. I could only pray for the receptionist to not piss Seth off too much or she'd end up with some nasty curse. With Seth, you never knew what he'd do when you angered him. Though because I had some control over him, I did not have to worry, but I still worried.

"Ah," the store manager said. "I presume, Sarah Knight?"

I turned to see the same portly man, bushy mustache, combed over hair to hide a progressing bald spot, in far better health than the last time I saw him. I needed to remember surprises would kill this man. He came out from behind the desk, waddled up to me, and shook my hand.

"Mr. Sels," he said in a baritone voice with a tinge of cheer. Mr. Sels seemed like the type who could pull off a convincing Santa Claus. I couldn't help but imagine him letting out the iconic ho-ho-ho. The mere thought put a smile to my lips, which is what I needed after the earlier attempt at this interview.

I returned the handshake and replied, "Sarah Knight. A pleasure to meet you, sir."

"Likewise." He returned behind the desk and sat down in the expensive leather seat. The sound of leather squeaked under the added weight. Mr. Sels grabbed some of the disarrayed papers on his desk and reshuffled them into a neat stack and glanced up. "You come highly recommended."

"Sir?"

"You friend. A Ms. Dawn, I believe, told me you were on the lookout for an opportunity such as this job." He splayed his hands about the room. "You certainly are lucky to know Ms. Dawn. I would give my life for her."

A niggling poke in the pit of my stomach made me swallow the bile that was rising up my throat. Mary might be nice to others, but me? Never. There had to be a catch to this job, but first I had to find out what this job entailed.

"I'm sorry, sir, but Mary did not tell me what this job was all about. Would you mind telling me the details of what I'm applying for?"

Mr. Sels blinked his eyes rapidly and sputtered. He coughed to regain his composure and leaned forward on the desk with his elbow and arms resting on top. "Ah, yes, no worries. The job you're here about is for a salesclerk position in one of my stores, The Glen, to be more precise. We need the extra hands. I do apologize, the position is nothing glorious like an office desk, but I promise you, if you work hard, you can move up and off the sales floor."

Outside the office door, I heard screaming and a loud crash. I winced. Please don't let the commotion be Seth. Mr. Sels was getting back up to go and investigate when I jumped in front of him and said, "I would love to take the job."

He reached out and pushed me aside. "Well, I have a few more people to interview, Ms. Knight, but I know Mary said you were eager to get this position."

Another loud crash happened outside the door. People were screaming about spiders. Oh, good lord. Mr. Sels was reaching for the door handle when I said, "Mary's right. I can even start this afternoon if you need me."

He stopped and studied me, even though part of him was distracted by the commotion. I pushed a little more. "What do you got to lose?"

"I like your moxie, Ms. Knight." Mr. Sels gave a half smile and reached out with his hand. "You're hired."

As we shook hands, the door burst open and gave us a wide view of the waiting room overrun with spiders and other odd things. It was curious he could do such things without me making a wish. Seth was on the floor laughing his butt off while the receptionist scrambled into the room, her hair frazzled, eyes wide, and hid behind Mr. Sels. She stuttered and pointed at the creepy critters. "Call an exterminator or an exorcist. That child is not normal."

I stood there and threw Seth a look which would have melted flesh. He abruptly stopped laughing and rubbed the back of his head. The little imp. I pointed at him and the room and said, "I wish…"

CHAPTER
TWELVE

AFTER THE WHOLE fiasco in the office upstairs, Mr. Sels magically held off for an hour before we met back up at the store to meet the rest of the staff. I was still puzzling out how Seth did his magic without my wish. And yes, I had to use my last wish for the day to erase everyone's minds of the display of magic. Guess my dream of buying a winning lotto ticket would have to wait another day.

Seth was pouting while we waited downstairs outside the locked doors. The store wasn't due to open until later in the afternoon. The Glen was one of those mid-scale clothing stores catering to the late teens to late twenties type of crowd. And the one thing this store did, that others didn't, was offer late store hours. It opened in the afternoons and closed in the mornings around three A.M.

I was looking at the mannequins in the store display and noticed how the clothing kind of suited my tastes, even though I was pushing forty. Hey, forever twenty-four was my motto. Your mind was as young as it wanted to be and your body was the only one which reminded you, you're old.

We were waiting at the entrance of the store in the mall. White tile lined the walkways with carpeted shoulders for weary shoppers to take a moment to rest. The other stores were open, with several patrons gladly buying wares from them. Seth was leaning up against the wall with a sour face. People had the tendency to walk a little more out of his way, so they were not on the receiving end of whatever temper tantrum he was about to throw.

I moved back to the bench beside him, sat down, canted my head to one side, and said, "Are you still mad I wished to undo your pandemonium upstairs?"

He shoved his hands deep into his pockets and hunched his shoulders more, eyes trained on the tiled flooring. I waved a hand in front of him and said, "Earth to Seth. Are you ignoring me?"

Seth turned away and huffed. So, he was ignoring me. Fine. Time to ask something which would get a response out of him.

"Does someone need a nap?" I asked in the most patronizing tone I could manage, like an owner did to their dog.

Man, the look he threw over his shoulder could have dissolved flesh. Good thing he didn't have that sort of power, or I'd be dead. I rocked the camera in my hand like a person with a treat bag or parent with an enticing toy for their disobedient toddler, while I held the most sarcastic smile plastered on my face.

He turned away and grumbled, "Demons don't sleep."

"Yeah, says the one who constantly says he's busy taking naps when I need his help."

"Piss off."

"Ohhh, someone is cranky."

"Careful. Remember, you gave me permission to do magic if I felt your safety was in danger. Don't make me remove your mouth because I thought you'd get in trouble for saying something stupid."

I tapped the camera. "Seth, in. Now."

With his arms crossed, he stared back and refused to budge. "Here? Right now? Did you forget to feed your hamster again?"

People continued to stream on by us, caught up in their own conversations. Some would look our way and do side conversations, but most of them were oblivious to our presence. I tapped the camera again. "I'm serious. You may have gotten away with being out all the time with Mrs. Smith, but I'm not her. You're cranky and obviously need a rest."

Mr. Sels' booming voice rang out as he held his arms wide like he'd greet a longtime friend. "Sarah, and Seth. So good to see the both of you." He beamed.

I bounced off the bench and greeted him. "The feeling's mutual, sir. I hope you don't mind I brought my nephew along."

"He's your nephew?" Mr. Sels asked.

"Yes." I bobbed my head and placed a hand on Seth's shoulder, who threw me another nasty look like I was going to pay for all this later on tonight.

"Ah, yes, I see." Mr. Sels turned to open the doors to the store. "I thought the young boy was your son, but no matter. My store can handle anything the troublemaker can throw its way."

A wicked grin grew across Seth's lips. I gripped his shoulder harder and bent down to whisper in his ear, "Don't you even dare."

"Spoilsport," he grumbled.

"The rest of the staff will be here momentarily." Mr. Sels carried on and invited us in before he rolled the security gate back down. "For today, you'll train with the day crew to get you up to speed on how to do your job. If you've ever worked at other retail stores, there isn't much difference. However, here at The Glen, we cater to the young crowd with a macabre twist. In the evening, we switch the products over to spooky merchandise. There's a whole dynamic to the setup and you'll get into the groove of things."

I glanced around the store and saw the regular things you'd see in other department stores, so I was curious as to the evening merchandise switch and how they pulled off the swap without closing the store. Not like they had the use of magic to snap their fingers to replace everything all at once. My wandering eyes caught Mr. Sels' attention, and he held his thumbs in his suspenders like a proud farmer getting ready to do his long spiel.

"Ah, I see you're trying to figure out how we make the switch without closing. We do the swap in phases. The customers have become accustomed to change in merchandise throughout the day. They have even been known to stop in from the time we open until we close to see the show. During the day they like to call this store The Glen, but at night they refer to the store as The Graveyard." He splayed his hands about the store. "At first I was appalled by what they were calling my store but as the word spread and more people caught onto the bizarre way

The Glen operated, we more than tripled our sales and gained super fans."

Seth had been wandering through the store and stopped to stare up at a mannequin. His eyes narrowed to slits, head cocked to one side and the next, while he chewed on the insides of his mouth. He moved onto the next one as well and examined the human-like statue.

I motioned at the mannequins and asked, "My nephew seems to be curious about those mannequins. Is there something different about them?"

Mr. Sels followed my gesture and noticed Seth getting closer to them. The man hustled over to where Seth stood, pushed him away, and said, "Easy, son. I don't need you breaking them."

"They're just store dummies," Seth replied. "Why get upset if I break one?"

"Because they're special."

"How?"

"I cannot divulge the answer, for they're a company secret and you do not have the clearance, young man."

Seth gave Mr. Sels a hard stare before he threw up his hand and walked away. "Whatever."

The sound of metal rattling caught all our attention, and we turned our heads to see the other employees trickle in to start their day of work. Two guys and a gal walked over to where we stood and introduced themselves.

"Hi, I'm Mitch," said the tall, slim, dark-skinned, young man with a perfect white smile and he pointed to the short girl who looked like his twin, with her hair in a ponytail and said, "She's Melissa."

"Nice to meet you." Melissa waved.

Mitch landed a hand on the other guy's shoulder and said, "And he's Jeremy."

Jeremy was at least four inches shorter than him, definitely not athletic like Mitch, with stark white skin and raspberry punk hair. The two were like night and day. Mitch had a warm smile where Jeremy's smile sent night crawlers across your skin.

Seth came by my side and glared at each of them before he pulled on my shirt. I bent down to listen to him. He said in a low voice, "I think we should leave. Something doesn't feel right."

Over the past few months after I got Seth, I learned to listen to him when he said things did not add up. Though, usually he had Mary backing him at the same time, so I could not easily say no and continue to plow on through with my choice. But when Seth said something didn't feel right, I took the moment to check my gut.

My stomach did a triple backflip, tied itself into a knot, and sent threats of bile up my throat. The waves were subtle, and one would not sense them if they were not trained to look out for them. I wasn't wearing my best poker face because Melissa asked, "Is there something wrong?"

I stood back up and, with a forced laugh, replied, "Oh no. Nothing's wrong. My nephew was getting bored and wanted to know when we'd leave."

"Ooh, he's your nephew?" Melissa gushed. "He's so cute. I bet all the girls at school practically throw themselves at you, little man."

Seth cut his eyes at her and answered with a slight growl.

"I'm not little. Nor do I attend school for such institutions are a waste of my time and talents."

Mitch asked, "Are you homeschooled?"

"Does where my education comes from truly matter?" Seth replied and arched his eyebrow.

Jeremy got between them and threw his hands up, forcing all of us to look at him. He said, "Guys, we've got to get the store ready and we're already behind schedule. Chop, chop, people."

Melissa and Mitch both looked at each other and said, "Oh shoot. He's right."

The two of them hustled toward the back room to get ready. Jeremy jerked his chin and said, "Hey new girl. You're with me and bring the squirt. He can help set up too, to keep him out of trouble."

Mr. Sels chuckled and said aloud, "Ah, good. Jeremy, please take good care of Sarah Knight, our newest employee. I know she'll get trained in no time with your capable hands."

"Of course, Mr. Sels." He nodded and continued toward the cabinets near the other side of the room. Mr. Sels said his goodbyes while Jeremy gave Seth and me the rundown of how The Glen switched out the merchandise during operating hours.

The entire time, Seth never stopped glaring at the two mysterious mannequins near the front of the store. My fingers itched to take a snapshot of them or to peek through the viewfinder to see what they truly were, but I didn't have time before the store opened and the crowd rushed in like the day after Thanksgiving.

CHAPTER
THIRTEEN

AFTER THE RUSH, the store quieted down enough for all of us to take a breather. Seth had taken to hanging out in the back room while the adults did their things. But in truth, he did not want to be put to work by Jeremy. So, instead he stole my phone to play word games while he waited on my shift to end.

I walked by the mannequins, straightening things up, swapping out the merchandise according to the store schedule when a chill crawled down my spine. I snapped up, whirled around, and stared hard at the suspicious mannequins. They were still in the same positions as they were before, but they definitely had creepy vibes emanating off of them in a big way.

As I lifted my camera to take a peek at them through the viewfinder, Jeremy called my name.

"Hey, Sarah." He tossed his jaw to one side. "Come here."

Um, hello? I'm not a dog. Who did he think he was calling me, like someone's pet golden retriever? Still, I let my camera go, the body swung on the strap around my neck. Mitch and Melissa were curious about my camera earlier, but we never had the chance to talk because we were too busy handling the customers.

"Now," Jeremy said, crossing his arms and tapping his foot on the floor. I hurried over to where he stood, which was another display. He pointed down and asked, "What is this?"

"Um, shirts," I replied and tucked a stray strand of hair behind my ear.

He let out a long sigh, picked up the t-shirts and shoved them into my arms. "I know this is your first day and all, but you're falling behind. These shirts were supposed to have been removed over an hour ago. And if I catch you trying to take selfies in the store again, I will take your camera and put the infernal device under lock and key."

Whoa. Who peed in his cereal? I frowned but kept eye contact with him. No way was I going to be pushed around by this insecure dickhole. I growled, "Touch my camera and die."

"Excuse me?" His eyebrows rose upwards.

"You heard me," I replied. "You lay one finger on this camera and you can kiss your precious life goodbye."

"Are you threatening me?" Jeremy's face turned all shades of red.

I stepped into his bubble, inches from his face, and replied, "You bet your ass I am. Don't fuck with me. I'm not your dog who comes when called or does every inane thing you ask. No. I'm a human being who will kick your ass if you push me too far."

He moved his mouth and pressed his lips into a thin line to the point they turned white. He finally found his voice and said,

"Consider this as strike one, Ms. Knight. I'm writing what you said to me down in your file."

Taking a page from Seth, I replied, "Oooh, not my file… I'm so scared."

Jeremy grabbed more shirts off the display shelves and shoved them at me. "Get back to work, or would you like to go for strike number two?"

I took the shirts and walked a few feet before I looked over my shoulder and replied, "Are you always this up tight? Maybe on your next break you can see about yanking the stick out of your ass and everyone can take a breather."

"That's strike two, Ms. Knight," Jeremy yelled after me. Mitch ran over to him and talked in soothing tones. I heard snatches of the conversation as I put the day clothing away while Mitch got Jeremy to give me another chance and to forget about the strike. I definitely liked Mitch.

In walked a teen girl who was so thin she'd blow away if you breathed on her. Behind her was a big burly guy with muscles upon muscles. The two wore dark clothing and makeup. I couldn't stop staring at the guy because he did not fit my idea of a goth.

Melissa ran up to the big guy and squealed, "Dawg. Glad to see you're here."

"I doubt it. You're only glad because you can leave in about fifteen minutes." The big guy, who apparently was called Dawg, replied.

The bony girl stood next to them, indifferent to their upbeat greetings, and only shrugged her shoulders when Melissa said hello to her. She grabbed the two by their hands and brought them over to where I was rearranging the merchandise on another display shelf.

"Sarah," Melissa said. "I'd like you to meet Dawg and Squeaks."

I dropped the shirts on the table and held out my hand. Dawg grabbed mine and gave a good squeeze and firm shake.

"Nice to meet you, Sarah," Dawg said.

"Likewise," I replied.

I turned to Squeaks and offered my hand. She refused to shake hands and only waved. Well, that was awkward. I still said, "Nice to meet you too, Squeaks."

Squeaks ducked her head and ran off to the back room. I watched her go while Melissa commented, "She's one strange duck. Dawg, you sure you want to keep on working with the weirdo? I swear she's up to something and it stinks."

Dawg rubbed his chin and watched Squeaks as she ducked into the back room and said, "Naw, I can handle small and bony. Ain't much to her, so she's not a threat to me."

Melissa swatted him. "Don't underestimate her because she's small. All of them serial killers are crazy smart and can fell even big guys like you."

"Ohh, I'm shaking in my boots." Dawg laughed and wrapped Melissa in a bear hug. She squealed and pushed away when her brother Mitch came up.

He eyed the two and asked, "You about ready, Sis?"

"Sure am." Melissa bobbed her head and ran to the cashier to grab her purse. As she passed me, she leaned in and said, "Seriously, watch out for Squeaks. I get danger vibes from the girl."

I tucked the strand of hair behind my ear and replied, "Got it. Thanks for the heads up."

Dawg looked between us and asked, "Is Sarah working the night shift tonight?"

Jeremy came up with Seth in tow. Murder was in Jeremy's eyes, and he yanked Seth up in front before he said, "No. She was just leaving with this piece of work."

Seth had the look of the cat who ate the canary, so I could only assume he did something to Jeremy, which was none too pleasant and enough for Jeremy to send us home early. I turned to him and asked, "What did Seth do?"

"Your son—"

"Nephew," I corrected him.

Jeremy gritted his teeth. "Your nephew smeared peanut butter all over my locker and on all my things within the locker. Where in the world he got peanut butter? I have no clue."

Don't laugh. Do not laugh. Okay, the situation was definitely hard not to laugh. A snicker escaped my lips. Oops.

"Not funny," Jeremy snapped. "How about you clean it off since the mess was caused by your brat? Unless you want to pay for the damages."

"Uh, how about a solid no? I'm not being paid to be your maid. Nor do you have proof of my nephew being the culprit," I said right back in his face. Jeremy was rubbing me raw. The laughter which I held at bay fizzled while the ire rose within me. Dawg stepped forward and placed a hand on Jeremy's shoulder.

"Dude, I've got this. Go chill."

Jeremy looked down and shrugged the hand off. "Don't touch me."

"Dude, take a deep breath. I'll handle the store for now."

"Fine." Jeremy turned, stopped, and whirled around to point directly at me. "You, be here early tomorrow to handle the cleanup before we open the store. I expect my locker to be sparkling by the time I get in. Capeesh?"

I rolled my eyes. "Jeremy, get a frigging grip. It's just peanut butter. And no, I'm not going to clean your damn locker. You have no damn proof Seth did the deed."

"If you want to keep your job, you're going to clean my locker. Or I'll ring up Mr. Sels and let him know you were caught stealing."

"Bullshit. He won't believe you."

"What makes you sure he won't, princess? We pull a background check on everyone. Trust me, he will fire you if given good reason."

"You son-of-a-"

He waggled his finger at me and said, "Uh, uh. Tomorrow morning, bright and early. Bring your best scrub brushes, princess."

"Fine." I grabbed Seth's hand and pulled him along with me. Jeremy headed to the back.

Seth called out to the crew, "See ya guys tomorrow."

Mitch, Melissa, and Dawg all waved before we heard Jeremy's high-pitched scream echo out from the back of the store. Seth cackled and we did not stop until we got outside to call for a ride. I most certainly did not want to know what else he did or get blamed for the evil deed.

CHAPTER
FOURTEEN

ANOTHER NIGHT on the cat pee infused sofa did not do wonders for my sleep. Instead, I awoke with puffy eyes because of my slight allergies to our domesticated feline friends. Of course, Seth offered to get rid of my allergies with the lowly cost of a wish. I simply ignored him as I grabbed my coffee and dumped an unhealthy amount of sugar into my cup.

Ivan had wandered into the kitchen about ten minutes after me and took a step back. He gestured at my swollen eyes and asked, "Cats. They bother you?"

"Slight allergy," I replied with a smidge of annoyance in my voice and stirred the sludge, which would send my heart into the running of winning the Kentucky derby.

He grabbed the coffeepot from the burner and poured himself a cup, and took a sip of the black magic brew. How he could handle the strong stuff this early in the morning with no sugar or cream was beyond me. After he placed his cup down with a satisfying sigh, he said, "That does not look like a slight allergy. Maybe we get you another room?"

I sipped my sugar laden coffee and arched an eyebrow. "Will Mary take part in making the decision on which room I get?"

"No." Ivan grinned and took a hearty gulp from his mug. "We need you healthy. Not sick."

"Thanks."

"Least I could do."

We both sat there in companionable silence and watched the sun rise over the horizon from the tall landscape windows in the living room. The kitchen was the open type, so whoever was making the meals would be included in the family fun happening in the living room. A feature I considered to be useful, and I would definitely want in my house when I finally got one of my own.

Other team members of Wings of Virtue trickled in to make their own breakfasts before they headed off to their normal day jobs. For anyone to be doing work for the organization full time was rare. Unlike the supernatural mafia, Wings of Virtue was a nonprofit organization and relied on donations to keep things afloat. Much like a church in some regard but less pushy when recruiting new members... most of the time.

"So, job," Ivan began. "Is good?"

"Somewhat," I replied while I sat hunched at the kitchen counter and my hands hugged my coffee cup for warmth. "Most of the people seem nice. Except the associate manager."

"There is always one." Ivan chuckled. "No job is without difficult people."

"Very true," I said and took a sip of coffee. The contents had cooled a bit, so I grabbed the pot to add more to my cup. "Today is day two and I'm kind of worried about going back in…"

"Seth?" Ivan asked in a knowing way.

I breathed out an exaggerated sigh. "Yeah, Seth. He did something and I was too chicken to find out. We hightailed out of the store before the associate manager had a chance to fire me."

Seth shuffled into the kitchen. His hair all askew like he slept hard, but I knew better because demons didn't sleep. Instead, I asked in a rather loud voice. "Hey sleeping beauty. How many shows did you binge on last night?"

Seth flipped the bird in my general direction as he snagged the coffeepot from the burner and took a huge swig right from the pot. Ugh, gross.

Ivan cleared his throat and said, "Use a mug. We are civilized under this roof, demon."

Again, Seth flipped the bird at Ivan and drank the entire contents of the coffeepot before he put the carafe back down and shuffled back down the hallway. I called after him, "Hey, you're supposed to refill the pot if you take the last cup."

With his signature move, Seth waved his lone middle finger back at me while he continued to shuffle down the hall to the room he holed up in to watch his shows. The djinn was one-hundred percent a premium and movie channel junkie. Nothing got between him and his shows unless there was a quote unquote internet issue interrupting the stream.

Ivan continued our conversation. "I would not worry about the associate manager. Keep doing your work. Mary will make sure you keep the job."

"Mary? Our Mary?" I asked, cleaning out my ear with my

finger and giving my ear a whack for good measure. "Are you sure you're talking about the same Mary we both know?"

A deep basso laugh rumbled from Ivan's chest, and he placed his hand on mine. "Yes, the same. She has a good heart and means well. We both feel this job will be good for you."

Suspicion bells rang all around and I felt the camera send trills right up through my nerves. I narrowed my eyes to small slits and asked, "This job isn't a ruse for something else, is it?"

Ivan worked his mouth and said, "No. It's no such thing. This job is not a Wings of Virtue mission. You've sworn those off. We'll respect your decisions."

"Um, Ivan, do I need to remind you it isn't my decision? Remember, Michael?"

"No, it is still your decision."

Uh, huh, and I'm Peter Rabbit. If Ivan had set me up with this job, I would trust what he was saying, but with Mary? Mary was entirely different, and my gut told me through several flippety-flops there was a fifty-fifty chance this was a Wings of Virtue mission. Or else why would she fight so hard for me to have this job?

Seth came back into the kitchen and threw something at me. The object thwacked into my face, and I realized I held a t-shirt. I looked at the shirt as my brows creased upwards.

"Go get changed. You got to get to work in like an hour or so, unless you want to be late," Seth said with exasperation, like a mother telling her child to clean their room over and over again, only to be ignored once more.

Ivan looked between us. "You're not using your wish to travel, are you?"

"That was the plan," I replied. "One wish to get there, one wish to get back, providing some imp doesn't make me use them up because of his foul play."

"No." Ivan waved his hand. "I will drive. Go get ready and I will take you. I want to see this place where you work. Seems interesting."

Seth glowered in the doorway with his arms crossed across his chest. "You better hustle Sarah. Remember, Betsy takes longer. So, you got five minutes."

Crap. He's right. I downed the rest of my coffee and headed off to my room to get ready. Seth stayed in the kitchen with Ivan, and I heard small bits of their conversation before I turned the corner. Details involving spiders left behind for Jeremy made me grimace and sent shivers up my spine. Today's shift was going to be oh so fun… not.

CHAPTER
FIFTEEN

THE FOOD COURT in the mall was more crowded than usual. But again, today was a Saturday and most people chose to loiter at the mall when they had nothing better to do. I made my way, balancing my tray overloaded with drinks and tacos, through the overpopulated seating area. Seth sat far away from where we ordered food, and I bypassed several open tables. Why, in the living hells, did he choose a table that far?

A grin plastered over his face while I nearly avoided teens who popped up from their tables without looking and I slammed into a woman who was dealing with a fussy child. The drinks tumbled from the tray and splashed all over the woman, followed by my tacos. Her head whipped up and threw the most searing stare one could imagine. Several tables away, Seth fell over, laughing. The little stink.

I stood there with my mouth held open before I found my tongue and said, "Um, sorry?"

The woman stood up and towered over me. Not just her height, which scared the bejesus out of me, but her bulk as well. She was not someone you wanted to mess with and here I just dumped soda and tacos all over her. On top of all things, she had already become irritated by dealing with her fussy kid.

Her lips were pressed into firm lines, the corners pulled downwards, and her eyes narrowed to slits. A low rumble emanated from her chest before she replied, "Sorry? You're sorry? No, you're not sorry. If you were sorry, you'd be offering to pay for my cleaning bill or buying me new clothes instead of gibbering some half-ass apology."

She bent down to get into my face, mere inches, before she growled. "No, you are definitely not sorry. But if I were you, I'd start coughing up some dough or something to make this right. Now."

The bottom fell out and my stomach followed. Under this woman's death glare, I felt small and helpless. I merely stared back, doing an impression of a deer caught in the headlights, before I felt the tug on my shirt.

With a glance, I saw Seth standing off to the side. A smirk still present on his lips. The ass was still enjoying every bit of this situation he, no doubt, architected. He pressed the camera into my palms.

"Either this or pay up."

Oh, good god, no. I couldn't. What Seth was suggesting was something I couldn't do, especially in the food court with witnesses. My eyes wandered and landed on the kid, who still watched all the events unfold right in front of them.

"I highly doubt a picture of me is going to make things up, young man," the woman sneered.

"She's right," I said and put the strap of the camera back on. The familiar weight brought some sense of control back into the situation. I glanced back at the woman and reached back into my fanny pack to grab my wallet and pulled the anemic leather fold out. The billfold unfolded and I reached in and grabbed three crisp twenty dollar bills out of the money Ivan kindly loaned me, handing them over to the woman.

She snatched them out of my hands, counting them, and said, "Sixty isn't enough. I need more."

"Um, sixty should be plenty," I argued right back. Where was the security officer for the food court? The woman's hand jutted in front and motioned a gimme hand sign. I sighed. Either this, or be pummeled, or snatch her life force. Seth leaned toward the life force solution, but I could not be that cruel, especially with a kid watching.

I reached back into my wallet and took out the last two twenties and handed them over. The interior of my billfold never looked so empty in a long time. The drink and taco infused bully took the money, yanked on her fussy child, and left the food court. Meanwhile, my stomach grumbled, reminding me I still needed to eat lunch. But with no money, I was out of luck.

"Come on," I said, moving on through the crowd without even checking to see if Seth was following. Lunch wasn't happening now since I didn't have any money. Seth caught up and offered his opinion. "You know you would still have money if you simply took her photo."

"She had a kid with her."

"You would have been doing them a favor."

I stopped.

He bumped into me.

"That's ruthless and downright evil," I said.

"Uh, hello? Demon here."

Right. Demon. One-hundred percent pure evil. They would do heinous things if you let them free to do so and they didn't care who got hurt or killed in the process.

"Hey Sarah," a guy called. I turned to see Nathan wave his arms. He loped over to where we were standing and gave me a hug. "Fancy seeing you here."

"Same," I replied and tucked a strand of hair behind my ear. "I'm about to head back… unless you'd like to buy me lunch."

Seth said under his breath, "Smooth."

Nathan chuckled. "Ah, yeah, I saw you earlier with a woman and how she practically bullied you for money. So, you need food, yeah?"

"Please," I begged. My stomach added groans and gurgles to further the point. Nathan laughed and dragged us back to the taco hut where he got us more drinks and oodles of tacos. I followed him over to an open table where we sat, and he divvied out the food.

Seth snagged the big drink and started sucking the soda dry, while I scarfed down three to four tacos before I said another word. Nathan merely sat there and watched Seth and me devour the offerings on the plastic tray like we hadn't eaten in weeks.

"So, Seth, you never told me if you're like a cousin or nephew… or…" Nathan began.

"Or Sarah's love child from a relationship gone wrong?" Seth offered.

I nearly choked on the taco's hard shell, slammed a fist against my chest several times to dislodge the dastardly death particle, and started coughing. My hands slapping the surface of the tabletop with each shuddering breath. I grabbed a drink to wash down the hard bits; the soda adding the necessary lubrication for my parched throat.

"Sarah?" Nathan asked, his brows rose together. "You okay?"

Clearing my throat, I replied, "I'm okay. Taco shell down the wrong pipe."

"Alright. Maybe slow down?"

"Yeah." I took another swig of soda.

Nathan licked his lips, leaned in closer, and said, "Uh, so, is Seth your son?"

Again, I nearly choked as soda went down the wrong pipe. Seth fell out of his chair, rolled on the floor, laughing his butt off while I fought for air. I gasped, "Gods, no."

The rest of my lunch hour was spent spinning a darn good yarn about why my nephew lived with me. The fates decided to throw another curveball my way when I heard my name uttered by another older male.

I turned to find my eldest brother standing there in a mall cop uniform, with a sour expression, like he sucked on a dozen lemons for the past hour. Nathan looked between us, at Seth, back at me, and then at my brother. The yarn I spun. Consider the tale now royally screwed.

CHAPTER
SIXTEEN

NEVER DID I ever expect to see any of my family in the town of New London. Especially my eldest brother, Jacob, who went by the name of Jake, standing across from our table in the food court with the most lemon puckered expression on his face. His long legs ate up the distance that yawned between us and snatched me up in a hug.

Um, not what I expected, but okay. I tentatively returned the hug because you can't just receive a hug and not return one back. Which would be weird. After several long minutes of my brother dishing out awkward hugs, I patted him to signal I needed air.

We both broke apart as he held me at arm's length, his eyes searching me from head to toe, and said, "Where in the seven hells have you been?"

"Away," I said through clenched teeth. He and I had never been on the same page when I decided to drop out of college and run off with my ex-husband, Walter. Hey, the loot the supernatural underground mafia offered was hardly irresistible. No one in their right mind would be able to say no to a pile of gold or the other expensive treasures the supernatural mafia used to lure in unsuspecting recruits. Well, maybe Ivan, but I doubted he would count.

"Sarah." Jake squeezed my upper arms, patted them, and let his hands drop to his sides. "Ma, was worried. You never called to tell us you were fine. One day you were in college and poof, the next day you were gone. If not for Debbie, we would have assumed the worse."

Gah, Debbie. I totally forgot about her. Of course, she would not have kept her jibber jabbering mouth shut. I narrowed my eyes and asked, "What did she tell you?"

"What did she not?" Jake's voice rose an octave. "If she didn't tell us you ran off with the idiot Walter, Da would have sent his ex-military friends after your butt. However, since Ma knew Walter's family was loaded, she was fine. Never mind, Da and I were absolutely against you going with the creep. But Ma said you'd be happy with a guy who made sure you'd never have to work a single day in your life."

Part of me cringed at the thought. Ma was totally okay with her daughter being a gold digger. I barely swallowed the hard lump down before Jake continued, "I thought I'd never see you again. Imagine my surprise to see you here, in this mall, working… and spinning lies."

Uh, how much of my story did he overhear? Nathan wore a frown, sat off to my side and watched the interaction between my brother and me play out. Seth propped his chin up on his hands, delight dancing in his amber gold eyes, and waited.

"Err, right." I massaged the back of my neck to ease some of the tension. "Well, surprise. Walter and I split up about two months ago… and I landed here to get a fresh start."

"I see." Jake crossed his arms. "Are you going to introduce me to your new friends?"

"Uh, yeah, sure." I waved at Nathan. "This is Nathan. He and I have only recently met. Nathan, this is my eldest brother, Jake."

"The same one who dumped your nephew on you?" Nathan asked. Jake grimaced and glared daggers at him.

Oops. I ducked. The corners of Seth's mouth pulled tighter, revealing a grin which would outdo even the Cheshire Cat.

Jake's eyes cut over to Seth, who was still seated and grinning from ear to ear. "Mind telling us who the kid truly is?"

Eep.

"Is he yours and Walters?" Jake added on, his arms uncrossed so he could rake a hand through his short blonde hair. "I'm shocked. Well, not really shocked, you never told us. You always liked keeping your family in the dark about monumental things which happened in your life."

Okay, time to stop this train of thought right here and now before everyone started calling Seth my son and thinking I had a kid with Walter. I held up my hand in the universal sign for stop in front of Jake and said, "No. Just stop right there."

"Then who is he?" Jake gestured back at Seth, who continued to grin like a maniac.

"Seth is not mine. Okay? I found him," I explained, pulling at various straws to make this a plausible story since the *'he's my nephew'* story fell flat on its face. "The kid was digging through the trash at my last job and looked half starved. So, I took him in."

"Sarah," Jake and Nathan chided me.

Nathan continued, "You should have taken him to child services. You're not qualified to look after him. He needs help."

Seth threw a broken piece of the hard shell from his taco at Nathan. Sour cream flecked onto Nathan's round glasses as the hard shell bounced off his cheek. He grabbed a napkin and wiped the sour cream off his face and glasses. "Seriously, you need to take him to child services. If you don't, you'll get into trouble."

I flapped my hand at him. "No, worries. Wings of Virtue signed off on letting him stay with me."

"Wings of Virtue?" Jake said each word slowly. "That vigilante group which was responsible for the mess downtown two months ago? The same one which was nearly bankrupted due to all the lawsuits? That group?"

Lawsuits? Ivan never mentioned the lawsuits to me. Probably another reason why Mary was super angry with me.

"Uh, yeah," I replied. "The very same. And they're not a vigilante group. They're a nonprofit organization dedicated to helping those in need. I, in fact, was one of those people they helped."

Jake stood there with a frown. Nathan mirrored the same expression. I stepped over to Seth and patted his head. "Now, I'm returning the favor."

"I'm not a dog," Seth informed in a low tone which spoke of danger if I did not stop patting him.

I didn't like the spotlight Nathan and Jake were giving me.,

My eyes darting around the area for a way to break free when I spotted the clock. I pointed at the clock face and announced, "Well, would you look at the time? My breaks almost over. Seth and I got to get back."

"Oh, I see," Nathan said, the tension in his shoulders dissipating as he rolled them both and worked his neck back and forth. He stood up, gave me a hug and a kiss on the head. "Stay safe and stop telling lies, okay?"

"Okay."

Nathan let go and rubbed Seth's head before he asked, "Hey, did you need a ride later?"

"Sure, if it's not too much of a problem."

"None at all. I like spending time with you and, yes, even Seth."

"Cool. I'll give you a call when I'm about to get off work."

"Sounds good." He walked over to Jake, extended his hand and said, "Nice to meet you, Jake. Hope to see you sometime later."

"Sure." Jake smiled and shook Nathan's hand. "Nice to meet you too, Nathan. See you around."

Nathan walked off and disappeared into the crowd. Jake still hung around. He appeared like he still had more to say, but the whole situation was getting awkward.

Seth cleared his throat. "You know, if we do not start back now, you're going to be late getting back."

Jake latched onto the conversation starter. "Come on. I'll walk you both back. Sarah, you can catch me up while we walk. But first off, which store are you working at?"

I snatched up my purse and the camera and started walking. I slouched and shoved my hands into my pant pockets while we walked. Seth in front of us, leading the way.

"Oh, I'm working at the new trendy store, The Glen," I said. "Why?"

My eldest brother stopped, his shoes loudly squealing to a halt on the mall tiled floor, eyes nearly ready to pop from their sockets, and only air escaped his mouth in a high-pitched keen.

Seth stopped too. He cocked his head slightly and asked, "Is there something wrong, officer?"

CHAPTER
SEVENTEEN

"THE GLEN?" Jake said. "You're working at, The Glen?"

"Yeah. So?" I asked.

He reached for my hand and pulled me back to where he stood. "You need to quit."

"No."

"I'm serious, Sarah. You need to quit... or something bad will happen."

I tucked a loose strand of hair behind my ear and frowned. "Why and what will happen if I don't?"

Jake glanced around the area. People turning their heads, gawking, pointing, or whispering as they walked on by. More than likely, they thought my brother had apprehended a criminal who was caught stealing. Which, of course, was far from the truth.

He leaned in and whispered, "There are rumors and reasons why the place is called the graveyard at night."

"Because of the goths?" My eyebrows quirked upwards. "And the macabre merchandise?"

Jake shook his head and let go of my hand. "No. Not because of the customers or what the store sells, but what has happened recently in the store in the past month."

"Which is?"

"Dead bodies."

I shoved his shoulder. "Get out. For real?"

He nodded. "Yes, really."

Seth interjected, "Dead bodies, you say? Like how they were found?"

Jake paused, his eyes darting down to where Seth stood looking up between us, and replied, "Um, I can't go into details, bud. But maybe you can help me convince my sister she should find another place of employment?"

With a wrinkled nose, Seth replied, "Oh, you don't want to spill the gory details."

"Well, you're young and you don't need to be hearing about such things."

"Try me," Seth said, crossing his arms across his chest.

"No, kid. You're too young."

Ha. If Jake only knew Seth had years on all of us. He may look seven, but he was most certainly not seven. Perhaps his attitude did match his appearance but, his brain was packed full of centuries of knowledge.

"Sissy," Seth said. "I bet you don't even know how they died."

"I do too," Jake retorted. "They were found beheaded."

"Really?" Seth's eyes lit up like fireworks at a big celebration.

Jake clamped his mouth shut to prevent further details from slipping. His lips pressed so hard together they turned white.

I placed a hand on my brother's shoulder and told him, "Look, I can't just quit. I need this job so I can get a place of my own."

Jake tilted his head and replied, "You can move in with me. We have a spare bedroom. Rebecca won't mind and Amelia would be delighted to have her aunt stay with us."

Eep. Not that I didn't love my brother, but the housing situation he offered sounded like a disaster waiting to happen. I kept a calm face, trying my best to not show wariness, and said, "Thanks, Jake, but no. I don't want to intrude and, honestly, I really need my own space."

"I'm serious, Sarah. You can totally come stay with me until you get another job. I don't want to lose you again." He stepped forward and embraced me in a bear hug. I struggled to breathe.

"Sarah," Melissa yelled as she ran toward us. My co-worker stopped, bent over, hands on knees to catch her breath. She inhaled another deep breath and exhaled. Her eyes were wet and wide. "We need you back, pronto."

I pushed my brother away. "What happened?"

"Dawg got hurt." Melissa's voice shuddered, tears brimming in her eyes, threatening to fall at any minute. She really cared for the guy.

"How?"

"He was working on the mannequins when he got cut, bad," she said between stifled sobs. "He's gonna need stitches and I need you to come back so I can go to the hospital with him."

"Uh," I replied. "Okay?"

Melissa grabbed my hand and started pulling me toward the store. Jake's eyes were dark, his mouth in a firm line. Seth had already gone ahead of us. He paused momentarily to see if we were following.

I waved at Jake. "See ya later, Jake. As you can see, I've gotta go. Bye."

Melissa jogged in front, and I scrambled to follow. Jake called after us, "Both of you should quit before you get hurt too... or worse."

"Love you, too, Jake," I replied while jogging backwards, turned back around, and picked up the pace. I didn't have time to deal with my overly paranoid brother. Dawg needed to get to the hospital, and Melissa wanted to be there with him.

We hustled through the front where an agitated Jeremy waited, with crossed arms, feet tapping, and the look of two weeks' worth of constipation on his face. He yelled, "Where were you? You're over an hour late coming back from lunch. I should give you a strike for being late."

Melissa stepped up to him and got right in his face. "Chill, Jeremy. Today's only her second day and no one mentioned we only get thirty minutes for lunch. So, cut her some slack, dude."

His mouth flapped open and closed like a fish. Melissa tapped his bottom jaw lightly to reset his mouth. Jeremy glowered at the both of us, did an about face, and headed toward the back. I glanced around the store. The late afternoon merchandise was being phased in and customers hung around waiting for other merchandise to switch out. Mitch was at the register handling customers, but Dawg was nowhere to be found.

"Where's Dawg?" I asked. "I thought you said he was hurt?"

"He was," Melissa said. "The emergency response team was already here and got him off to the hospital."

"Wait. I thought you wanted to go with him."

"I do. But I can't leave Mitch to manage the store by himself. Which is why I needed you back here… to help Mitch."

"Oh."

Melissa went over to the registers and snagged her purse out from behind the counter, hefted the strap to the bag onto her shoulders, waggled her fingers at us, and said, "Bye."

I watched her glide out of the store faster than she normally walked. Potentially eager to get to her dear friend's side at the hospital. She passed by the front windows and was full on running. Seth stood near the front over by the mannequins which laid on the floor unfinished. He paid no mind the area had been taped off. In the thick of the scene, he bent down and peered at the puddle of blood which needed to be mopped up.

Wheels of the store mop bucket squeaked behind me and got closer. Jeremy's stuffy nose whistled, because of crusted boogers, announced his presence before I saw him. I turned, and he shoved an old mop in my hands, and said, "Get mopping and afterward I want you to clean every surface. Maybe a little hard work will teach you for being late."

"Sure." I took the squeaky wheeled bucket and mop over to where Seth stood, removed the ridiculous tape cordoning the area off and got to cleaning. As long as I was working on something, mister stick-up-his-ass kept off of mine.

The amount of blood which covered the floor was alarming. I highly doubted Dawg had a mere slice. This looked serious. The mannequins were on the floor with clothing partially on them.

One mannequin laid in pieces but had blood smeared against its lips. A primal urge to flee from this spot kept on making my skin erupt in goosebumps.

I adjusted the mop; the pole leaning against my shoulder so I could take a peek at the area with my camera. Seth kept silent, but his eyes were on Jeremy. Flipping the switch so the camera was turned on, I lifted the viewfinder up to my eyes to see if I could uncover the mystery of these mannequins.

Seth stepped over to me, elbowed me in the side before I heard Jeremy screech.

"Just what are you doing?" Jeremy said in a loud voice. All the customers in the store stopped and looked my way. I let the camera go to dangle on the lanyard.

"Cleaning this mess up," I replied.

Jeremy huffed and puffed his cheeks while he fast walked over to where Seth and I stood. He pointed at my camera and back at me. "No, you weren't. You were taking pictures again. Which is against store policy. No social media."

Seth snarked. "Dude, you need your eyes checked. The camera is so old, the piece of junk was born before the internet."

"I don't care." Jeremy sliced the air with his hand. "No pictures. Sarah, you will need to put your camera away while you're on duty."

"No," I said and jutted my jaw out in a stubborn fashion. "And you can't make me."

"How about, put the camera away or you're fired," Jeremy retorted with a face smacking smirk.

"No," I said again, and added, "You can't fire me because

you're short staffed. Fire me and you'll have Mr. Sels to answer to… do you want to tell him you fired me over a stupid picture?"

Jeremy stood there for a moment, his jaw working back and forth, grinding his teeth, breathing hard through his blocked nasal passages. "Fine. But no more pictures. I mean it. And clean this mess up. Now."

He walked away when I mumbled under my breath, "Of course, your royal whininess."

"What did you call me?" Jeremy whirled back and stabbed a finger in my direction.

I shrugged. "Nothing."

"That's what I thought." He readjusted his collar and walked to the back of the store to do whatever he did back there. I blew out a sigh of relief when he was out of sight. Seth kept an eye on Jeremy before he said, "Take a look now while he's in the back."

I nodded and brought the camera's viewfinder up so I could look through to see the area. The blood and mannequins gave faint traces of magic, but nothing jumped out. I let the camera dangle once more when I told Seth, "This area gives me the heebie jeebies, but the camera isn't showing anything."

"Figures." Seth sighed. "You know, seems like every time you try to investigate this area while Mr. Sels or Jeremy are around, they stop you. Like they know something. My demon sight sees something, but the signature is so faint. Almost like there is a dimensional portal around this area."

I did a double take. "A portal?"

"Yeah," Seth said and frowned. He kicked the bucket and motioned to the back, where Jeremy emerged. I got to mopping up the area and acted busy. No sense in attracting mister stick-up-the-ass over here.

I whispered, "Do you think we should tell Ivan?"

"No." Seth narrowed his eyes. "Not yet."

I chewed on the side of my cheek while vigorously scrubbing the dried blood off the floor. "You know, I have a hunch Mary knew about this."

"No, not a hunch. You and I both know she knew," Seth corrected me, his golden fiery eyes shining brightly in the LED lighting of the store. "And tonight we're going to get her to confess."

CHAPTER
EIGHTEEN

"WHATEVER YOU GOONIES are looking to get outta of me, you ain't gettin nuthin." Mary sat on the blue microfiber couch, face scrunched up into a pout like frown, with her arms and legs crossed, leaning as far back as she could possibly lean into the thick cushions. Her feet dangled strappy sandals from the toes, which she could easily use as a weapon if push came to shove. Mary's amber eyes darted between Seth and I as we sat on either side of her, blocking any potential escape route.

Seth leaned forward onto his arms and hands to push his point. "We'll sit here for as long as it takes until you fess up to why you sent Sarah on a mission."

"I did no such thing." Mary's eyes still searched for other means of escape.

"Did too."

"Hey, Blondie, don't you owe me a wish or two?" Mary turned her head my way. The muscles in her jaw flexed.

I snuck a glance at Seth, who shook his head. "No, I don't. Besides, I already used today's quota."

"On what?" Mary demanded. "More lazy requests for refilling your bowl with cereal?"

"Hey," I protested. "I'll have you know cereal is a wonderful snack and a great go-to meal. There's no shame in asking for more."

"Getting off topic here." Seth crawled onto the cushion of the couch and crept closer to Mary. "Did you, or did you not send Sarah on a mission?"

"Yes, alright." Mary's mouth puckered into a scowl. "I've been casing Mr. Sels' stores at the mall for a while. There'd been stories goin' on 'bout people who worked the night shift gone missing. Not to mention the mannequins always getting swapped out. The place reeked of supernatural shenanigans, though I could never catch what was truly goin on. Mr. Sels and his goons are sneaky sons-of-guns. But, before I was about to give up, here comes Blondie, who I knew would blow this case wide open because she had perchance of attracting trouble like ants at a picnic.

My jaw hung wide open. No words came to mind at her confession.

Seth looked back over his shoulder at me. "She does have a point about you attracting trouble."

"Shut up." I swatted him and denied the very truth of the matter. "I do not attract trouble."

"Are you sure?" both Mary and Seth asked in unison.

My hands rose in a placating manner. I said, "Fine. You're both right. Happy?"

Mary's eyebrow quirked upwards, weaving her head side-to-side and hummed. "Mmm-hmm. And that's why I sent you on a mission, Blondie, because you attract all kinds of trouble."

"Well, how can I trust you now, Mary? Sending me on a mission with no info, which is stupid, by the way, and could have gotten me killed. Aren't you supposed to be helping me?"

"Shit." Mary spat. "Why da hell do you care? You've always been reckless, and I figured since here mooching off our kindness—"

"Oh, you mean like you putting me and Seth in the room with the cat-whizzed infused sofa. How fucking kind of you."

"Hey, there's a cardboard box in the back. You can go sleep there if the sofa is too good for your sorry ass. At least I keep my promises and don't leave my friends hanging."

"Nah-uh, no. You cannot throw me leaving the organization back in my face," I shouted back at Mary, arms going wide. I leapt to my feet and paced the room. "You of all people know I had no control over what the supernatural mafia did."

Mary showed her clenched teeth. "That may be true, but you could have at least stayed."

"Not wanting to put you guys back in their sights was the main reason why I left."

"Fuck. You're here now." Mary gestured about the room. "With another shit pile, I might add, and want *us* to clean the mess up for you."

"No." I stomped over to the couch, got up in her face, mere inches, enough to smell the spearmint wafting from her mouth. "I'm here because I have nowhere else to go. Give me another week and I'll be gone… and the troubles should follow… or so according to you they should."

"Blondie, you're so full of shit, you reek. I know you're here to get Ivan and me to clean up whatever tangle you're in and you're just chicken about the accidents at the store as and don't wanna find out the truth."

My hands shot out before I could stop them. They made contact with Mary's shoulders and pushed her so hard the couch flipped over. Time slowed, her eyes went wide, Seth yelled something, the couch progressed upwards and over until bam.

Mary and the couch landed on the floor with a thud. She cried out with a yelp when her head smacked on the hardwood floor. I peeked over the overthrown couch to see her reach behind her head to pull away with blood.

"Oh, hell, no," Mary mumbled right before she fainted. Crap.

Seth was already running down the hallway yelling, "Ivan!"

We were only trying to find out if Mary set us up, and we did. Never was the interrogation supposed to end in violence. She'll never forgive me for this because if anyone could hold a grudge, it was Mary.

CHAPTER
NINETEEN

MARY ONLY NEEDED to have five stitches, but stitches, nonetheless. Ivan was super disappointed in all of us for resorting to violence during our argument. So, we bunked down in the bedroom with the stinky sofa until morning and snuck out of the house before Ivan or Mary got up. I did not want to face either of them. Not after our fight.

Mary was right. I did attract trouble like a super magnet. Raking my hands through my hair, I shook my head. They'd be way better off the sooner I got enough funds for my own place. Also, the faster I was out of their hair, the less likely Michael was going to smite Ivan and me for disobeying his orders.

Seth and I were hoofing our trek to the mall. The entire time, he was at my side with a sour look. Either he didn't like us walking or he was displeased we were also hitchhiking.

"You know, you could just wish yourself to work." He kicked a rock further down the road.

"And scare the daylights out of my fellow co-workers? No, thank you."

"Maybe the scare will get Jeremy to talk."

"More like a heart attack, and dead men tell no tales."

"That depends."

"Depends, how?" I asked, knowing better than to discount anything the demon said. Sometimes he told the truth, but you just had to know where to look or how to decipher his messages.

"Your camera." He gestured at it dangling from the strap around my neck. The dormant magic and hunger hummed within the case, waiting to be unleashed to devour unsuspecting souls for their life force. "The camera can see and talk to spirits."

I stopped.

Seth walked on ahead and called back, "You still have to get to work. Standing there won't get you there."

Jogging up to him, I said, "You're lying. The camera only eats life forces, reveals the true nature of things, and of course supposedly controls demons. So, now, you're saying the camera can talk and see spirits?"

"Of course, dumb-dumb." Seth took longer strides. For a djinn in the shape of a seven-year-old boy's body, he was abnormally faster than me. I ran to smack the backside of his head for his snide comment.

Rubbing the back of his head, he threw me a dirty look. "Hitting people because they told you the truth isn't socially acceptable. Now, apologize."

"Why on earth, you chose to use the form of a young boy is beyond me. Your vocabulary does not match one." I sighed and ignored his demands for apologies. We both continued our walk down the tall dry grassy shoulder of the road, avoiding trash thrown from speeding vehicles, like discarded cups, fast-food paper bags and more. There was even a bevy of dirty diapers strewn over one section. We both had to hold our noses and run fast to avoid gagging.

Seth cleared his nose and wiped the excess on my jeans. I jumped to the side. "Ewww."

"There. Young enough for you?" he teased.

"Yes." I grabbed leaves to help wipe the boogers off my jeans. "That was perfect behavior for a seven-year-old."

"Good." Seth held his head high and strutted.

"So, why seven? Why not take on the hot bod you had almost three months ago?"

"People let their guard down around children." He cut his eyes toward me. "And you don't deserve my smolten bod. Not after you bound me against my will."

I shoved him. "Get over yourself."

"Only if you release me." He glowered. "And stop shoving people. You got into trouble for pushing people around last night, remember?"

"Don't remind me." I frowned. The hum of tires droned behind us, and I stuck out my thumb, walking backwards, and plastering on a false smile.

The car slowed down, saw both of us, and sped off. I shouted after them, "Jerks!"

"Have you learned nothing?" Seth shook his head. "That's part of why you attract trouble."

"What are you talking about?" I said and placed my fists on my hips. "Calling people jerks is not why I get into trouble."

"No." Seth gestured to all of me. "But this does."

"You gestured to all of me," I replied, eyebrows rising. "Are you saying I'm entirely the reason why trouble follows me around?"

"Well, aren't you?" he asked, eyebrow arched upwards, kicking another rock down the road. "Since I've known you for these past few months, it's been disaster after disaster. I'm not even going to go into the whole gremlin issue at your last apartment."

"There were gremlins there?"

"Oh, right, I forgot you're not too bright." He sighed and rolled his eyes. "Yes, there were gremlins in the last apartment. How the hell did you think the camera was satisfied for so long?"

"Uh, those were cockroaches, dude." I dragged my hands through my hair again. I should have put my hair up in a bun or ponytail to keep stubborn strands out of my face. Seriously, I needed a haircut, but I needed money for such luxury and I wasn't trusting no one with scissors near my hair over at Wings of Virtue.

Seth cocked his head to one side. "Those weren't cockroaches."

"Yeah, they were. I'm pretty sure I know what cockroaches look like." I splayed my hands. "And the dump was a full on cockroach motel."

"No, those were gremlins parading around as cockroaches. Did you or did you not look at them through the viewfinder with the camera?"

"Uhh." I paused. "No, I never did. I saw the vermin, pointed the camera at them, and took the shot."

Seth slapped his forehead, stumbled backwards, and shouted, "Hades, you're such a moron sometimes!"

"So what if I didn't look through the viewfinder first before I took pictures? What's the big deal?"

Seth let out a pained sigh.

"I should take the camera from you and let the cursed thing eat your soul," he grumped. "You should never, ever, take a shot with the camera without looking through the viewfinder first. Otherwise, you might take a snapshot of something which won't take kindly being captured or having its entire life essence stolen."

Cold rushed through me. I gripped the camera to feel its reassuring pulse, but the warmth did not stop my teeth from chattering. I turned to watch Seth, who strode by my side while we walked.

"Are you telling me, Seth, this camera doesn't kill the entire being with one snapshot?"

"Yes, it's exactly what I'm telling you. Did you put your hamster into overtime to finally connect the dots?"

I rolled my eyes and let out a long, exasperated groan. "No, my hamster is fine. But that piece of information would have been useful. Why didn't Mrs. Smith tell me?"

"She's a dragon. She probably hoped you would have tried to capture something which wouldn't take kindly to you trying to steal their life force and thus die by their hands. You know Mrs. Smith wants the camera back, bad."

"Right. Okay, from now on, I'll look before I take a snapshot."

Seth bobbed his head. "Thanks. It's all I ask. I have no inclination to becoming Mrs. Smith's slave anytime soon, again."

We walked further down the road, both of us in silence, when something occurred to me. We never finished talking about the camera's ability to talk to ghosts. I cleared my throat, tucking hair behind my ear, and asked, "So, the camera can really talk to the dead?"

"Yes," Seth replied. "And we're going to use the camera tonight to get to the bottom of these mysterious accidents."

CHAPTER
TWENTY

NO, we did not walk the entire way to the mall. I gave up halfway and wished our butts to the parking lot, close to the trees, so we did not scare any unsuspecting normal people who didn't know magic, is in fact real. Jeremy was in a colorful mood today, sniping at Melissa, Mitch, and myself for putting the wrong product out on the shelves. Mr. Sels made an appearance earlier to check in on his staff before hightailing out of there when questions were asked.

If you asked me, I believe Mr. Sels and Jeremy were in cahoots. I wouldn't doubt if the two were behind the troubles the store was having with their employees. Why would anyone suddenly get hurt swapping out the clothes on mannequins? Or worse, die from doing anything with those mannequins. Not to mention Jeremy being super huffy puffy about me trying to take pictures of two mannequins. Did he suspect my camera having superpowers?

Mitch and Melissa were hanging out at the cashier counter talking when I came up. Seth was busy playing in the clothes rack and chose not to take part in my chores at work. Instead, he made my work harder tonight by making messes. I placed the bundle of dark sweaters from last night's showing to the right of me before I asked the two, "So, what's the story with those mannequins?"

"Which ones?" Mitch asked.

Melissa added, "You mean the ones Dawg was messing with?"

"Yeah. Those mannequins," I said.

Mitch and Melissa exchanged a knowing look. An unsaid conversation passed between the fraternal twins before Melissa cleared her throat.

"Ain't nothing with those mannequins. Dawg got hurt because he wasn't paying attention, that's all," Melissa said.

Mitch leaned forward on his elbows on the counter. A slight smile played upon his lips, but didn't reach his eyes. Both of them were tight-lipped about the mannequins and about Dawg's accident yesterday. Time to try another tactic.

"My brother said there were murders here. Is it true?"

A small laugh escaped Mitch's mouth. He glanced my way and said, "Your brother, the security guard? He's a real piece of work."

"Yeah, he might be, but you're dodging the question. Were there murders? My brother says we should quit."

Melissa shook her head. "No, no murders during the day. You're fine if you don't work the night shift."

"Melissa, shhh. We're not supposed to talk about the murders, remember?" Mitch said, his brows furrowed upwards.

His sister flapped her hand at him and said, "She's lasted two days, bout time we tell her what's up. Well, while mister stick-up-the-butt ain't around."

Mitch walked around from the counter, gathered the dark sweaters into his hands, tossed his head over his shoulder, and said, "Well, I'm not going to stick around to get my butt chewed off by Jeremy with you telling our newbie store secrets."

"Oh, get out of here, sourpuss." Melissa waved her brother away. "I'm gonna tell Sarah all about the shit going on so she can protect herself, especially from Squeaks."

"Wait, Squeaks, the wisp of a girl is a suspect behind the murders?" I interjected.

"You can't prove Squeaks did murder anyone," Mitch called over his shoulder and walked off.

"Whatever," she called back, rolling her eyes and letting out a huge sigh. "Brothers. Can't live with 'em and can't live without 'em."

"So, you suspect Squeaks is behind the murders?" I asked.

Melissa waved her hand. "Hold up. I've gotta give you the full story before you come to the same conclusion. But I can say this about Squeaks. She's too weird to not be a serial killer. I mean, I get gooseflesh whenever she is hanging about me."

I nodded. Seth stopped messing around in the clothes rack, came over and hopped up onto the counter to listen in on Melissa's story. He motioned his hand with a flourish for Melissa to continue telling her story.

"Okay, the first murder happened about maybe four or five

weeks ago. Mitch and I were new, so we stayed on the day-evening crew while Batty and Squeaks took on the night shift. Now, I see you wanting to ask about their names and I'm gonna stop ya right there because I ain't got time to discuss why they call themselves those names."

Melissa held her hands up to stall any of us from asking questions. "Anyways, those two gals were scheduled to do the night shift, and all was going good, according to Squeaks, but when closing time got close, things shifted sideways. Squeaks swears she was out back throwing out the trash when she heard Batty screaming bloody murder. And she swears she tried to get back into the building, but the metal door had somehow pushed her doorstop out of the way and locked her out. Squeaks says the screams were horrific, followed by splatters and gurgles like Batty was choking on her own blood or something. When Mr. Knight, the mall security guard, came around and let Squeaks back in, they discovered the body. They found Batty's remains, well what was left of her... because her head was missing, right at the feet of the two mannequins in front of the store. Squeaks emptied her stomach right there, along with Mr. Knight. Those two were questioned by the police, but were let go because Squeak's story checked out. She was found outside by the trash bins by Mr. Knight around the time of Batty's attack."

"And what about the other murders? How many more were there before or after Batty?" Seth asked.

Melissa tapped her chin and looked upward. "I would say they were a week apart after the first one. Well, the ones in this store. I don't know much about the other stores in the mall. But rumor says there were mysterious disappearances of employees with only bloodied clothes left behind. Mr. Sels hired Dawg after the third one, since Squeaks seemed to be the main witness."

"Okay." I held up my hand and lowered my head. "You're saying only when Squeaks was working, these murders happened? If there has only been three murders in this store that we know of, a week apart, why hasn't she killed again?"

"Because," Melissa's lips broke into a wide grin, "my Dawg is so strong and awesome he can thwart any serial killer's attempt."

"Uh-huh," Seth said in an unamused tone. "Then what was yesterday's issue?"

Melissa's smile faded. "Um, he was just clumsy from lack of sleep."

Clumsy and lack of sleep, my foot. Part of me wanted to point out there was something hinky about those mannequins. I pressed the issue. "How'd he cut himself on those mannequins if he was only swapping out the clothing? Kind of seems strange if you ask me. Especially if he ended up needing stitches."

"Oh," Melissa said and blinked. "He was removing the tags with a knife and his hand slipped."

"That's all?" Seth asked. "Nothing weird?"

"No." She shook her head, light colored curls bouncing with each shake. "He was just distracted. Said he saw something but decided whatever he saw was nothing, really."

We were getting nowhere with this little interrogation. Either we got more questions or were stopped dead in our tracks. Guess Seth was right. We needed to work the night shift to get our answers from the dead.

"So, if I wanted to work the night shift," I said and continued, "how would I go about requesting the change in schedule?"

Melissa's eyes went round like an owl, sucked in her breath, and laid a hand on her chest. "After I told you why you should not do the night shift, you still want to take on the shift? Are you crazy?"

"We're still figuring out if we should," Seth snarked.

I swatted the back of his head. He ducked out of the way, so I thumped his thigh in retaliation. A smirk plastered on the kid's face.

"Yeah, I want to work the night shift. I'm curious about how everything plays out."

Mitch came back around the counter and said, "You're nuts if you want to work the night shift. Especially with Squeaks. Word is, Mr. Sels suspects she's behind the murders, which is why he had Dawg watching her."

"I'm a big girl. I can take care of myself," I retorted. "So, how do I get on the night shift?"

"You talk to Jeremy," Mitch and Melissa both replied in unison. Speak of the devil, mister stick-up-the-butt came waltzing out from the back room. He scanned around before his eyes landed on the three (or four, if you count Seth) of us hanging at the register. He stomped over to the counter and said in a vicious tone, "You lazy louts get your asses in gear. Mr. Sels isn't paying you to stand around and gab all day. No, he's paying you to move products. And from what I see is the merchandise is an hour behind."

He clapped his hands together for emphasis. "Get going, people. Chop-chop."

Mitch and Melissa ducked out of the cashier area to wrangle up the past-the-hour products and to put out the timely merchandise. I took this opportunity to sidle over to where Jeremy stood. His fingers tightly clutched a clipboard he retrieved from under the counter, his other hand with a pen, and ticking off boxes on the list.

Okay, either now or never. "Hey Jeremy."

He paused but didn't look up. "You should be out on the floor, helping switch out the merchandise and not standing here bothering me."

"Yeah, yeah." I flicked my hand. "I wanted to know if I could work the night shift."

The pen in his hand stopped mid stroke, and he lowered the clipboard, tilted his head to one side, mouth opened and closed. Words failed to come to his lips as he stood there looking at me like I had suddenly sprouted another one.

He finally sputtered, "You want to work the night shift? Are you nuts?"

My brows creased. "Uh, no? Why can't I work the night shift?"

"Because," Jeremy replied. "That's why."

Seth snorted. "Such an adult answer."

Jeremy rounded on him. "Shut your trap, you little snot. I know you were the one behind the peanut butter prank with my locker, and if I were you, I'd not utter one peep if you don't want to be locked up for vandalism."

He shrugged and pushed back on Jeremy. "I'll back off on the pranks if you just let Sarah work the night shift. Unless you want us to go to the authorities and tell them you and Mr. Sels are in cahoots and are the true perps."

Jeremy jerked back like he was slapped hard. He threw a

steely gaze back at Seth and rubbed the bottom of his jaw. The cogs obviously churning in his head. His hand dropped from his jaw as he blew out a breath. Jeremy said, "Okay, fine. Sarah, you can work the night shift tonight."

"Cool." I crossed my arms and leaned against the counter. "Can I go until my shift is about to start?"

"No," Jeremy said and looked like he took a bite out of a sour lemon. "You're still working your day shift, too. Now get back to work."

"Wait, what? So not cool," I groaned. Seth hopped off the counter, took my hand in his, and dragged me off to go tend to the merchandise, which needed swapping. My feet felt heavy as we plodded along to the various display racks to swap out products. If I was expected to work two shifts, I was going to need an ultra-caffeinated beverage on my next break to make my way through the night.

Or I could make a wish…

Err, wait, never mind. Seth was giving me the biggest Cheshire Cat grin, and considering the cantankerous mood he'd been in lately, I wasn't going to risk the potential chaos. Tired or not, I needed to power on through this day… with lots and lots of caffeine. Maybe Squeaks would take pity on me and decide to skip out on her killing spree… maybe… we'll see.

CHAPTER
TWENTY-ONE

JEREMY WAS MORE than happy to wish me the best of luck for tonight's shift with Squeaks. I swear the dude literally did a skip hop when he left the store at the end of his shift. Asshole. Maybe I should pay Seth to do another peanut butter job on the dude's locker to take him down a peg.

Seth and I were fully prepared to take on the night shift with Squeaks, but we did not expect to see Dawg swagger in about halfway through the shift. He waved at us and moseyed his way onward to the registers. Squeaks returned his wave with a half-smile. She did not look happy with his sudden appearance. But again, if he was hired to keep an eye on Squeaks, it meant Dawg had to keep her on her toes. Especially with unannounced appearances when he wasn't supposed to be working.

Dawg muscled his way behind the cashier counters and removed his leather jacket showing off his newly bandaged right arm. Wounds still fresh with antiseptic. He leaned on the counter and nodded my way.

"Evening," he drawled, the purple streaks in his silver close-cropped beard gleamed in the store lighting. "Never thought you'd work this shift."

I finished scanning in the customer's items for purchase and rang out the total. Once the customer was taken care of, I replied, "Yeah, me neither. Y'all got my curiosity up."

Squeaks noticeably stiffened and walked off. Seth watched her from his perch over by the mannequins. He wanted to investigate them more since they seemed to be the source of the eerie energy.

"Why's that?" Dawg asked, examining the cuticles on his fingers. Picking at the dead skin and flicking the discards toward the ground. I wrinkled my nose.

Turning around and leaning on the counter, I gestured at his crude habit. "Will you stop? You're disgusting."

"Better than picking my nose." He picked off another piece of dead skin, flicking the discarded flesh to the floor. "You going to tell me why you're working tonight?"

"I'm curious. Heard rumors. That's all," I replied. "Why? Is it a crime?"

Dawg pushed himself away from the counter with a chuckle. "Naw, jus' means I got to look out for you now, considering what's been going on and all."

"Mind cluing me in?" I asked, watching new customers stream into the store, perusing the spooky merchandise. One thing about The Glen was once you set out the stuff for the night shift, you didn't have to shuffle the products in and out on the hour, you were set for the rest of the night. Certainly, made the swaps tons easier on whoever did the redeye shift, for sure.

Dawg rubbed his chin and stroked his short beard, twirling the strands between his fingers, combing the hairs forwards and back. "Not much to tell you. You wouldn't be working the night shift if you didn't already know the dangers."

"No one said anything about the dangers," I lied, cutting my eyes toward him, hugging my shoulders as a chill went through me. "I know about the murders, but no one said anything about the existing dangers."

He leaned in closer, pointing toward Squeaks who was straightening up the display racks, and whispered, "Squeaks. She's our prime suspect. Three murders while she was on duty and every time, she claims she was somewhere else. There weren't no one else in the store at the time these murders happened."

"What about the mannequins?" I said, pointing over at the two suspicious mannequins. "Those things creep me out. Who's to say those things aren't possessed? Would you have noticed?"

A heavy rumble erupted from Dawg, his laughter starting deep within him, shook your entire being while he laughed out loud. He wiped tears from his eyes and said, "Now, there's some crazy stuff right there. Those mannequins had nothing to do with the murders, nor could anyone convincingly hold a pose all night without someone noticing a shake or slight movement."

"But you got hurt the other night while you were swapping their clothes. Melissa said you sliced yourself with your pocketknife, but why would you even be using a pocket knife to dress mannequins?"

"No, I got cut on one of the mannequin's attachment pins. I wasn't watching what I was doing and got sliced. Bad enough to leave a ton of blood on the floor and to get twelve stitches."

"Oh," I said. Maybe they were onto something about Squeaks. She seemed odd, but I couldn't discount what Seth said about those mannequins either. Every time I got close to them, the feeling like someone danced over my grave would rush through me.

Dawg leaned in close, held up his hand to one side to cover his mouth so no one could read his lips, and whispered, "Look, stick with me. Don't go anywhere with Squeaks alone. 'Kay?"

"Sure." I nodded and glanced over at Seth. He was keeping tabs on Squeaks but occasionally whipped his head back toward the mannequins like they moved or did something strange. Could Seth be setting me up for one big prank? He's done such things in the past, so this whole bit with the mannequins was a huge possibility. Now I thought of how he kept on pointing back to the mannequin the more the situation smelled of shenanigans. I mean, hell, my camera couldn't reveal any more than small traces of magic with those mannequins.

I felt Dawg's big meaty hands pat my shoulders as he walked behind me to get out from behind the counters to go help Squeaks keep the products straightened up in the store. This time of day didn't stop people from picking up stuff and dropping the item in a disheveled mess.

Seth waved his arms at me, motioning for me to come over. I took a quick look for any customers who might want to check out, but the store was clear for the time being. I hustled over to where Seth sat under the mannequins, crouched down to his level, grasped my camera, pulling the viewfinder up to look through the lens.

His hand covered the lens, his other hand held up one finger against his lip, ushering for me to keep quiet. He kept low, winding his arm for me to follow him. We stuck close to the other side of the store and snuck into the backroom. The djinn closed the door and engaged the locks, letting out a long exhale.

"I've got a feeling something is going to happen tonight." He leaned up against the locked door. "Those mannequins are giving off tons of power."

"Why didn't you want me to look at them?" I asked.

His eyes narrowed to slits. "And give away we're on to them? No, way."

"What are you talking about?" My brows creased upward; my lips pursed. "Who?"

Seth rolled his eyes. "The mannequins. Duh."

"I thought we were watching Squeaks?"

"Have you noticed she avoids the mannequins like the plague? She's afraid of them. And no, I don't think she did the murders."

I raked my fingers through my hair. "So, are we still going to ask the dead about what really happened?"

He held one finger up. "That's the thing. I don't feel any ghostly activity around here. At all. You can't talk to spirits if there aren't any spirits."

Crouching down to his level, I leaned in, narrowing my eyes before saying, "I think I smell a lie. A big fat one. I don't think my camera has the ability to talk to spirits or even see them. Hence why you're saying there aren't any."

Seth shrugged. "You can either believe me or not. I'm not going to waste my breath to try and convince you about your camera's capabilities."

Turning the camera over in my hands, I did glance at the dials for the various picture modes. There were a few symbols on the dial. I had no idea what they meant. They weren't covered in my photography classes in college.

Thus, another reminder I needed to take a day to really get to know my camera or hit the archives in Wings of Virtue to see if they knew anything about this camera. Mary, Ivan, and Seth were all pretty closed lipped about what my cursed camera could do until the well-timed scenario presented itself and boom, my camera suddenly was the solution to the problem. Every time I asked why they weren't saying anything, they suddenly had something else more important to do. And, no, I was not going to go visit Mrs. Smith, the dragon, to get more details on the camera. Such actions begged to be eaten or tricked into servitude for the old lizard.

"Can I at least look?" I frowned, turning the camera dial to one looking like a ghost. "Maybe there's one in this room."

"Knock yourself out." Seth gestured at the room, still leaning against the only exit out of this room. A sheer fire hazard, if you asked me.

Pulling the camera's viewfinder up to my eyes, I moved around, looking for anything out of the ordinary. No trace of energy could be seen. Everything seemed normal, for now. When I lowered the camera, I caught movement to my left. I turned the camera to see a lone rat, ick. The camera pulsed in my hands, itching for me to press the shutter button.

My camera was hungry. Several days had passed since the camera's last meal and the sight of a lowly creature whet its appetite. My index finger caressed the shutter button until the camera pulsed again and forced my finger to click the button. A flash went off in the room, followed by the last squeak of the poor rat, when pounding on the door sounded.

Screams erupted outside in the store. My heart rate picked up, mixing in with the rush of the camera processing the consumption of life force, as Dawg pounded on the door, yelling.

"Guys, let me in, let me in. Oh gawd. Don't let them get me."

A woman was screaming. We could only guess the scream came from Squeaks, followed by crashes, as the screams moved across the store. Something inhuman chittered, which sounded like a recording, followed by more screams. Dawg continued to pound on the door.

"Let me in!" Dawg screamed, rattling the doorknob. A high-pitched inhuman squeal ruptured the room and was close to the back door. Dawg whimpered, "Oh, gawd, no."

CHAPTER
TWENTY-TWO

I SHOVED Seth out of the way, unlocked the door, and whipped the door open. Dawg came crashing in as his hand went to go pound on the door once more. He fell to the ground, and I watched him roll over, hands wrapped around his stomach.

Dawg's shoulders shook as his mouth opened with laughter roaring forth from within. The bastard was laughing? Outside the door, a high-pitched giggle wafted into the back room. I peered around the door to see Squeaks with her arms around her stomach as well and almost doubled over, laughing her butt off.

"What the hell?" I shouted.

Seth smirked, "Fooled ya."

I swatted the backside of Seth's head and frowned at Dawg, who still laid on the floor chuckling. He wiped the tears out of his eyes and said between guffaws, "Man, you were right. She was so easy to fool."

"Seth?" I growled. "Want to tell me something?"

The djinn stepped away from me, hanging out of arm's reach, and replied with a snicker, "Like what? Such as you're way too easy of a target?"

Rolling my eyes, exhaling loudly, I mimed a fake laugh. "Oh, ha, ha. You got me. Real rich, guys. Now, will you all knock it off?"

Dawg sat up. I grabbed his hand and hefted him back up. He patted my shoulder and sidled back out into the room where Squeaks waited. Seth still hung back, knowing full well I wanted to swat him another for his foolish prank. Demons can't live with them. No, seriously, you can't at all.

After I slugged Seth real hard in his arm, we both followed Dawg into the other room. The two were whispering when we entered. Dawg looked up and waved us over.

"Sorry, Sarah. This was all Seth's idea. He cornered me and Squeaks the first day you all were here," Dawg said, rubbing the back of his head. "Actually, Squeaks caught him peanut buttering Jeremy's locker. He convinced her to not tattle and cajoled her into helping to pull this prank on you."

I shot Squeaks a look. She jumped and hid behind Dawg. He twisted, trying to see where Squeaks hid, and pulled her back out from behind him. Dawg continued, "And I happened to have walked in at the time he was talking to Squeaks. Seemed like a harmless prank and all."

A scowl took up residence on my face. The sneaky bastard. I should have followed my instinct about Seth being up to no good. I pinched the bridge of my nose to ward off the incoming migraine from too little sleep, not enough caffeine, and the sheer adrenaline rush happening at the moment.

"And the murders? Were any of those true?" I asked.

Squeaks cleared her throat. Her soft soprano voice barely audible. "Only Batty's."

Dawg interjected, "Me and Squeaks go way back. The nonsense Melissa told you about Mr. Sels hiring me to watch over Squeaks was to throw you off Seth's trail."

"Melissa and Mitch were in on the prank too? Even Jeremy?" I asked.

"Melissa and Mitch, one-hundred percent. Jeremy? Not sure, but I think he was on board too. Nothing like a little hazing to bring the team together," Dawg said while he stroked his closely cropped beard.

I glanced over at Dawg. "What about your accident? Was your accident even real?"

"You can do a lot with corn syrup." He unraveled the bandage on his arm to reveal the unscathed arm. Oh, good grief. I knew it was too much blood for a cut on the arm. Ugh, how could I be so stupid?

Seth had come out of hiding, patted my back in a patronizing manner, and said, "Aw, don't take this too hard, Sarah. We were just playing."

"Seth, I swear you are going to be so grounded," I said between clenched teeth. My other hand opened and closed into a fist. Blood pumped hard through my veins.

The little brat chuckled and danced away from me, chiding in a sing-song voice, "Oh, I'm so scared. You can't do anything."

"Alright buster, no more premium movie channels or streaming TV for you. You're on a no-internet based punishment." I shook my fist at him.

For once, Seth stopped, his bottom jaw fell open, his eyebrows skyrocketed into his hairline, and he slumped forward. He whined in protest. "You can't."

"I can and I will." I crossed my arms. "And I just did. Think about next time you want to pull a prank like this on me again."

"That's not fair!"

Thrusting my jaw forward, I said, "Life's not fair."

Dawg let out a shrill whistle. We stopped our back and forth to turn our attention to him. Dawg tapped his watch to show us the time. Closing time. Delight danced right through me, giving me a third wind since the adrenaline died down.

"Alright, Squeaks, you and Sarah take the trash out. Seth, I'm gonna make you the door guard to make sure these ladies don't get locked out. I'm gonna go make the final rounds in the store to close up and make sure things are ready to go for tomorrow."

Squeaks raised her slender hand. Dawg nodded. She asked, "Dawg, don't you think we should all help prep the store for tomorrow? If we all pitch in, we'll get things done faster."

"Fair enough." Dawg nodded. He clapped his hands together and divvied out the sections of the store for each of us to manage. Seth was the lazy lout who sat on the counter over by the registers to watch us work. A small pout still present on his little boy lips. Good, sulk, you little brat. Maybe this time you'll learn not to pull shit on me. I couldn't believe it. I mean, I should have seen this coming, but no, I had fallen for the joke, hook, line, and sinker.

Taking another look at the mannequins, their mere presence sent chills dancing down my spine. I shook to rid myself of the chills. All of this made sense now. Jeremy's constant hassling me about taking a peek at the mannequins with the camera, Melissa and Mitch's questionable tight lips about events within the store, and so much more. But, still, those mannequins kept on drawing my eyes.

Lifting the camera up to take a peek through the viewfinder, I heard Dawg make another whistle. I blew out an exasperated breath and let my cursed camera dangle from the strap around my neck. Turning, I saw Dawg and Squeaks near the back door leading out to the trash bins.

"Hey, Sarah, remember? You and Squeaks are gonna go handle the trash tonight, yeah?" he hollered at me.

I waved at him. "Yeah, I remember. Coming."

On my way over to where Squeaks and Dawg waited, I hooked an arm around Seth and dragged him off the counter. He begrudgingly followed two steps behind. Seemed like a certain djinn probably needed more than no internet. He needed a serious timeout within the camera.

We came up to the two waiting, and Squeaks handed me two overburdened trash bags. She picked up the other two and hustled them into the cart outside the door. Thank goodness there was a cart because hell if I wanted to carry this stinky trash on my back all the way down the hall and outside to the trash bins.

I turned to Seth and asked, "You've got the doors, right?"

"Duh. Of course, I remember." He folded his arms across his chest. "Not like I have the attention span of a squirrel, like someone else I know."

With my hand, I smacked the backside of his head as we hustled out into the hallway. Squeaks moved the cart at a marginally slow pace. Dawg popped his head out the door and mentioned, "Don't take too long. I'm hoping we can all leave soon. This place gets pretty creepy once there aren't any more customers in the store."

Squeaks ducked her head and smiled. "Sure thing, Dawg. We'll be back before you know it."

"Cool." He grinned right back at her. "If you hear me screaming, you all come a running, cool?"

That got a giggle out of Squeaks. Seth rolled his eyes, commandeered the cart, and pushed the bin faster down the hallway. He grumbled between a huff and a growl. "Let's go people. We don't have all night."

"Seconded." I helped him push the cart faster down the hallway. Squeaks skipped to catch up. Her hands landed on the handle and gave added force to the cart's momentum.

The door to the store stayed open with the help of a piece of wood from one of the display racks. Part of me wanted Seth to stay behind to guard this door, for my stomach continued to swirl with butterflies. Ever since I latched eyes on the mannequins, before we left for our garbage tossing jaunt, things felt darker. Hard to explain, really, but the sensation of an event about to happen still lingered in the air.

Seth still wouldn't look at me. Since I took away his shows and movie privileges, he avoided eye contact. I cleared my throat. "Seth, maybe you should hang back and make sure the door to the shop doesn't shut us out."

"And who's going to watch the door out to the trash bins?" he said.

"I will."

Squeaks licked her lips and said, "No, I can't handle throwing these bags into the trash bins myself. I need help. Normally Dawg handles the trash for me, but he's doing the final sweep in the store. You're gonna have to help me, Sarah."

"But the wood holding the door open doesn't look sturdy."

Seth groused. "If the wood worked for them several times over, the wood will work tonight. Quit being such a worry wort."

"Says the little imp, who caused me to be doubting everything tonight."

"Look," Squeaks said. "With your help, we'll get these bags in the trash bins quicker than just one of us. We can hurry on back to finish closing up shop."

"She's got a point." Seth pushed the cart harder. "Let's get this over with and go home."

"Fine." I grumbled. Clearly, the two were dead set on me helping with taking out the trash. I could only hope the sinking feeling in the pit of my stomach was dead set wrong.

With the three of us pushing the cart, we made our way to the trash bins in record time. Down three sets of metal stairs, Squeaks and I hustled the bags into the bins. Seth held the door open while we handled the trash. The two of us were climbing back up the steps when a loud yell echoed down the hallway.

Seth turned. His eyes grew wide, my hand automatically seizing the camera, as Squeaks and I ran the rest of the way back up the stairs. All three of us dashed down the hallway back to the store. We were almost at the store's door when another blood curdling scream erupted.

An eerie sound, like that of Styrofoam rubbing against more Styrofoam, scrawled into the night air. Dawg, his voice hoarse from screaming louder than usual, eked out a cry of desperation, "Oh, gawd, no, no, no, please, no."

High pitched chitters, clicks, and scrapes sounded on the tiled floor followed by metal on metal sound. Our hands reached for the doorknob to push the door open. But Squeaks held onto the door to prevent us from opening the door wider. Sheer terror shined in her eyes. Dawg yelled, a sickening crunch and squelch overshadowed the tail end of his scream, followed by silence.

I shoved Squeaks out of the way and barreled into the room. On the floor in front of us was Dawg, or at least his body was. His head was nowhere to be found. Squeaks let out a shrill, bursting my eardrums.

Lifting the camera, I scanned the room. Nothing. Wait… a quick movement happened close by. The temperature dropped immensely, sending violent shivers through me. Even Squeaks hugged her arms and rubbed them for warmth. I swung the camera in the general direction of Dawg's fallen body. Floating over the corpse was his own spirit. His eyes shone with terror, and mouth hung open in a perpetual scream.

Huh. I guess Seth was telling the truth. Speaking of the devil, Seth moved in close, rose his hand to point at the vacant space above Dawg's deceased form and whispered, "I see dead Dawg."

Hefting the camera in my hands, I strode forward, for we needed to have a little chat with our dead friend.

CHAPTER
TWENTY-THREE

"NO, DON'T," Squeaks yelped.

Seth and I stopped in our tracks and whipped around. Squeaks' eyes darted around with a wild flare like she was ready to bolt at any moment.

"Mind cluing us in on your sudden outburst?" Seth asked. "We have a viable spirit to talk to, and you're only delaying us."

Squeaks pawed at the air, motioning for us to go back to where she stood, which was well away from the deceased on the floor. Seth and I both glanced at one another and tilted our heads to one side. A silent conversation—something weird was going on with our fellow co-worker Squeaks.

"This is all a crime scene," she squeaked. "You can't touch nothing. Not unless you want me to go to jail."

Seth and I both had our brows creasing, narrowing our gaze at Squeaks. Why in the world would she be dead sure she'd be arrested for this murder? She was with us… wasn't she?

I took another scan with my camera, going up and down, side to side to make sure there was not any weird entity that had attached itself to Squeaks. Aside from the minor aura of magic, Squeaks was, pardon the pun, squeaky clean. However, off to the side of the room, I recognized the other figure with the big dark feathery wings.

The Valkyrie from the night when my friends and I fought against being turned into Avarice's zombie slaves. She gave me the choice to bow out of all of this, accept my death, but in exchange, the world would burn. Instead, like the stubborn woman I am, I chose to live. In hindsight, maybe I should have accepted death.

She glided across the floor with shadows gathered at her feet. Seth watched her with his fiery eyes and held a menacing glower pointed in her direction. The Valkyrie bent down at Dawg's corpse, reaching deep into his chest to pull out a cream-colored jewel. The gem sparkled in the cool lights of the store.

I stepped forward. The Valkyrie leapt backwards, while Dawg's spirit continued to hover over his dead body. Waving the camera, I asked, "Can you hear me?"

"Of course." The Valkyrie nodded and pointed at Seth. "I see you followed my advice."

Seth charged at her, his hands and arms splayed out at his sides. "So, you're the one. The sneaky raven wench who couldn't keep a secret. *You* are who I have to thank for my current predicament."

The Valkyrie frowned. "Don't push this on me, djinn. Without me you would have failed your purpose, again."

"Seth, what is she talking about?" I placed a hand on his

shoulder. He shrugged my hand away, whirling around to point back at me.

"If you weren't so stupid and actually used that brain of yours, I wouldn't be subjected to everyday humiliation. Do you realize all I have to deal with? Being bound to the likes of you…"

"That's not how I saw things," the Valkyrie mused. "You were bawling your eyes out over her only a few months ago. Just like you did those several thousand years ago."

"Can it." He sliced his hand in the air. "She was different… nothing like this, this idiot you see here and now."

"Hey," I scowled. "I'm right here."

Seth looked me up and down. "Are you? Really? I swear you're off in la-la land almost twenty-four seven."

"Whoa." I held up my hands. "So this is why you've been mister snarks-a-lot lately? Because I bound you?"

"Yes," he growled. "You didn't even ask me. You simply made the wish with no thought of how I felt. Of course, you barely have any thoughts so, why the hell am I expecting you to even bother to think ahead?"

The Valkyrie got between us, pushing us apart, looking at the both of us, with a mean scowl plastered across her dark blackberry lips. She glanced down at Seth and said, "Djinn, deal with it. You knew you had to be bound for any of this to work. I merely gave Sarah the information she needed to succeed."

"Thank you, uhhh," I replied and added, "Um, what is your name?"

The Valkyrie kept her gaze pinned on Seth as they held a staring contest between each other. She tossed her hair back and said, "Erin. You can call me Erin."

"Thanks, Erin."

"Anytime." She smiled and turned back to Dawg's spirit. She motioned for the ghost to come close to her. Dawg floating a foot off the floor, glided over to Erin, and stopped. He continued to look around the room, his eyes still wide with terror and shock.

Because I was still holding the camera, it allowed me to see and hear the whole scene play out. Dawg clutched his enormous arms and rubbed them for comfort, his shoulders hunched, body slumped over. When he talked, his voice was high, like he was still yelling. He asked, "Am I dead?"

Erin nodded with a frown. "Yes. I'm afraid you are. Come with me."

"You're too pretty to be the Grim Reaper," he said, nose crinkling, reaching out but hesitating. "Are you the Grim Reaper?"

The Valkyrie chuckled. Her laugh like the sound of wind chimes blowing in the evening breeze, long dark hair tumbling down her alabaster shoulders. "No, I'm not, but I am still here to guide you to the other side. If… you're willing."

Dawg's eyes glistened in the store light when he turned his head toward Squeaks. She was still standing over by the door, away from his dead body. Seth and I clustered close to him. Squeaks' bottom lip trembled as she watched the scene unfold. Only thing was, she was only seeing me and Seth talking to nothing.

With her friend recently deceased, two people talking to air, one using a camera like the thing was some glorified ghost busting artifact, we certainly looked crazy to her. The wide startled eyes, her shaky legs, were some signs the girl was either going to faint or bolt. Seth hustled over to her to make her stay put.

Dawg said aloud, "I can't leave her. No one understands her like I do. They'll blame her for my death."

Erin grabbed his hand while her other hand held the cream-colored jewel. She worried her bottom lip and said, "I'm sorry, but you cannot stay. You have to come with me."

Wiping his face with his other hand, he tugged at his beard and choked out, "But who will take care of her? Who?"

"Sarah will," Erin said, gently tugging on Dawg's hand.

My head snapped up at the mention of my name. I interrupted the touchy feely scene and objected, "Whoa, whoa, whoa. When did I volunteer to look out for Squeaks?"

"Ever since you took possession of the camera." Erin tossed her head at the cursed camera in my hands. "Whether you want to or not—"

"Can it, feathers," Seth interrupted Erin. "Sarah is not going to watch over Squeaks. She's got enough troubles as is, without adding more."

Dawg gave me the biggest puppy dog eyes in the history of puppy dog eyes. My heart melted, a little, in the moment and couldn't stop my mouth from uttering the next few words, but Seth, somehow knowing what was about to tumble from my lips, was at my side in a blink of an eye. His hands slapped themselves over my mouth.

"You say anything about watching Squeaks and consider your daily allotment of wishes to become one and only one," he sneered. "Simply pathetic on how puppy dog eyes can melt mortal hearts."

Excuse me? Who the hell did he think he was? I was the master, not him. Blood thundering, I ripped his hands away and said, "Fine, I'll watch out for Squeaks."

"Great. Just bloody great. You're down to one blooming wish a day and you're probably going to waste the wish getting to work on time or worse, refilling your stupid cereal bowl." Seth tossed his hands up in the air. "Tell me why I'm bound to you again?"

"Because, deep down, you know I attract trouble and chaos, and keep things interesting," I snarked right back at him.

The Valkyrie and Dawg smiled at Seth and my verbal jousting. Erin tugged on Dawg's hand once more, who nodded his head and followed the Valkyrie. Wind rose in the store, bringing feathers, leaves, and shadows into a small whirlwind. The two vanished from sight.

Silence covered the room in an eerie blanket as a lone black feather drifted to the floor. Squeaks even watched the feather float downwards to the tiles to land in the pooling blood. My fingers still clutched the camera.

Seth let out a huge sigh, breaking the spell of silence. "You do realize you missed your chance to ask Dawg, who murdered him, right?"

I smacked my palm against my head. Crap.

CHAPTER
TWENTY-FOUR

GHOST OR NO GHOST, we still had a problem which was cooling on the tiled flooring. Needless to say, Seth and I had to call the cops because Squeaks was incapable of doing such actions. She was in shock. Who could blame her? The only person who probably got her was murdered in cold blood while on the same shift. Not to mention she was already prime suspect numero uno with the previous murder which happened on her watch at The Glen. If I were in her shoes, I definitely would not want to call the cops down to the store so they could hassle the crap out of me.

However, we had a dead body on the floor oozing rapidly cooling blood all over the white six by six tiles. At least the grout between the tiles was black, so we did not have to worry about staining them with blood.

Seth cleared his throat, yanking on my shirt to grab my attention. I bent down so he could whisper into my ears. "I'll go keep an eye on the girl. She looks like she's ready to bolt any minute. And if she knew the police were on the way, she'd leave before they got here. Which would only paint her guilty in their eyes."

"You've got a point, Seth," I said, bobbing my head. "Guess I'll go make the call so we avoid suspicion."

"Right." He shuffled over to where Squeaks sat upon the display booth for daytime skinny jeans. Several tissues were gathered in her hands to stifle the flood of tears running down her cheeks. The bold mascara and eye liner ran down like watered down paint, giving her a more abstract makeup feel to her goth look. Squeaks glanced up, her eyes red from all the crying, breath catching in shudders while she tried to stop more sobs. The dark eyes followed my trek over to the wired phones behind the cash register.

Dialing 9-1-1, I was immediately connected to an operator who asked me what I needed. I simply told her the situation and was given the response the police would be on their way. In addition, she told us all to stay put and not to touch anything until the authorities showed up on the scene. I thanked her and hung up.

Off to my right, I heard Squeaks ask, "You called the police?"

"Yeah," I said and gestured at the dead body on the floor. "Kind of have to in this situation. If we didn't, things would have gotten worse."

"Oh, gawd," Squeaks whimpered and crumbled to the floor. She held her face in her hands, sobbing, barely able to speak but still said between breaths, "Ah, geez. This is the last straw. I'm going to jail."

Seth frowned down at her, forming a crease between his eyebrows, and said, "Why would you be going to jail? You didn't kill him."

"They won't care," Squeaks wailed. "They still suspect me for Batty's murder."

"You weren't really there for Batty's either. You were out back throwing out the trash," Seth tried to reason with Squeaks. "Tell me, how are they going to pin this on you? You don't possess a single weapon on you that could cut a head clean off. Anything you would have had would have left jagged marks and a great mess."

Squeaks snorted a great snort to pull back the extra mucus running out of her nose. She looked past Seth at the dead body on the floor, really squinted her eyes, and widened them. Squeaks inhaled sharply and declared, "You're right. The cut is too clean."

"Of course I'm right." He hooked his thumbs in his belt loops, tossed his head in my direction and said, "Now if you can convince Sarah I'm always right, I'll make you my favorite."

That got a chuckle out of Squeaks, who used the tissue in her hand to let out another great blow from her nose to clear her nasal passages. She chose to stay put on the floor while I waltzed on over to Seth and snagged Squeaks' original perch on top of the display booth. Of course, I shoved the jeans out of the way so I did not have to leap as far from the floor. When you're in your late thirties, your body just won't cooperate anymore. Even great leaps can tire you out or worse, cause unwanted injuries where you ask yourself where you got the mysterious bruise winking back at you from the bathroom mirror.

It wasn't long before we heard footsteps approaching the mall entrance of The Glen. Outside the metal gates stood the cops and my brother the mall security guard. I leapt off the booth, landed where my ankle rolled to one side, making me wince, and hobbled my way to the gates. Reaching down, I unlocked the gates from the inside and rolled them upwards to let the cops and my brother into the store. There was no need to close the gates since the cops needed to get the dead body out of the store.

I held back as they walked past me. My brother pulled me to one side, the corners of his mouth turned down, brows furrowed downward with concern. He first drew me into a hug, but drew back. He asked, "Are you okay?"

"Yeah." I tucked some hair behind my ear. "Besides rolling my ankle, I'm fine. Though I think Dawg is done for…"

Jake followed my gaze and saw the body on the floor with the ever-growing pool of blood. He inhaled and held his breath for a moment, exhaled through his mouth, and repeated the process. Jake's mouth pressed into a thin white line, and he said, "This isn't funny, Sarah. A man is dead and you're making jokes at his expense?"

"Uh, yeah," I replied. "Or go screaming down the halls. Which would you prefer?"

Jake exhaled again. "Fine, fine. But can you tone your excitement down some? At least have some respect for your late co-worker."

"I've only known the dude for what, three days?"

"Yes, and you should still show some respect."

"Okay." I sighed. "For you, I'll reign in my sarcasm."

While Jake and I talked, Jeremy came rushing into the store.

His eyes locked onto me and stomped the rest of the way. I mumbled under my breath, "Great, just what we need. Who called that asshole?"

Jake whispered, "I did. Mall policy is to call owners or the main manager if a major event happens in their store and they're not present."

Jeremy's hands flew up, eyebrows lowered, making his eyes dark and beady, his mouth twisted before he yelled, "I knew it! You're always making trouble. Give me a reason why you shouldn't be fired?"

I set my jaw and leaned towards him when Jake stepped in between us, holding his hands up and asked, "Whoa, calm down, sir. Sarah had nothing to do with—"

"Shut up." Jeremy shoved my brother out of the way and jabbed a finger into my chest. "You're in cahoots with Squeaks, aren't you?"

Part of me wanted to grab his finger and put him in a hold where all I'd need to do was do another tweak and he'd be nursing a broken digit. Instead, I batted the finger away and said, "I did nothing wrong. And Squeaks did nothing wrong. Go bother the police to get the full story before accusing me of such shit, jerk wad."

Jeremy's eyes widened while his mouth struggled to form an angry line. His nostrils flared with a deep breath when one of the police officers moseyed their way back to the gate. I really was not in the mood to be asking or answering any questions, but if answering meant I could get away from Jeremy and I could go home, then sure, fine, I'd deal with their little interrogation.

"Are you Sarah Knight?" the approaching officer asked.

Jeremy sneered, "Lady, you're gonna have to wait. I'm busy asking my employee why she didn't call me first before she called the police."

The female officer arched an eyebrow and rested a fist on her hip. "Is there a reason why you're requiring your employees to call you first before the authorities?"

"Company policy," he said.

"Uh, huh."

"Now, if you'll excuse us, we're busy." He made a shooing motion with his hands.

"Sir, I need to ask the witness what she saw. Why don't you go speak to my colleagues while we're talking? We'll only be a moment or two."

Jeremy squinted his eyes and looked between us. He shoved past me and said, "Fine. But don't let her go home. I have my own questions for her to answer."

Oh goodie. I stuck my tongue out at Jeremy behind his back when my brother elbowed me. He muttered, "Be nice."

Holding a hand on my chest I said in mocked surprise, "What? Me? Never." Then snorted.

The officer cleared her throat and asked, "Are you Sarah Knight?"

"Yes. What do you need, officer?" I replied. My brother chose this moment to go talk to the other cops who were talking to Jeremy, Seth, and Squeaks so he could keep the peace. Some big brother he was, leaving his little sister to deal with the big bad cops on her own. At least the cop saved me from Jeremy.

"Can you walk me through what you were doing at the time the victim was attacked?" she asked, pulling out her notepad with a rather nice sturdy looking pen. I had a thing for a good pen. They were far and few between. I'm talking about pens working no matter what the circumstance. The officer clicked her pen and snapped me back to the present.

With a sigh, I launched into the story, starting from when Dawg and Squeaks showed up to work up until this point. From there, the officer had more questions, which I felt obligated to answer, hoping the question would be her last one for the night.

The female officer tapped her pen against the pad, trying to jog her memory for one more question, when a voice I had not heard since college let out an elated yelp. I cringed before I turned around to see yet another person I least expected to see.

"Oh my god, Sarah? Is that you?" a rather familiar feminine voice exclaimed.

CHAPTER
TWENTY-FIVE

WITH A SLIGHT WAVE of my hand, I welcomed my old college roommate, Deborah Jones, who liked to be called Debbie. She stood there in green scrubs, taking in the store's scene. Other emergency personnel followed, pushing a gurney in front of them. Swallowing, to help get moisture back into my mouth from answering all the questions, I replied, "Hey Debbie, long time, no see, girl."

Debbie rushed forward and gathered me into a bear hug. She was slightly taller than me, had far more curves, that guys adored, shoulder-length wavy golden-brown hair, and twinkling hazel gray eyes. Debbie released me from her crushing hug, worried her luscious lips as she looked me over and reached out to pinch my arm.

"Ow." I swatted her hand away, rubbing the sore spot, and threw her a look. "Why'd you pinch me?"

"You never called me back," she said, hands on her hips. "Do you realize how many times your family literally grilled me to find out where you went? AND how many times I had to swallow my tongue, so I didn't spill the beans about you running off with Walter? Like, you left me hanging, girl. I thought you were my friend."

Still rubbing the sore spot on my arm, Debbie could give you a mean pinch. She even gave children who pinched each other on St. Patrick's Day a run for their money. I said, "Sorry, but I wasn't in a position to give you a call back then and things kind of got out of hand."

"Mmm-hmmm." She arched a slender, well-manicured eyebrow. "A likely story."

"Well, the story is true," I said, raking my fingers through my unkempt hair. The day's dirt and grime stuck like clay and made me feel gross all over. I seriously needed a shower.

Debbie closed her eyes, pinching the bridge of her nose, and shook her head. "Tell me, Sarah, do you ever get tired of lying?"

"But I'm telling you the truth," I half-lied to her. Part of the story was true. The rest was because I didn't want my past life prior to my relationship with Walter and the supernatural underground mafia to intermingle with my current mess. There was no need to drag my friends and family down with me into the darkness.

"Yeah, right," she said, dropping her hand and glancing around. "Well, now I know you're here, don't think your brother didn't tell me. You and I have some catching up to do."

Not going to happen, Debbie. Sure, she was my roommate, but there was only so much cheerfulness one could take before wanting to gouge out their own eyeballs and stab their own eardrums to drown out the joyfulness. No, planning on ditching family and friends was not bad. More like better for my own mental health and wellness. Also, even better for them, so they didn't get tangled up in the crazy trouble magnet Seth and Mary insisted I possessed.

The sound of latex snapping caught my attention and my head snatched up to see Debbie putting on a pair of white latex gloves. She smirked in my direction. "What? You thought I was here to look pretty? Pfft. Please, hun, this is why you and I need to go to a cafe to catch up. Tomorrow. Don't worry. I'll come pick you up."

Just like Debbie to not leave me a way to wiggle out of forced socialization. Ugh. I watched her pick up the black bag she left by the door. Only one hand had a glove on so she could carry in her tools with the ungloved hand. Debbie hustled past the display cases and booths to get to the dead body.

She sucked in air so quickly I was worried she was going to faint. Instead, she stooped down, opened her bag, and went to work on studying the corpse on the floor. Seth hung back with Squeaks but kept his keen eyes trained on her. Using this opportunity, I moseyed on past the female officer, who was caught up in tidying her notes. She didn't notice me sneak on by her.

Upon coming up behind the officers I overhead one of the guys mention this was at least the fifth incident this month. Same markers and everything, with the headless victims and the missing mannequins, only piles of dirt were left behind in their place. Though, he remarked, this store was the only one to be hit up twice. The officers leaned in closer, whispered amongst themselves, and tossed wary looks over at Squeaks.

Squeaks didn't miss the rabid glares sent her way. She ducked down behind Seth, who returned the glares with more oomph. The officers suddenly had the urge to look elsewhere in the store. One of the officers noticed me lurking close to the scene. He threw up his hands, stepping close and said, "Miss, you're going to need to step back. We don't need you contaminating the crime scene here."

"Um, well, you should know my ward, Seth and co-worker Squeaks, were all over this store today. You'll probably find traces of our hairs or other bits of DNA mixed in with your scene."

He shook his head. "You still need to step back. Let us do our job. Have you already talked to Officer Lendy?"

"Yes."

The male officer gestured at the counter where Seth and Squeaks sat. "You can go wait over there. We would like you to stay just in case we have any more questions."

Jake came up behind the officer and said, "I think my sister and her friends have answered enough questions for tonight. Maybe you should let them go?"

"Not until we're done here." He let out an exasperated huff. "Look, bud, why don't you go over there and keep them company too?"

My older brother hooked an arm around my neck, dragging me back from the officer, and said, "Of course, officer. We'll just be over here."

I followed begrudgingly. Jake let go once we reached the

counter, and I plopped my rear end onto the counter. Seth still watched Jeremy give the officers a run for their money, with all of his screaming. He also kept an eye on the officers' every move, including Debbie. Seth pointed at her.

"Who's she?" he asked.

Chewing my cheek, I said, "An old college roommate. Her name is Debbie."

Jake narrowed his eyes at Debbie and spat out, "She was never honest with us. I always had a feeling she knew where you were, but didn't want to tell the family."

"She did."

Jake's eyes widened, stepping back, gasped, "I knew it. Ma didn't believe me. Told us to leave her alone. To stop harassing her. I swear she would have told me where to find you, Sarah, if Ma didn't stop me."

"Debbie might have... or she would have kept tight-lipped about my whereabouts. I was the one who begged her to keep me eloping with Walter a secret and to not tell anyone where I ran off—" I said.

Seth frowned. "Wow, just when I thought I knew how low you'd sunk, I only learn more about how despicable you absolutely were."

"Like you're any better, Seth."

Squeaks was watching the fight happen between Jake, Seth, and me. Completely oblivious to the presence of the police. Which is what she needed.

Things were quieting down. The officers were talking to the other medical techs on the scene as they lifted the body onto the gurney so they could remove the deceased. Debbie continued to scribble down notes in her notebook.

Officer Lendy, the female officer from earlier, walked over to us. She jerked her thumb back at the scene and said, "Once we get the deceased out of here, we'll only have a few more questions, and you folks can finally head on home. We already have the number to Mr. Sels to inform him of what happened in his store though, I believe Jeremy, the store manager, will inform him before we have a chance. Just hang tight for a few more moments."

We all nodded our heads and thanked Officer Lendy for the update. The time was well into the early hours of the morning. After the double shift I had done, my eyes were ready to close shop on their own and leave me sleeping on the counter. Seth poked me a few times when he noticed me nodding off.

Jake, Seth, and I discussed the best types of caffeinated drinks to keep one up for long hours when a low whistle belted out an eerie tune. Creepy music was not something I ordered to shock me back awake. I sat on the counter, back ramrod straight, straining to listen for the next clue as to who was behind the tune.

Obviously, none of the officers, but the tune was certainly familiar. My hackles were on end, nerves jabbing pins and needles, while I clutched the countertops so hard the ends bit into the skin of my hands. I knew who was behind the tune of terror.

CHAPTER
TWENTY-SIX

A SMOOTH, deep, velvety voice crooned around the corner, the whistling abruptly stopping. The person's long shadowy silhouette paused in the doorway before he waltzed in, a smile on his punchable face, and overall aura sent my jellies running into hyperdrive for a little of horizontal one-on-one with him.

"Hi Sarah," Vincent said. "Did you miss me?"

Cold rushed through me, like a bucket of ice thrown all over me. The camera sent pulses through my entire being and fought off Vincent's sexual charm. As I shook my head, the mindless fog cleared, and I looked past him. If Debbie, Jake, and Vincent showed up, the odds were pretty high Walter would come plodding through the front.

Vincent's demure expression faded. He turned to look behind him, turned back, and asked, "Are you expecting someone else?"

"Maybe," I replied. "With all sorts of people just showing up tonight, I figure Walter would appear any moment now."

Jake got in front of me. Seth sidled closer to block Vincent from getting access. Both of their lips lifted, revealing teeth.

Jake held out his hand with a stopping gesture. "Whoa, man, close enough. Who are you and why are you here?"

Vincent was not in uniform but pulled out his badge, which hung from a lanyard, so it was on display on top of his civilian clothes and reached for a card in a top pocket. His shirt was the type found at a high-end men's department store paired with expensive dark slacks. The belt he wore was more than I made in the past few months, even with doing odd jobs for Wings of Virtue. And his shoes were polished dark black alligator skin with squared off toes. The man was definitely not a normal patron of The Glen, nor did he appear to be with the police.

The sex demon handed my brother the card. Jake turned the card over, inspected the text imprinted on the heavy-set paper, and pocketed it. A sly smile tugged at the corners of his lips. Jake said in a nonchalant manner, "Detective, huh? Explains the clothing, but doesn't really explain why you're here."

"I'm here for her." Vincent nodded toward Squeaks. She jumped and tried to hide behind all of us to get out of Vincent's leering gaze.

I jutted my jaw outward, showed my teeth, and replied, "She's not going anywhere with you."

"You can't stop me." Vincent walked over to where Squeaks was hiding. My brother Jake stepped in front of the detective, blocking his advance toward Squeaks.

Jake gestured at the rest of the cops milling about in the store, doing cleanup of the crime scene. "The choice is up to them. They were here first."

"I can pull rank if needed," Vincent replied, his mouth forming a grimace. "But I don't answer to any mall security cop. Out of my way. The girl is coming with me."

Jake pushed himself into Vincent's inner space. I grabbed ahold of my brother's wrist and pulled him back. He had no idea what Vincent could do, and I certainly did not need my brother turned into a sex craved junkie.

My brother tore his hand away from mine, continued advancing on Vincent, and poked him in his chest. His words were on edge, with a razor-sharp tone to them. "I may just be a mall security officer, but these people's well-being and safety are my top concern. Therefore, I will ask you again to back off and leave the girl alone."

Vincent's eyes flashed dark. Uh-oh. I knew the look. But, to my surprise, Vincent rose his hands and stepped back. Jeremy's squeal broke the tension. "What are you doing here?"

The sex demon turned to Jeremey and said, "My job. I was about to take this young lady down to the station."

"No." Jeremy said and stomped up to Vincent. "Your people already have things handled. Why don't you leave?"

The corners of Vincent's mouth turned downwards, throwing Jeremy a rather nasty look, straightened his shirt and replied, "I don't think you have the authority to tell me where I can and cannot go. In fact, I believe you might need to come down to the station with me."

Jeremy shrunk back; his hands held up in front. "No, no. I don't think we need to do that, sir. I'm going to go call my boss."

With his phone in hand, Jeremy hustled off to a far corner to call Mr. Sels.

Officer Lendy came over to see what we were fussing about and to see who the newcomer was. She motioned at Vincent to get his attention. "Detective, why are you here?"

With a fluid motion of his hand, Vincent grabbed the female officer's, bent down, and kissed the back of it. Her cheeks flushed, along with the very tips of her ears, while she looked away, doing her best to hold in the sudden need to squeal aloud.

She regained her composer and fanned herself, trying to relieve the sudden heat, and said, "Ah, ahem. Detective, are you here in response to the accident?"

"I wouldn't call this accident a singular event." Vincent's eyes darkened. "Too many of these have happened in the mall as of late. I suspect a serial killer is on the loose."

At this moment, Seth pulled on my shirt. I walked back a step, leaning down so he could whisper in my ear. "Seems kind of convenient Avarice's lapdog is investigating these scenes. She might have lost control of some zombies."

I whispered in reply, "If zombies caused these murders, how come the flooring wasn't messed up to show where they entered?"

Seth chewed on the side of his cheek, scuffing his feet on the tiled floor, obviously thinking about the missing evidence pointing to a zombie attack. His fiery eyes latched onto mine, and he nodded toward where the mannequins were once standing. They were absent. "What happened to the mannequins?"

Peering over at the booths, I noticed the mannequins were gone and their absence was worth investigating. The camera in my hands hummed as though pleased with our deduction, wanting us to gather more clues in the vicinity of the missing mannequins.

When I took a step in their direction, my brother grabbed my arm and said, "Don't be going anywhere, sis. I don't like the detective and the way he sizes you up like you're a seven-course meal. He gives me the creeps."

A warm smile crept over my lips, and I replied, "Same, but I'll be fine, Jake. I've dealt with Vincent before and know what to do if he gets too chummy with me."

I waggled my camera at Jake. A deep crease formed in the middle of his brows, his eyes tracing over my ancient camera. Rubbing the back of his neck, Jake remarked, "Sis, I hate to point this out, but, taking pictures of your assailant isn't going to do much. You need more firepower than a few pictures to take down creeps like him."

Seth tamped down on a vicious chuckle while my cheeks heated up, when I realized my brother did not know this camera's true capabilities. I'd been dealing with the supernatural for so long, I totally forgot my brother, as well as the rest of the family, were normal and had no clue the supernatural even existed. To them, all of this was only a good story on TV and nothing more.

To regain some composure, I snapped back, "I know. But have you felt how heavy this thing is? You must admit this camera would do some serious head trauma if used to bash someone's head in, right?"

The vacant look in my brother's eyes, told me right there why I got teased about the hamster in the wheel so much. I witnessed my brother overthinking what I said before he barked out a laugh. "You're so right, Sarah. Ah, okay. Go on and do what you need but, stay out of the officers' way, okay?"

"Yeah, yeah. Got it." I got on my tiptoes to look around my brother for Seth. "Seth, you coming?"

He nodded and skipped over to where I stood. He chirped, "Sure."

Both of us strode off toward empty booths where the mannequins were last seen. Under my breath, I said, "You sure this could be the work of Avarice's zombies?"

"Possible," he replied. "You know how slippery she can be."

A sick feeling shuddered throughout me. The one wish, when I wished the zombies to go away, and Avarice appeared, was the one wish I wished I'd never made. Ever since that wish, things had gotten more and more difficult for me, my friends, and for Wings of Virtue.

The big booth the mannequins were last seen came upon us. Seth and I both paused our conversation regarding our suspicions about zombie involvement and took to looking for clues. We found the booth was still in its original position. But piles of dirt were scattered where the mannequins once stood.

"We need to move this booth aside to see if the display is hiding anything." Seth motioned for me to come around to his side of the booth to help push.

A glance over at the officers to make sure they were staying put eased the tension, but only by a fraction. Seth and I both put our hands to the booth and shoved. The wheels underneath groaned and slid at a snail's pace.

Vincent's voice sounded, "Hey, what are you doing?"

"Moving this booth back," I said, turning to lean up against the booth. Sweat trickled down my back from the minor exertion. Geez, I needed to work out more.

His hands sliced the air and pointed back at the counter where Jake and Squeaks waited. "Both of you need to go sit over there and wait."

I was about to reply when Seth snagged my hand and pulled. "C'mon. No need to argue, Sarah."

Snatching my hand away, I walked over to Vincent and got into his personal space, aiming the camera down to his precious jewels. With a growl in my voice, I said, "Back off, or kiss your boys goodbye."

"You wouldn't dare," he said, baring his teeth.

"Try me."

Seth grabbed my hand again, yanking really hard, making me stumble backwards, only catching myself just in time to follow Seth. The djinn continued, glancing back over his shoulder at Vincent as we made our way back to the counter.

Curious. This was not the Seth I knew at all. Rarely did he ever back down. I got close and whispered, "What's going on with you?"

"The less he knows, the better," Seth said with a grimace. "And I'm tired of dealing with his crap. If only you could hear his lurid thoughts. Ick. What a total sleaze."

Err, what? Seth had my full attention, and I asked, "Seth, are you telling me demons can read each other's thoughts?"

"No." He paused, tossing me a look. "I can hear others. A rare gift among our many races of demon… and the camera gives me an extra boost."

"Interesting." My mouth pursed, eyes hooded, while I processed this new information.

Seth waved his hand in front of me. "Hey, Sarah. Can you tell your hamster to take a rest, so we can get a move on?"

Shaking my head out of the sudden trip to la-la land, I motioned for Seth to lead the way.

Officer Lendy was already talking to my brother.

"So, we're going to get in touch with Mr. Sels. But we do not think this store will be opened tomorrow. Will you make sure this store stays closed tomorrow, Mr. Knight?" Officer Lendy asked.

Jake bobbed his head. "Sure, can do, no problem."

Squeaks was clinging to my brother's side like a baby opossum, fear showing on her pale face as she watched the officers continue to process the scene. The gurney for the body had long since left, but Debbie hung back to ask more questions of the officers and to reassure them she would call them when the autopsy was completed.

With a final nod, Debbie gathered her things, taking her gloves off one by one, the latex snapping as her hands slipped free. She turned from the cops as her eyes caught mine, and she hustled over.

Debbie wrapped me in another one of her famous bear hugs. Upon release, she clasped my shoulders, staring directly in my eyes and said, "A little birdie told me this place is closed tomorrow. Sounds like the perfect opportunity for you and me to catch up. What do you say, roomie?"

"Uh." I tucked a loose strand of hair behind my ear. How deep was Debbie into all of this? Would she believe in all of this woo-woo nonsense? Or was she aware of the supernatural?

Jeremy yelled at the officers, "Close the store? Close the store?? Are you crazy??? No, Mr. Sels is not going to close the store tomorrow. You just need to finish your little investigation now and be done with it. We don't need all of you tromping around this place all day tomorrow. What else could you possibly glean from this horrific mess?"

A male officer responded, "Sir, this is a crime scene, and we need to come back and ensure nothing was missed. Besides, it's only a day."

"A day without profits, officer." Jeremy sneered.

Vincent stepped in front of the other officer and replied, "too bad. The store is closed. Tell your boss that if you even think of opening the store tomorrow, then you both will be thrown in the slammer for blocking an active investigation and for tampering with evidence."

Jeremy's throat bobbed up and down as he gulped. His skin visibly grew more pale while Vincent held his stare.

"Fine." Jeremy huffed and stomped toward the front of the store. He shoved Debbie and me aside, only pausing to throw a hard glare my way. He inhaled through his nose. "Don't think you're getting out of this work. I expect you to be here tomorrow."

Jake came to the rescue and ushered Jeremy onward. "No, the store is closed tomorrow. So she won't be here, and I advise you to leave my sister alone."

Jeremy dug his heels into the ground to try to stop my brother from pushing him out of the store. He tried to shrug Jake's hands off of him. "Unhand me."

"Sure." Jake let go of him and pointed at the front. "Now leave."

Looking from my brother to me, he scowled. "Don't think this is the end of it, Sarah. Just you wait."

With that, he spun on his heels, phone in hand, and marched on out the front. His nasal voice echoed down the empty mall hallways as he informed Mr. Sels the store would be closed tomorrow for investigation.

My old college roommate whistled low. "Wow. What a tool."

I laughed.

Debbie grinned, reached out and shook my shoulder, egging me into agreeing to a meet-up. "C'mon, Sarah, what do you say? It's totally been ages and I'm dying to get caught up. We can even meet-up at The Coffee Bean. My treat."

Yech, my last place of employment? Is she kidding? I rubbed the back of my neck. "I dunno."

Seth bounced between us, rocking back on his heels, wearing a tremendous Cheshire Cat grin on his face. My hands couldn't reach his mouth fast enough. He inhaled deeply and replied, "Sounds like fun, we'll be there."

CHAPTER
TWENTY-SEVEN

SETH SAT across from me at the table, slurping up the double whipped cream on top of his hot chocolate. Whereas I sat sipping my plain black coffee with no sugar. The coffee was bittersweet because it was the morning blend. If you wanted more caffeine in your coffee, it was better to go with the lighter variety. Don't be fooled by others saying the dark was the way to go for more caffeine. They were dead set wrong. I should know because I once worked here at The Coffee Bean.

So far, Debbie hadn't shown up. Maybe she would be a no-show. Which would be great, for I was not looking forward to all the pointed questions she probably had written down in a small notebook. Debbie was one of those organizational freaks and liked to keep a small notebook to keep track of things. So technically, she was a logical, organizational, control freak. One of the reasons why people scratched their heads at our friendship. We were complete polar opposites of each other.

Yet, she and I got along fine. I scanned the cafe looking to see if she came in, didn't see us, and sat down in a booth. Nope, still not here.

Seth reached over to the end of the table and snatched a paper straw. He unwrapped the paper sheath, balled up the wrapper, and threw the wad at my head. I smacked the projectile aside and glowered back at him.

He took his paper straw and dipped the sipping utensil into his hot cocoa, taking tentative sips. Guess the cocoa was still too hot. A car drove by the window and slowed to a stop. The person inside double checked the paper bag they received from the drive-thru window to make sure they got the right order. Sigh, still no sign of Debbie.

Bubbles brewing and popping caught my attention, and I whipped my head back around. Seth was busy blowing bubbles into his hot chocolate. Seriously, he may look like a seven-year-old, but this was taking it a bit far. A slight smile pulled at the corners of his mouth. He knew he had gotten under my skin.

Snatching his hot chocolate away, I asked, "Did you want more whipped cream?"

He ran his tongue over his lips and smacked them, eyes bright as he eyed the thick forest green ceramic mug in my hand. "Hell, yeah."

"Language." I frowned at him. "A young boy doesn't curse… well, they don't curse in front of grown-ups."

"Duly noted." He held up an index finger. I turned and headed back to the counter. Since I had worked here, we still had the privilege of getting ceramic mugs. Also, lifetime customers, those with snazzy little cards, got ceramic mugs too. Mine was a dark sea blue.

Clara, behind the counter, waved at me. She took the mug from my hand, grabbed the whipped cream container from the small fridge under the counter, and loaded the top of Seth's hot chocolate with another round of whipped cream drizzled with dark chocolate and caramel. I had no idea demons had such sweet tooths.

The bell above the shop's door dinged, followed by the high-pitched squeal of my old college roommate calling out my name. "Sarah."

"Debbie." I gave her a waning smile. Clara behind the counter grabbed a yellow mug and filled the mug to the brim with some coffee. My roomie bounced over to us, gathering me into a hug. Did I mention she's a hugger? Because she's a hugger.

I motioned for Debbie to follow while she snagged the yellow mug and moseyed on over to the table we were sitting at. She slid in beside Seth, pulling him into a hug, and tousled his hair to boot. He ducked out of her arms, pushing her away enough to throw a nasty look.

"Watch the hair," he complained.

"Sorry, little man. I got carried away."

"I'm sure." He continued to give her a sideways look until he noticed the overloaded hot chocolate in my hands. He reached out, opening and closing his hands, and said, "Gimme."

I slid the green mug over to him, the content slightly sloshing over onto the table. He pulled the mug the rest of the way to him and licked a healthy portion right off the top. "Mmmm, so good."

Debbie's eyes twinkled while watching Seth devour the

whipped cream. Uh-oh, she, like everyone else, thought Seth was mine and Walter's love child. I gave her about another minute before she asked about him.

She leaned back in the booth, her arms resting high on the back of the booth, tilted her head toward Seth, and asked, "So, who's the kid? Is he yours?"

I nearly gagged on the coffee I was sipping. Sure, I was prepared for her to ask me who Seth was, but something about the question always seemed to catch me off guard. I coughed, choking, while dabbing napkins at my mouth and chin to clean up the coffee dribbling down my face.

Once I wasn't wheezing for nonliquid air, I replied, "No, he's not mine and Walter's kid, if that's who you thought he was, but he is my ward."

Debbie cocked her head the other way, her face screwing up, and said, "Maybe you might want to start at the beginning."

"It's a long story." I took another sip of my coffee.

"We've got time."

And so, we did, but I wasn't in the mood to be telling her what happened after I left her hanging, covering for me while my family continually hounded her for my whereabouts. Debbie moved one arm off the back of the booth to snag her yellow ceramic mug for a gulp of coffee. Her nose wrinkled at the unsweetened drink. She placed the cup back down on the table, grabbed six packets of sugar, and four containers of creamer. All of which she dumped into her coffee.

I gestured at her mug and said, "Want some coffee with your cream and sugar?"

"Shut up," she said, her mouth quirking up at both ends.

Seth stayed hunched down sipping his hot chocolate, not willing to make Debbie remember he was here too. She took a long pull of the drink and let out a loud, gratifying sigh.

Her fingers drummed on the tabletop. "Well, if you're not talking, I guess I will, but it's been so long. I don't know where to begin."

I smiled. "How about after I left? Tell me what happened."

"Everything? Or just some of what happened?" Her eyebrows rose, both hands encasing the mug before her on the table.

"Sure, why not? Like you said, we've got nothing but time."

"Okay." She sighed. "You asked for it."

An hour passed, Debbie still going strong, covered all the things which happened over the past years after I ran off with Walter. The more I listened to her, the angrier I was with my family. The lengths they went to, harassing my old college roomie for answers on my whereabouts, definitely made my blood boil. How could they?

Seth had finished his hot chocolate and declared his need for several more. To keep the twerp in line, I went ahead and retrieved another mug. He slurped down two in record time. Debbie was still nursing her first cup of overly sweetened, too creamy coffee. I, on the other hand, was on my fifth cup. The signs of being overly caffeinated shown, through the jitteriness of my hands to my unrelenting tapping of toes.

On the final gasp for air, Debbie wrapped up her story and gestured at me. "So, there you have the full story. Now, mind telling me what happened from your end of things?"

"No, not really," I said, stirring some sugar into my dark brew. "My side of things was too boring. Not much to tell. Walter and I ran off, eloped, did boring marriage things, something happened between us, we divorced, end of story."

Debbie's eyes narrowed to slits. "You missed the part where you picked up your ward."

"Seth?"

"Yeah, Seth. When did he come into the picture?"

"Oh, he ended up on my doorstep at the last apartment complex about two months ago. The nonprofit organization, Wings of Virtue, helped me with the necessary paperwork to make all the stuff legal and all."

"Why do I get the feeling you're leaving out some really important details, Sarah?"

"Because I am." I held up my hand to stall her questions. "No, I cannot tell you. Consider them classified."

Her gold eyebrow arched upwards. "Are you some kind of secret agent?"

"In a way, yeah," I lied.

"Hmmm."

Ivan's truck pulled up outside the cafe. I had secretly texted him to save me from my roomie's interrogation. He beeped the horn, signaling my meeting with Debbie was over. Getting up, I gathered my phone and fanny pack and motioned for Seth to scoot on out of the booth. Debbie stood up and out of his way so he could wiggle on out.

With another crushing hug, she said, "Been nice catching up with you, Sarah. We need to do this again, real soon."

"Yeah, sure. Especially since you weren't here to pay for my coffee earlier."

"Oh, right. Whoops." She laughed.

Ivan beeped Betsy's horn again, prompting Seth to skip on ahead of me and out the door. I disentangled myself from her arms and hustled on after him, but Debbie followed.

"Sarah, wait."

Pausing for a moment, I waited for her to catch up. She handed me a card. "Your brother told me how he didn't like you working at the department store, The Glen. He said there was something weird going on. Either way, we have an opening for a photographer."

"Doing what?"

"Taking pictures, silly." She laughed. "Please consider taking the job. Way better than working retail."

"I'll think about the offer," I said and placed the card in my back pocket. Ivan beeped the horn again. Turning, I waved at Debbie. "Love to stay and chat, but I've gotta run. See ya."

Debbie returned the wave and called after me, "Text me later, okay?"

"Sure," I said, knowing full well I would probably forget to send her any text and jumped into the passenger side of the truck, squishing Seth between me and Ivan. Betsy shifted into gear, lurched forward with a loud backfire, a plume of smoke rising from her tailpipe, dousing the patrons outside The Coffee Bean in a cloud of smoke, and leaving them all hacking from the fumes. Seth and I laughed as we rode down the road with Ivan yelling out the window, "Sorry."

CHAPTER
TWENTY-EIGHT

ON THE WAY back to headquarters, we stopped by our local Peking Chinese restaurant and ordered the crew several different types of dishes. Seth surprised me by ordering three times his normal amount. Where the kid put all the food was beyond me. But hey, this was supposed to be a relaxing day after what we dealt with last night.

The card Debbie gave me burned in my back pocket and I was curious as to what photography job she was talking about. Not to mention, with today's technology, I wouldn't have to worry about knowing the proper way of developing film. Nope, all pictures were one-hundred percent digital now.

Seth's hand waved in front of my face. "Earth to Sarah. Come in Sarah."

I blinked, shook my head, and peered over at Seth.

He said, "Ah, there you are. Ivan wants to know what else you would like. They're out of orange chicken."

"I can go for some simple chicken fried rice… with the tiny green peppers to make the dish super spicy." I licked my lips at the mere thought of the tasty dish. The hot peppers would ensure no one else would be snatching any off my plate back at the house. Except for Seth. Heat in food never bothered the djinn.

Seth gave me the thumbs up, leaned over to the window, cupped his hands to his mouth, and hollered, "She'd like the extra spicy chicken fried rice."

Ivan stuck a finger in his ear, twisted his finger, and pulled his finger out. He bent down to the window and said, "You don't need to shout. I'm right here. Sarah, did you want spring rolls or egg rolls?"

I waggled my eyebrows at him. "Why don't you get a dozen each? You know how everyone loves those things. Oh, and some Crab Rangoon while you're there, too."

"Good idea." Ivan smiled, his hand running through the bottom of his short, black and white, peppered beard.

Shoving Seth, I motioned for him to follow Ivan. "Go help him."

"Is this your wish?" Seth threw me a look like he was about to take my hand off if I touched him again.

"Maybe. Go help. Quit being a twerp and go help."

Seth rolled his eyes, let out a humongous sigh, and said, "Fine."

He scooted over on the bench seat of Betsy, opened the driver's side door, and hopped out. He slammed the door shut and said, "I'm going to count this as your daily wish."

I winced at the loud sound of the door closing. Pinching the bridge of my nose, I exhaled, shooing him with my other hand. "Okay, sure. Just go."

"Wish granted." He smirked, turned, and ran after Ivan, who stood at the top of the stairs holding the door open for Seth. A silent chuckle moved Ivan's shoulders up and down, with a twinkle in his eyes. Ivan always seemed to have a soft spot for Seth, even though Seth was a demon.

I leaned back on the bench seat, resting my suddenly aching head, the overly caffeinated high compressing down on my temples and sinuses. Betsy was still running and pouring heat out the vents. The heat and fumes from Betsy didn't help me much either, even though I stripped out of my coat. Should not have drunk so much coffee. The light from the sun setting blasted into my eyes. Even with my eyelids closed, the migraine gained a solid hold on my cranium. Ugh, maybe I should not have wasted my wish on Seth helping Ivan.

The birds outside the truck, chirping their fool heads off, weren't doing me any favors, nor was the loser riding around in his cruddy vehicle with the bass on high. Please make the torturous migraine stop. I was resolving into a whimpering puddle of pain.

Time weaved in and out, switching between hours and minutes. Footsteps sounded on the stairs coming down to the truck. I heard Seth stop.

"Uh-oh," he said.

Ivan asked, "What? What is wrong?"

"Sarah has another one of those massive headaches. I guess I should have stopped her after the third cup of coffee. She's not going to be much fun on the way home now."

"Nonsense. If we keep our voices to whispers, we can still have fun but not make her worse. Besides, we have food. Food always makes things better."

"So, you say." Seth let out a small huff.

The passenger door opened. Ivan's presence could not be missed. He whispered, "Sarah, I know you had too much caffeine, again, which is why you have a headache. But I need you to hold the food."

I reached out with my hands, still keeping my eyelids shut. Light was not something I wanted to deal with at the moment. Seth crawled in on the driver's side and with the last bag in place, Ivan closed the door gently.

He said something to Betsy in a low voice I did not catch. Ivan engaged the clutch and shifted Betsy into first. Betsy, out of character, purred and allowed for a smooth transition between gears with no backfires or anything.

Okay, I think I can handle this, if everyone kept their voices low and if I didn't get queasy. Ivan shifted gears and took a turn too wide. One of the Chinese takeout boxes stumbled out of Seth's hands and landed in my lap. The heat from the box made me leap up in my seat enough to hit my head on the cab of the truck. Ow!

Whatever plopped onto my legs had a too sweet smell to the substance and I started gagging. My hands reached out to the manual handle to wind down the window. The familiar knob caught in my hand, and I tried to wheel the window down. Unfortunately, the handle broke off on mid-crank. Ivan took another turn too wide. My stomach rolled with the turn.

The cabin of the truck, with all the food, was getting hotter, along with the smell of the spilt food and no fresh air. My belly was rebelling. With the pounding migraine, nothing but coffee from earlier swirled with each swerve and turn of the truck on the road.

Ugh, nope, not going to happen. I swallowed the bile down only for the swell to double in size. Nothing was going to keep my stomach from making a statement. My cheeks puffed out, a feeble attempt to stem the inevitable flow of belly juice.

Seth knew what was coming and yelled, "Watch out! She's gonna hurl."

And hurl I did… on dinner. Gross.

CHAPTER
TWENTY-NINE

"I CAN'T BELIEVE you did that," Mary said. She reached into the pizza box, the food we got to replace the ruined Chinese take-out and pulled out another slice of buffalo chicken pizza. The ooey gooey cheese made strands as she pulled her chosen slice away and inserted the delectable piece into her mouth. She made a deep moaning sound, savoring every single bite.

"Oh, she totally did," Seth piped in, reaching across me to snatch another meat lover's slice. He bit into the piece like a velociraptor tearing apart prey. Part of me shuddered. He was, after all, a demon. A minor one, but a demon, nonetheless.

I groaned, leaning my head into my hands on the counter. Throwing up earlier was not my intention at all. The entire situation was the perfect storm for my stomach to evict all contents out onto our Chinese take-out and on poor Betsy's already stained carpet. What surprised me was Ivan was a sympathetic vomiter.

"I didn't know Ivan would also throw up." I groaned. The memory, in tandem with the smell of the pizza assaulting my nostrils, threatened to curdle what remained in my stomach.

Seth let out a loud laugh. "Oh, man, the puke fest was awesome. He blew chunks everywhere. The windshield, the seats, the floor, I never saw someone puke so much. At some point, I thought he and Sarah were having a competition on who could vomit the most."

Mary couldn't help but titter at Seth's comment. She tried to school her features into a serious face, but the corners of her mouth were quirking upwards.

"Now, you both know," she said, taking another bite.

Another chuckle rumbled from Seth, who asked, "I wonder if I can get him to puke again?"

"Don't you dare," Mary and I said in unison.

Seth let out a long sigh. "Fine. I'll leave the big guy alone. Where'd he go anyways?"

"He went to go wash up," I said, massaging my temples, willing the queasiness and migraine to go away. No such luck.

My djinn sidled up to me, leaned in, and took in a big whiff before he leaned back, waving his hands in front of his nose. "Don't you think you should go do the same?"

"I don't have any clean clothes, genius."

"Uh, yeah you do."

I held up one finger and corrected myself. "No clean clothes which fit, genius."

"Ohhh, Blondie is spicy tonight," Mary chimed in. "Look at her throwing zingers at you, genie."

Seth, obviously ignoring Mary, snapped back at me. "And

who's the dumb-dumb who ate all the junk food without working out?"

Burying my head in my arms on the counter, I groaned. "Can't I wish myself fit, have clean clothes, and not have this over-caffeinated induced migraine and nausea?"

"You already used your wish for today."

"Sure, right... I don't recall officially making a wish, Seth."

He shrugged. "Dems the rules."

"Your blatant back ass rules you like to change on a whim based on your mood."

"True."

My head was pounding. I couldn't do verbal battles with the little twerp tonight even if I wanted to, not with my stomach swirling and this terrible headache. The world was spinning, and I wanted to get off. In response, my stomach lurched and flopped, sending another stream upwards. Leaping off the chair, I rushed down the hallway toward the bathroom.

The world tilted and upped the ante on my ability to run or even make my way to the toilet to properly dispose of my angry stomach contents. I slammed into the hallway wall, sliding down to the floor, I righted myself onto my hands and knees, crawling, swallowing back the rising bile, refusing to let my stomach win this round.

In the background, I heard laughter filter down the hallway, Seth and Mary laughing at my expense. Determined, I scrabbled on the floor, inch by inch, pulling and clawing the light-colored carpet onwards to the bathroom. The door was blessedly left ajar. Sweat poured down my backside, arms throbbing, hands aching.

Never had I ever had this bad a reaction from too much

caffeine. Part of me wondered if I had caught a stomach bug. Another twist and turn of my guts propelled me forward on the floor. Tears flooded my eyesight as my end goal got closer. The bathroom was nearly within reach.

Heavy footsteps came from the other end of the hallway. The black combat boots stopped in front of me, big thick hands wrapped themselves under my arms and helped me up. Ivan bent down and aided me to the bathroom.

"I'm here," his thick Russian accent whispered in my ear. "Lean on me. I will take you."

Nodding and regretting the motion because my head spun even more, I leaned into him as we hustled down the hallway to the opened bathroom. He helped me over to the toilet and stepped back.

"I would stay, but you know what happens," Ivan said, stepping outside the bathroom, holding the door ajar mere inches before he added. "May you feel better soon."

The door closed with a distinct click. I sat there on the floor holding onto the porcelain steering wheel, feeling my stomach twist and turn, unsure if my stomach truly wanted me to puke after all.

I leaned forward, forehead against the cool seat, feverous arms clamped around the sides of the porcelain god's body. The contents shifted inside me, sending my vision into pure white, hot burning pain erupted while everything rushed forward and emptied into the bowl. More contents followed, pounding into overdrive. I cried out and sobbed.

Long, stringy drool pooled from my lips into the bowl below me. This was the worst over caffeinated migraine I'd ever had, worse than alcohol poisoning when I was in my early twenties. This couldn't be from being over caffeinated, I must be sick. Most probable explanation for the fever, chills, queasiness, and all-over achy body. At least I know I'm not pregnant, thank God.

A knock sounded at the door.

"Go away," I moaned between vomit laced spit.

The door opened, and Seth walked into the room. He had a stack of clothes in his hands and placed them on the towel hamper beside the shower stall. Sitting down on the floor next to me, he softly rubbed my back in up and down patterns.

Shuddered breaths escaped my lips, followed by tears. I croaked out, "Why are you here? And why can't you make me feel better? You're my genie, so I should get wishes."

"Shh." He continued to rub my back, patted, and then stood up. His footsteps padded over to the shower, and he turned the water on. A few minutes passed when hot steam built up in the room. He reached over to the handle on the toilet and flushed the contents down.

Seth motioned for me to move away from my porcelain sanctuary. "Come on. Once you get cleaned up, you'll feel better."

"I'm not getting undressed in front of a seven-year-old." I glanced over at him, my head pillowed on my arms resting on the toilet seat.

He rolled his eyes and huffed. "Seriously?"

I shrugged, tossing his earlier statement right back at him. "Them's the breaks."

"Fine." He stood up, held up his left hand, and snapped his fingers. A plume of golden smoke covered his entire being, dissipating, revealing the handsome hunk I remembered seeing so many months ago.

A different sensation plummeted southbound and was for sure not queasiness. I stayed put, letting my eyes drink in the glorious hottie standing before me, right in front of a delicious hot steamy shower, yum, yum. He stood there with one arm propped on his hip, staring me down, while I kept my position in front of the toilet.

Seth bent down, dragged me over to the shower, and grumbled, "Oof, you weren't kidding. You do need to go on a diet."

"S-s-shut up." I did my best to not melt in his arms while he manhandled me over to the shower.

"This would be easier if you stood up, Sarah."

"Can't. Too dizzy."

"Have you even tried?"

"No. Too dizzy."

He exhaled another heavy breath. His strong arms pulled me upwards, holding me close, before he placed a kiss on my head. His hand reached behind him into the shower. The sound of water muted the rest of the household. Glancing up, I saw his eyes crinkle at the corners, an impish smirk plastered on his lips before he shoved me back into the stall.

Cold sluiced over my skin. I nearly fell over and broke my neck when I jumped forward, foot catching on the lip of the stall. I screamed, "Seth, you asshole. When did you switch it to c-c-cold??"

"Ah, better now?" His ever-delicious dimple in his right

cheek deepened with the slight smirk he wore while he watched the freezing water torture the sickness out of me.

"I hate you," I said between chattering teeth. "So much."

"No, you don't." Throwing me a mock kiss before he snapped his fingers. A plume of golden smoke once again enveloped his body, this time revealing the seven-year-old boy form he favored.

Seth walked toward the door, paused, pointed at the pile of clothing on the hamper. "After you're done washing up, be sure to put some clean clothes on. I worked a bit of magic for you, so these should fit."

"Oh, how kind of you," I said in my most sarcastic tone between the chattering of my teeth due to the freezing cold water.

"De nada." He waved, closing the door after himself.

"Jerk." I turned the faucet back to hot, stripping out of the wet clothing to get clean. On the bright side, I no longer felt sick, so maybe Seth did grant my wish.

While sudsing my hair up with shampoo, Mary barged into the bathroom. She huffed, "We've gotta talk."

CHAPTER
THIRTY

WITH MY HAIR IN A TOWEL, and clean clothes on my freshly scrubbed person, I followed Mary back out into the living room and sat down on the couch opposite from the counter. I noticed the camera was on the counter. Ivan or Seth must have put my camera there. She scooted out a bar stool and sat down.

The two of us played chicken with our stares, daring the other to speak first. Mary caved in with a great big sigh and said, "Blondie, you need to quit your job."

"Yeah, I know. You're not the only one to tell me to quit my job," I said, and added, "Did you talk to my brother?"

"Who?"

"Jake, my brother. I'm pretty sure you've met him before. Is he putting you up to this?"

"Naw, Blondie. Your brother has nothing to do with why I'm telling you to quit. Seth told me."

My eyes widened. "Seth? What did he tell you?"

"One, you have Vincent sniffing around and two the mysterious headless victims with no real leads as to who or what is committing the killings." She leaned against the counter, propping up her elbow, and leaned her chin into a cupped hand. "It'll be only a moment before trouble marks you as the prime suspect in this whole fiasco."

"Umm, Seth forgot to mention we did get some clues. We both saw Dawg's ghost. Sure, yeah, we were unable to question Dawg because Seth was busy arguing with the Valkyrie. He didn't tell you about that, did he? No, I'm going to assume he left that part out. Either way, I'm not going to quit when I'm close to uncovering the truth."

"Shit, Blondie. Do you always have to make things difficult? I'm trying to help you walk away from all this and here you are diving headfirst into the oncoming crap storm. Are you stupid?"

"You and Seth seem to think I am, so why do my actions even surprise you now?"

Mary stood up from her seat, exhaling loud, dropping her shoulders into a slumped over position. In slow motion, she gently whacked her head against the stone top counter several times. A frustrated half-scream, half-groan escaped her lips.

I shifted on the couch. "Feel better?"

"No." Mary stood back up, rubbed her forehead between her eyes. "Now, I have a headache, thanks."

"Happy to oblige." I grinned.

Mary leaned against the counter, arms draped over the edge, her lips in a firm line. She said with vinegar in her voice, "Alright, look, I promised Seth I'd talk to you about quitting. And I did. So, if your stupid ass wants to keep on playing with fire and get yourself arrested or, worse, killed, I won't take responsibility for your stupidity."

She pushed herself away from the counter, strode a few feet before tossing her chin over her shoulder with a look of sheer annoyance. "Oh, and Blondie?"

"Yes?" I shifted my head to one side, grabbing a better vantage point.

"Don't say I didn't warn you. Have fun."

Upon her final word, she turned her head back and strode down the hallway until she turned out of sight. The fact Mary was again trying to get me to quit spoke volumes. Her spook-o-meter was probably raising all sorts of alarms. Not to mention she had more information about what was going down since she initially scouted the joint and got me the job to snoop around for her. Part of me wanted to tackle her and make her give me all the details, but did she really know who were the real supernatural baddies at play? Especially when she and I went to blows, the last time over her trying to get me to quit.

Another suspicion was Seth asking her to talk to me about quitting. Strange, my djinn did not want to ask me himself. No, he had to go get the one person who hated my guts to talk me out of my job. Or was this his directive? Knowing full well I'd do the exact opposite of what Mary told me. Like he was lighting a fire under my butt to push further for clues.

Curiouser and curiouser. I needed to get back into the store to search the area, at least see if I could find and talk to the ghosts, ones the Valkyrie had not claimed yet. Which meant we needed a fresh death, or to set a trap.

Not wanting to move, I yelled at the top of my lungs. "Seth. Can you come here for a minute?"

His snarky voice trailed from down the hallway. The same area Mary disappeared only moments ago.

"I'm busy."

"Your shows can wait. That's what the pause button is for," I replied.

"Ugh. Can whatever crisis you're going through right now wait? The show's just getting to a good part."

"No. Get your butt in here, now."

"Last I checked, you already used your wish for today and tomorrow. Try again the day after tomorrow, Sarah."

"If I recall, you aren't supposed to be watching any shows because you're grounded. And if I have to get my butt off this couch to come grab your sorry rear end, you're not going to like what happens."

"Ohhh, I'm scared," Seth said in a mocking tone.

Mary and a few others from down the hall laughed. My blood shot up in temperature, almost to boiling.

"Alright, enough." I launched myself from the couch, snatched the camera from the counter, and stomped down the hallway. I had a djinn's butt to go whoop. Wish me luck.

CHAPTER
THIRTY-ONE

SQUEAKS and I had the night shift again when the store opened up the next day. The police were able to do their intensive investigation and called in their clean-up crew so the store could open back up, per Mr. Sels' insistence. The store was packed to the gills with many customers wanting to buy gear from an alleged crime scene.

You'd think people would want to steer clear of such places, but no, the amount of patrons grew as the hour went by. The main crowd usually showed up during The Graveyard hours multiplied by at least two or three. And only Squeaks and I were there to manage the large crowd.

Sure, during the day we had Mitch, Melissa, and Jeremy. Though those three promptly skedaddled once, the clock struck six o'clock, leaving poor Squeaks and me to fend for ourselves in the mad mob when we arrived for the night shift. The entire situation was absolutely nuts.

Though, to be fair, I was glad to be rid of Jeremy. He had been an absolute thorn in my side all day long and whining I was too slow in switching out the merchandise. Jeremy was such a tool.

With the store back open, people were compelled to taking selfies throughout the store, some in front of the questionable mannequins, which were not there the other night but somehow were miraculous back again in their booths. Other patrons took their selfies where people rumored the last victim died. We sold more dark sweaters and hoodies for this night and had more than enough made up for the store being closed for one day. The amount of people we had was so much, Squeaks and I barely had time to switch out the merchandise. The whole situation was certainly an exercise in a delicate dance of supplying proper stock, at the right time, while giving our customers quality service in tandem.

Sure, I could have wished for more help, but Seth was in time out. I locked him inside the camera until his snarkiness was dialed down to a two instead of a twelve. Besides, wishes I made with him never turned out good. Unless you counted a refill for a bowl of cereal, though you'd still had the chance of getting roaches or some creepy crawly slithering out of the refilled contents.

Nonetheless, tonight was crazy. End of story. I wondered if tomorrow would be just as bad or perhaps the whole *'I was at the murder scene of The Glen'* shenanigans might wear off. I blew out the lungful of air I was holding and called over to Squeaks, "Hang in there. We have ten more minutes before we can close for the night."

Squeak's wide-eyed expression darted my way, her black lips crooked upwards in a wane smile as she gave me a weary thumbs up. She was manning the register, helping customers ring out for the night, while I raced around the store, taking care of the merchandise. We traded off every half-hour, so neither of us grew tired of the tasks at hand.

The line to check out was ridiculous. Never had I seen the line snake around the room three times. People continued to take selfies and videos while they waited in line. The Tok'ers were explaining the history of The Glen, aka The Graveyard, and why the store would live on in infamy because of the two mysterious but tragic murders of previous employees. One Tok'er got my attention.

He wore all black, an oversized hoodie, jet-black hair with electric blue highlight, pale makeup with black around the eyes to make him look like a skeleton. He was panning around the room to show his followers the craze of people wanting to be at the spot where the murders happened in The Graveyard.

I listened to his somewhat pleasing voice while I refolded the clothing at one of the booths as he announced, "Hey gravers. Bones here, at The Glen, aka The Graveyard, the day after they've reopened, to investigate the mysterious untimely death of our friend, Dawg."

Bones took a moment to wipe imaginary tears from his eyes. The line shifted forward, and he followed. He pulled the camera in close and whispered, "Now, what y'all don't know is Dawg was found decapitated. They never found his head and, as you all know, I find that fact rather peculiar. Could demons be behind all of these nefarious murders? Inter-dimensional beings? His jealous past lover, Squeaks? Who knows, but Bones is gonna find out."

I pretended to be refolding the shirts and sweaters on the display booth close to him to hear his theories. At the mention of Squeaks' name, I jumped but recovered by acting like I had dropped one of the shirts, hunkering down behind the booth. Why did everyone suspect Squeaks? No way she'd be in league with any evildoers.

"That's what you thought about Walter," Seth replied.

I banged my head against the booth. Totally forgot, Seth could hear my thoughts when he was in the camera and my skin was making contact with the case. I rubbed the sore spot on the top of my noggin and regained my footing, folding shirts and sweaters so I could listen in on Bone's Tok video.

Bones continued his dialogue, "So, we're getting closer to our prime suspect." He panned his phone toward Squeaks.

The guy was fifth in line and Squeaks saw him. She literally jumped back, like the register shocked her, and called out, "Sarah, time to switch."

"I'm a bit busy," I replied, refolding the same sweater for the fifth time. "Are you sure you need to switch?"

"Absolutely." Her voice high-strung. "Pee break. Gotta go, like now."

Some of our customers chuckled at her bio-break admission, but I knew she was trying to avoid the Tok'er from interrogating her. I discarded the sweater in a sad heap on top of the others and hustled through the crowd to the register. Squeak's eyes were still trained on Bones, her body rigid and not fidgety like someone who needed to pee really bad.

I waved her off. "Go. I've got this."

Squeaks grabbed her purse and left a blazing trail toward the back. Bones broke out of line and tried to follow her, but I called out to him, "Sir? Sir, you need to pay for that."

He paused and panned the camera back to himself. "See? All of these employees are in on the conspiracy. They won't let me near the prime suspect behind all these murders."

I marched out from behind the register, customers groaning their complaints, knowing I was the only one left to process their purchases. My feet stomped on the tiled floor while I made my way over to Bones. His phone's camera trained on me the entire time. I put on my best 'try-me' face and in a voice that would fry an egg, I said, "Turn your camera off. I've been listening and I don't like what you're implying."

"I'm just sharing the truth with my followers," Bones argued. "You can't stop me. This is my right, freedom of speech."

A forced smile worked itself onto my lips as I replied, "Sure, we're all about freedom. And I have the right to ask you to either turn your phone off or leave."

"What are you hiding?" Bones stepped into my personal space. "Do you know the truth behind these murders?"

"No." I stayed put, not willing to let this dude bully me. "Now, leave. You're upsetting the other customers, who are about to lose their patience, waiting to be checked out."

Bones eyed me, his lips forming a hard line, arms crossed, and back ramrod straight. Finally, he rolled his eyes and said, "Fine, I'll go, but don't think this is the last you'll see of me. My fans demand the truth, and you can't keep on hiding the truth forever."

"Whatever." I shooed him off with my hand. "Bye, now."

Not wanting to let me have the last word, Bones stormed off a few feet before he looked over his shoulder, narrowed his eyes and said, "I'll be back."

CHAPTER
THIRTY-TWO

THE DOORS to the store did not close on time. In fact, the doors were an hour late closing because Squeaks had literally up and left me. She never came back from her supposed pee break. Once all the customers were checked out, I raced over to the mall gate and rolled them down. There were some late comers who were miffed I would not let them into the store. A few choice words were exchanged about proper store hours. Guess who did not care what they thought?

With Squeaks nowhere to be found, my only option for extra hands was the very person who was being confined due to bad behavior the other night. I caressed the camera's body and said, "Seth, I need your help."

"Do you? Or are you making a wish?" Seth replied.

"Either one." I grimaced. "It's late, I'm tired, and I want to go home. So, if you can magic all my store chores to be done, that would be wonderful."

"Are you sure you want to waste your wish on such mundane things?"

"Why the hell does what I want to wish for matter to you?"

"No, what you wish for is of no concern to me... all I care is if there's enough power to supplement your wish."

"Don't tell me doing my end of shift chores is going to drain your powers." I groaned, massaging between my eyes. "Are you pulling my leg?"

He let out a large sigh. I imagined him rolling his eyes, too. *"No, I'm not pulling your leg. Making your one wish to handle your end of shift chores is not going to drain me. Though, might I recommend you wish to remove the necessity of you needing to make a wish? Maybe you could wish for me to assist you without the formalities of 'I wish' and together we could do so much more."*

My brain hurt, trying to process what Seth had proposed. Somewhere in the suggestion screamed an escape clause which would spell bad juju if I did not properly pen the agreement on paper. I shook my head and replied, "No. Not tonight. Can you just, please, take care of tonight's chores?"

"You gotta say 'I wish' for me to make such things happen," Seth said.

"Fine." I grumbled, knowing in the past I haven't needed to say 'I wish' to make one, and said, "I wish for my end of shift chores to be—"

A scream happened in the back hallways. I ran to the door in the back of the store and yanked the door open. Another scream erupted further down the hall. My sneakers squeaked on the recently washed vinyl flooring, more screams, blood roared in my ears while my arms pumped in a mechanical motion while I fled down the hallway toward the source of distress. My breath labored because I truly needed to work out more.

With a screech, I hopped on one foot to manage the added inertia from turning the corner too sharp and banging into the wall. A muffled scream drew my eyes. Squeaks was bound, her feet and hands tied with nylon rope. She sat on the floor next to the pile of cardboard ready to be thrown out with the trash, with a rag stuffed in her mouth with duct tape. Hovering over her prone form was Bones.

I shouted, "Hey. Get away from her."

Bones swiveled back around with his phone in hand, a smirk plastered on his face, and said, "Oh, look, here's the other one. Maybe she'll be more willing to talk."

The guy took a step forward, and I held up the camera and said, "Stop. Come any closer and I'll be forced to use my camera."

He barked out a laugh, bent over while he still held his phone up in my direction. Between snickers he replied, "Oh no. Don't take my picture. Heaven forbid you take my picture with grandma's camera."

Uh, right. Not everyone knew my camera was a vessel of bad juju which could steal your life-force. If I was in his shoe, I would not be intimidated either. Great.

Though, again, this dude was into the paranormal, maybe I should demonstrate the camera's powers.

"Not a good idea, Sarah," Seth chimed in. I batted at the camera like a bug was crawling over the case.

"You investigate the weird and paranormal… you investigate the truth, right?" I asked Bones.

His laughter died down enough for him to stand back up. He blinked, straightened his shirt, the knowing smirk still present on his lips, and replied, "Yeah. I do. Are you willing to talk about the murders?"

"Sure," I said, my hand itching to press the shutter button.

Bones nodded and took another step toward me. I held up the camera, and Bones' smirk grew into a full-on grin with teeth. A chuckle echoed in the hallway. His laughter was reminiscent of a Hyena's laugh.

He replied, "That camera of yours won't save you."

"Oh, you have no idea." I returned the smirk and motioned at Squeaks all bound up on the floor and said, "I advise you to release my friend before we have our little chat."

Bones paused mid-stride, glanced back at Squeaks, and looked at me. "Naw, she seems cozy."

"Don't make me use my camera." The itch in my index finger intensified. "Release her."

"Ah." Bones rubbed the back of his neck, his eyes darkened. "How about no?"

Squeaks let out a yelp and scooted to one side. A rat hiding in the cardboard near her ran out into the hallway, and I seized this moment to take the picture of the rat. The lights flickered overhead, an eerie green glow emanated up and away from the rat into the camera, while the poor creature let out a final ear-piercing squeak as the glimmer of life faded from its eyes.

Bones and Squeaks both became very still, eyes grew wide and unblinking. They were both so still, the whole scene appeared to have been put on pause. Next moment, Bones let out a huge laugh and exclaimed into his phone's camera, "Did you see that?"

Uh-oh.

"Told you," Seth chirped.

CHAPTER
THIRTY-THREE

CRAAAAAAAP.

Which was an understatement of what we were dealing with at the moment. All of Bones' Tok followers literally saw my camera snatch the rat's life-force, *live*. I mentally reached out to Seth, my hand still clutched around the camera's body, and asked, *"Do you have enough power to undo my mistake?"*

"I told you," Seth said in a smug 'I told you' fashion of a wife berating her foolish husband. *"And yeah, I could take care of said issue but—"*

"Wait, you have enough power to deal with undoing a live video on social media? I thought your powers had limitations." My brows furrowed, and I kept my eyes trained on Bones. who was going on his own monologue for his channel, saying now they had proof magic did exist.

Seth cleared his throat and said, "Humans are skeptics. My powers can tweak a video enough for people to call what they saw faked.

But, you need to decide, either doctor the video to push the followers into disbelief or finish up your end of shift chores."

"Can't you make an exception?" I literally whined in my head, right back at Seth. Squeaks was on the floor, watching my face and posture, her eyes still wide from the camera's demonstration of power. Bones? He still continued on about how the man kept magic under wraps and did not want the people to have access to such power. Neither of them could hear the conversation I had with Seth.

"No. One wish per day. No exceptions," Seth chided me.

With the roll of my eyes, I exhaled loudly, dropped my arms down by my side, and hung my head. Seth was being rather stubborn about the one wish decree. I replied back, *"Fine. I wish for you to take care of the video for me, please."*

"Done."

Bones yelped. He flung his hand like something bit him, his phone sailing through the air, and shattering on the floor. Squeaks cringed from the pieces flying her way.

"No, no, no, nooo!" Bones dropped to his knees and sifted through the remains of his beloved phone. "Just when things were getting good. Dammit."

I took this opportunity to hustle over to Squeaks and untie the ropes. The knots were pathetic. Obviously, Bones was never in the scouts, otherwise he'd have done a better job on tying Squeaks up. No matter, I was able to get Squeaks free and clear in a flash.

Offering my hand, she grabbed ahold, and I helped her up. Bones was still crying over his shattered phone when we edged around him. He turned and glared, his finger pointing right at me, and said, "You did this."

"Me?" I held my hand close to my chest and looked around. "What did I do?"

"You performed a spell or something to make me drop my phone," Bones sneered.

Squeaks let out a high-pitched, timid laugh, and I joined her. The guy glowered while we cackled. I replied, "Dude, magic ain't real. What you saw was a trick of the light. I highly suggest you get out of here before I call the cops."

He continued to glower at us. I pointed at the fluorescent lighting above him and said, "The lights back here flicker, a lot. So, your eyes were playing tricks on you."

"Explain what killed the rat." He pointed at the dead rat in the middle of the floor in the hallway. He clearly wasn't scared of me calling the authorities.

I replied, "Rat poison."

"Bullshit. You performed magic and now you're trying to cover things up," he spat back. "I bet you're behind the murders."

Squeaks jumped back when Bones mentioned murders. I turned and asked, "Do you want to get going on the closing chores?"

"Yeah." She tucked a loose strand of hair behind her ear. "You're coming right?"

"Give me five more minutes with this bonehead," I said and pointed back at Bones on the floor, who threw daggers from his dark eyes.

"Sure." Squeaks bobbed her head and hobbled off, clearly

favoring her left foot. Upon sight of her injuries, I turned back to the idiot on the floor, clutching my camera with more strength than needed. I waited until she left and turned my attention back to Bones.

I held the camera up, my blood roaring in my ears and said, "Alright, bonehead, yes, magic is real. Yes, my camera killed the rat. And yes, I am going to use my camera on you if you do not get the fuck out of here since you don't have enough common sense to scram when I mention the cops."

Whatever confidence Bones was building immediately drained out of him. His pale skin went even paler when I pointed my camera in his direction. I held the camera up higher to emphasize I meant business. Bones threw his forearms over his head and shouted, "Wait, wait, wait! Please wait."

"I'm listening," I replied.

Bones opened his mouth, but a loud scream echoed down the hallway, coming from the direction of the store. My feet moved before I had registered. I was running toward the screams. Heavy boots scrambled and thudded on the floor behind me. The two of us rushed into the store, hairs on my arms raised in warning, and Bones' muffled cry behind his hand as he covered his mouth, "Oh gawd."

A shrill scream erupted in the room once more. Squeaks' body was suspended between two enormous insect like beings standing upright, with long slender necks, triangular faces, humongous multi-faceted eyes, enormous mandibles, and spiked grasping forelegs. The creatures looked like mantises. Squeaks let out another bloodcurdling scream. She struggled to get free, but the creatures yanked and pulled her in opposite directions. A slick wet rip sounded, and her screams abruptly ended, followed by her juicy innards plopping down on the tiled floor.

One of the creatures, which had Squeaks' upper half, promptly bit down. Loud crunching echoed in the room before the creature shifted its head to one side and detached Squeaks' head from her body. The creature loosened its hold and dropped the remains of my once co-worker.

I held my breath, not daring to bring their attention to our arrival. I tugged on Bones' shirt and motioned for both of us to tiptoe out the back door. The kid was even more pale, with beads of sweat forming on his forehead. He wiped his mouth and stepped with me.

We were almost to the door when Bones bent over and threw up.

Crap.

The mantises snapped to attention, leaving the shredded remains of Squeaks on the floor and turned their heads our way. Mandibles clicked and clacked as each one skittered across the floor to where we stood. Double crap. On reflex, I lifted the camera in front and pressed the shutter button.

CHAPTER
THIRTY-FOUR

GREEN LIGHT FLASHED, eerie keening screeches lingered, and the mantis closest to me went poof, showering us with bug dust. The one behind the creature backpedaled and dove behind the booths. The racks and booths moved as the creature crawled away, toward the front of the store, where I noticed the two mysterious mannequins were absent.

Keeping my camera trained on the movements made by the various clothes racks and booths, I made an educated guess to where the mantis would emerge. The entire time, the creature hissed and chittered with each knock against the objects within its escape route. Meanwhile, Bones continued to spew the contents of his stomach onto the floor. His retch filled the voids when the creature was silent.

Closer and closer, the mantis made its way toward the booth of the missing mannequins. Heart pumping faster, breathing intensified, flesh prickled. I waited for the mantis to pop up, ready to snag the bastard's life force with the camera. The creature was not going to get away with murder, not this time. I saw the last booth move to the side, camera primed with my finger on the shutter and ready to shoot.

A lone shadowy figure with a triangular head rose from the floor. Mandibles clacked and clicked. As the creature reached out with spiked forearms, a blue round miasma formed before the creature. With the creature distracted, my finger began to press down when someone rattled the mall roll down cage door. The mantis let out an ear-piercing shriek, and I whipped my head over to see my brother on the other side. His eyes wide, mouth opened, and whole body frozen in place.

The mantis dismissed the blue miasma and shot toward my brother. My feet moved before I had the opportunity to think things through. Hands still grasped the camera in a death grip, and I thought to Seth, *"Need you out here, like now. I can't battle this creature by myself."*

"On my way," Seth said, surprisingly, with no snark. His golden mist streamed from the front of the camera, his shoes hitting the tiled flooring with a squeak while he ran beside me. I tossed my head at the mantis and Seth veered off to grab the huge insect's attention.

While I ran at my brother and yelled, "Get the hell out of here!"

"What the fuck is that thing?" he said, pointing at the mantis.

"Not your problem. Now go," I replied and flapped my hand at him.

Jake took two steps back, hesitated, and asked, "Why aren't you running? You have nothing to kill—"

I threw my most 'Shut the Fuck Up and Do What I Said' face at my brother. He closed his mouth, and I waggled my camera at him. "I've got this. Trust me. I need you to go call the police."

Jake's brow furrowed upwards, and his hand rubbed the underside of his jaw.

Knowing he was about to ask another question, I cut him off at the pass and shouted, "Just go. Ask questions later."

My brother nodded, turned, paused once more, and said, "In case things don't go as planned, sis, know I love ya."

Warmth flooded through me. But I squashed the feelings down. Now was not the time for the warm and fuzzies. The situation at hand was life or death and I dearly wanted the life portion of the equation. I scanned back to the room. Seth had the creature chasing him about the store. Booths, racks, and merchandise were strewn everywhere.

Bones had taken the moment to hide behind the counter with the registers. I let out a breath; the pressure eased a bit, and I took in another long breath. Blood still pumped fast through my arteries and veins, urging me to move. I readied the camera, finger ready to press the shutter button, and dove back into the action.

Seth noticed my movement and changed trajectories, where the mantis would be in line of site with the camera. He didn't have to worry about his life force being removed because he was a servant of the camera.

The mantis got closer to the target and stopped dead in its tracks. My finger had the shutter button pressed halfway when the creature turned its triangular head my way and backed up. The creature motioned in a circular pattern with one of its spiked forearms. A blue miasma whirled into being right beside the huge bug. In the blink of an eye, the monstrous mantis was gone, and the blue miasma winked out of existence.

I dropped the camera from my hands, the strap around my neck yanking because of the sudden force, and I stood there. My mouth flapped open and close a few times before I asked, "Did the creature actually stop in its track, cast a portal spell, and leave?"

Seth walked right up beside me and replied, "Yup."

In the back of the store, the metal door sounded shut. I darted my eyes to where Bones was last seen, but the slimy bastard wasn't behind the registers anymore. Crap. My feet automatically started up again to run after him when more footsteps, likely a group, haphazardly slapped the mall tiled floors.

Someone rattled the mall cage door and shouted, "Open up! Police."

I halted in my tracks, let my head fall back, eyes rolling toward the ceiling, an exasperated groan escaping my lips, and said, "Craaap."

CHAPTER
THIRTY-FIVE

ONCE AGAIN, the police were here, at The Glen, investigating yet another gruesome murder. Based on the green coloration on their faces, the cops were not expecting such a violent scene. The remains of my co-worker, Squeaks, were strewn across the white tiled floor with guts, blood, and more smeared because of the chase Seth had with the mantises.

Jake, who had arrived not but five minutes after the cops, stayed by my side. His lips pressed firmly into a hard line. Not a single word was uttered. The tense way he held his shoulders told me his current attitude. Mine flinched when I saw Jeremy turn the corner.

"What the hell, Sarah?" Jeremy yelled as he surveyed the massacre. His arms and jaw slack as color drained from his face. I gave my brother a side-eyed look and he merely shrugged his shoulder. The cops all stopped to look at Jeremy who was making a huge fuss. One of them hustled over to take his name and whatever other information they needed.

Why was it always Jeremy? Why didn't Mr. Sels show up? Kind of odd if you ask me if the owner of the store doesn't care to show up when not one but two murders in a row happen? Why Jeremy? Does he have something to hide? Is he behind all these murders? Or is he merely a pawn in this whole grand scheme of things?

Seth hung back with me and did not wander too far. He probably picked up on my suspicions about all of this, or maybe he wanted to keep the various forms of assholes away. His keen eyes gave scowls and death glares, which sent chills down the spines of Jeremy and the cops who dared to wander over here.

Speaking of hackles, mine rose when the familiar laughter emitted outside of the shop. Officer Lendy, the female cop from the other night, and Vincent, turned around the corner, hand in hand. In Vincent's other hand was a large coffee. He sipped his beverage when he disengaged his hand from Officer Lendy. She pouted, swiveled her head toward the action, and hustled over to her posse. Vincent continued his leisurely stroll over to where I stood.

He took another sip, smacked his lips, and said, "Lovely night, tonight, right, Sarah?"

Jake's mouth turned downward, eyebrows following suit, when he turned toward Vincent.

I replied, "Someone died."

"Oh, is that what that god awful smell is?" Vincent deadpanned.

"Ass," I retorted. "You knew what you were walking into, so

don't try to play 'I didn't know this was a murder scene' with me."

"Are you admitting to the murder?" Vincent rocked on his heels, sipped his coffee, wiped the excess from his perve mustache.

Jake jumped in and balked, "No. My sister would never murder anyone. Especially not like how the poor girl died."

"You obviously don't know your sister," Vincent said, looking off to the side and taking another sip.

My brother tilted his head to one side and asked, "What's that supposed to mean? And how do you know my sister?"

Vincent lowered his paper cup, along with his sunglasses, and stared right back at Jake. His dark eyes glittered when he replied in the smooth baritone voice, "We've known each other for a long time now. You can say I've been there to bail her out of trouble from time to time. Which reminds me, she does owe me a few favors."

My nose wrinkled at the slightest mention of favors owed to Vincent himself. He was, after all, a sex demon and owing favors to a sex demon was not good. Though, in this case, I owed him none.

I was about to reply when Seth said, "Hands off. Sarah owes you nothing."

Vincent's lips pursed, sunglasses pushed back up the bridge of his nose, and a chuckle devoid of warmth vibrated from his chest. He took another swig of coffee and replied, "Has she wished them away? No? Last I checked, they were still there."

Seth glowered at him.

Vincent waggled his finger at him and added, "Ah yes, I

remember. Avarice told me a juicy bit of gossip the other day. I believe your powers are hindered. Am I right?"

"Keep pushing, sex scum, and you'll be dog doo," Seth growled, fire flashing in his eyes.

The sex demon detective barked out a laugh. "I doubt it."

Jake's eyebrows creased together, his head bouncing back and forth between Seth and Vincent's banter. Finally, he thrust his hands forward and called out, "Enough. I don't care at this point about some woo-woo bull crap. All I care about is my sister and making sure she can leave after you ask your questions."

Vincent and Seth both cocked their eyebrows upwards. I merely caught Vincent's attention, tapped the camera hung around my neck, and motioned at his prized jewels. The sex demon frowned, moved away, and said, "I'll go see about speeding this along."

"Good idea," I said with a smug grin. Jake let out a heavy sigh right beside me. Seth surveyed the bevy of police officers and waited for the next one to brave their way over to us.

Officer Lendy broke away from the group, with Vincent's leering eyes trailing after her. Jeremy saw the officer make her way toward me and he jumped, screamed, and pointed at me, "That's right, officer. Lock her up. All this didn't happen until she was hired on. She's the murderer."

The female officer stopped, glanced over her shoulder, and said, "Calm down, sir. Let us do our jobs. We'll get to the bottom of all this." She smirked at Vincent and asked, "Vincent, can you take care of him while I'm talking to Ms. Knight?"

Vincent nodded and returned her smile as he strolled over to

Jeremy and placed a hand on him. Jeremy stopped screaming and visually relaxed under Vincent's hold. The female officer shook her head and stepped up to me. She readied her notebook and started asking her questions. Seth moved in close and took my hand in his to continue his charade as a young boy in front of the officer.

She must have peppered me with at least fifty questions, mostly the same questions, but asked in a different way. Officer Lendy asked me to tell her the story of how I found Squeaks, if we knew who the shifty character in black was based on our description, where I thought he went, and why I did not hear the screams if I was in the back hallway throwing out the trash. Of course, she poked holes in my story, for the trash cans in the store were still full and not emptied. I did not tell her about any of the paranormal woo-woo stuff because I didn't think further explanations would paint me in any better light.

My brother kept his trap shut. Even though he did see Seth play 'toro' with a gigantic praying mantis like creature. Though, he was probably still processing tonight's events, too. I know later either Seth and I would have to wipe his mind clear or read Jake into the whole supernatural world. Both I didn't feel like dealing with anytime soon.

The female officer worried her bottom lip, made more notes in her notebook, and pocketed the book in her back pocket. She unhitched the cuffs from her belt and brought them forward. Her eyes held a sincere look in them and said, "Ms. Knight. I'm afraid we'll need you to come down to the station to answer more questions."

"Are you arresting me?" My brows shot upward.

Jake gawked and sputtered, "T-t-tell me you're not arresting my sister."

Officer Lendy gave a sympathetic nod and said, "I am."

"You can't," Jake said, his hands splayed outwards. "You have no proof."

"I can," Officer Lendy said and added. "I can detain her for twenty-four hours for more questioning and to prevent her from leaving. She is a person of interest. Ms. Knight, if you please."

I turned and held my hands behind me.

Jake cried out, "Sarah, no. You didn't do this; they have no proof."

Cold steel snapped around my wrists. I glanced at my brother and Seth and said, "Seth, go with Jake. Call Ivan."

Seth bobbed his head, knowing full well his radius from the camera was still pretty decent, so we did not have to worry about him disappearing into thin air in front of my brother. Jake had enough about the paranormal tonight. The last thing he needed was another paranormal incident to happen. Especially since we did not have the talk yet.

The floor kept my attention while Officer Lendy read me my rights. More footsteps echoed out in the mall area; squeaky wheels followed in tandem. Debbie's voice grew louder as she approached the store with her crew. Officer Lendy took my arm and led me out of the store. The wheels of the gurney ceased to squeak, and Debbie asked, "Sarah? What's going on?"

"Nothing. A misunderstanding." I did my best to keep my voice level. Tonight's adrenaline levels threatened to take a dive and push my calm into a tearful breakdown. Slight wobbles rifted my speech, though not enough for Debbie to notice.

She frowned, hands promptly went to her hips and gave Officer Lendy a stern look. "You have the wrong person. The Sarah I know would never commit these hideous murders."

"Sorry," Officer Lendy replied. "She was found at the scene of the crime and her story simply does not add up. So, I'm taking her in for questioning."

"But did you have to arrest her?" Debbie argued.

"She's our prime suspect," Officer Lendy snapped back. "Of course, I had to arrest her."

Before Debbie could reply, the officer whipped away from her, yanked on my arm, and I hobbled to catch up. The female officer was sure in a hurry to put some distance between her and Debbie.

I glanced back at my old college roommate, who shouted, "Don't answer anything until you've talked to a lawyer."

"Not to worry. I know just the person," I replied and stumbled once more when Officer Lendy yanked on my arm again. She led me out to her squad car, tucked me in the back, got in the driver's seat, started the vehicle, and drove to the police station.

CHAPTER
THIRTY-SIX

WE ARRIVED at the station with minimal traffic. Officer Lendy brought me in through the side door. Many officers waved or said hi to her on our way through the bullpen to the back, where they processed criminals. We approached the tall desk and stopped.

Officer Lendy's keys jangled. She undid the cuff and the cold metal slipped away from my skin. Circulation rushed back into my extremities. The officer behind the counter came out with a white plastic bin and pointed, "Wallet, purse, phone, keys, shoes, belt, jewelry, camera, all in the bin, please."

"Sure, but not my camera," I replied, still rubbing my fingers to work the lingering tingles out of them.

The officer merely lifted an eyebrow and replied in a nonplused tone, "Wallet, purse, phone, keys, shoes, belt, jewelry, camera, all in the bin."

I shook my head. "No, I can't put my camera in there."

"Lady." The officer sighed, pinched the middle of their brow, and said, "Put the camera in the bin."

"But this device is my emotional support camera."

"Your emotional support… what?" The officer blinked several times.

"That's right. My emotional support camera. I cannot be parted with my camera, or I'll go off the deep end. And no one wants me to have a sudden break down because my camera was taken from me."

Officer Lendy moved in front of the other officers, motioned with her hands for me to remove my camera from around my neck and said, "That's the biggest load of bull I've ever heard. Put your camera in the bin. You'll get the camera back, promise."

"Do you tell all your detainees that?" I asked, pouring on sarcasm.

"Only the pigheaded ones."

"Fine." I glowered at her.

At least I tried. I hoped I wouldn't be detached from the camera for too long. Yes, I'm able to not keep physical contact with the camera for quite a long period but if I go for more than two days, the camera steals my life force.

The other officer rolled their eyes and said, "Wallet, purse, phone, keys, shoes, belt, jewelry, camera, all in the bin."

I removed the camera with a cringe, along with my purse, keys, belt, phone, shoes, and placed them into the bin. Turning back to Officer Lendy, I held my hands on my hips and asked, "Now, can I call my lawyer?"

CHAPTER
THIRTY-SEVEN

FOR WHAT IT WAS WORTH, Nathan was one hot lawyer. He had my bail set within a matter of minutes instead of hours, and I didn't even need to see a judge. And he did all the magic over the phone. The dude had some connections, and I started to think maybe us crossing paths wasn't a sheer coincidence. To be completely honest, I was glad I met him.

Nathan was unable to come down to the station personally, but the police station already knew him. So, when I was asked to call my lawyer and mention his name, the officer in charge of the infamous one phone call actually dialed his number for me. Crazy, huh?

Nathan mentioned to me he would pass a note on to my friends Ivan and Mary over at Wings of Virtue headquarters. He'd already got a bail set, so all they had to do was bring the money. Talk about knowing the right people to make sure things get handled quickly and efficiently.

He told me I was not to go back to the store. The Glen was off limits and if I even showed my face at the mall, I would end up back where I was right now. So, I thanked Nathan for the heads up and told him I'd be sure to stay clear.

I sat in the meager holding cell. The plain wooden bench bit into my knees as I swung my legs back and forth. A few women threw nasty looks my way, but I didn't give no shits about them, if they stayed right where they stood. Unfortunately, one decided to push themself away from the wall. She was rather tall for a woman and pushed others out of her way on her trek to the bench. Then towered over me, arms held at her side, hands in tight fists. With one hand placed on the wall above me and leaned over, furthering her intimidation strategy.

I craned my head back, saw her menacing glare, and said, "Um, can you go do your lurking somewhere else?"

"Move outta my way," the woman growled.

"How about, no," my mouth replied before checking in with my brain.

Her fingers and knuckles popped into her already tightened fist. The woman sneered and said, "Think yer sump thang, huh? Well, yer not. Now move before I smash yer bones into jelly."

"I don't take kindly to threats. Have you thought of asking nicely?"

Her hand slammed into the wall above me and vibrated. The bench bounced from under me. I refused to budge.

The woman glowered and hovered over where I sat. I continued to throw daggered glares right back at her. Down the hallway, more voices sounded as officers led another person to the holding pen. The towering woman straightened up, so the cops did not catch her harassing the other people in the cell.

But it wasn't another prisoner for the night. Instead, Mary's argumentative voice sent a wave of relief through me. Grateful I did not need to deal with Ms. No-Manners no more, I hopped from my seat and jogged a few feet over to the door and waved. Mary wore an 'I am not amused' expression.

The officer called out my name, "Sarah Knight?"

"That's me," I replied, a grin tugging on the ends of my lips. Happiness or relief sent a rush of energy through my limbs, making them jittery.

The door to the holding cell opened, and I was let out. I bounced on my heels and said, "Glad to see you, Mary. Where's Ivan?"

"He's busy," she replied, the cold dripping off each word. Her entire body gave off the icy aura of not wanting to be here right now, bailing out a once friend. Though I hardly blamed her because I did lie to her and couldn't tell her the real truth as to why I left. It is frustrating to not let her in on the secret. Not to mention the various fights we had since I showed back up on Wings of Virtue's doorsteps did not endear me any more as a friend she could count on.

We were led back up to the front, where my belongings were returned to me, and the cops also gave me the same instructions Nathan had told me over the phone, which was to not go back to The Glen. I nodded, thanked them, and grabbed my stuff. Her eyes were dark, a scowl plastered on her lips, toes tapping her impatience.

I hustled over to where Mary waited and followed her in her

wake, trying my best to catch up to her long-legged strides. The old truck, Betsy, sat in front of the station, idling in all her glory, and backfired in greeting. Mary unlocked the passenger side before she moved to the driver's side and got in.

Upon opening the door, I saw Seth sitting in the middle of the old bench seat, shoulders hunched, and eyes trained on the floor. He could sense Mary's foul mood. I kept my mouth shut. A rare occurrence, I know, but I kept my mouth shut, nonetheless.

Mary did not wait for me to put on my seatbelt before she shifted Betsy into gear and who hobbled down the parking lot. I clicked the buckle into place right as Mary swerved onto the road, cutting several cars off, their horns honking their displeasure at her reckless driving. She paid no attention and kept her eyes on the road.

After a minute or two went by, she said, "What were you thinking?"

"In regard to what?" I asked.

"Tonight. All of it," she replied, the words hot enough to sear flesh.

I glanced over at Seth. "Um, Seth, a little help here?"

"Oh, don't be asking him for help, Blondie. He's already told me his version. I want to hear your side of the damn story. And why in god's name are you pulling Wings of Virtue back into your crap? I thought you were done with us? Or were you lying?"

I winced for only a moment, but fury settled in my chest, searing away the sense of guilt. Mary was being an outright bully. Who the hell did she think she was lecturing me about what happened? My jaw set and formed into a scowl. "I did not expect any of this to happen tonight. The events simply unfolded on their own with no help from yours truly."

"And Bones?"

"One hundred percent did not mean for him to find out either."

"Your reckless behavior revealed magic to thousands of people online," Mary jeered.

"But Seth took care of—"

Mary threw me a look. Her hand shifted Betsy down a gear as we turned onto the dirt road, and said, "Yes, he did. Thank the heavens for his interference. Ivan and I were relieved when we saw Bones' followers call shenanigans on the live feed. Now, no one believes what Bones captured. But if you did not have Seth, the whole situation could have turned for the worse."

"What did you expect me to do? Let him continue hurting Squeaks?"

"You could have called us," Mary replied, her white teeth bared.

I ran my fingers through my hair and let out a long sigh. "I thought you didn't want me to involve you anymore."

"For other people, yes. For you Blondie, oh, hell, no."

"Fine, but you're being super confusing right now. I'll call you next time even if you're not gonna help. Happy?"

"No." Mary's hands tightened on the steering wheel. "What about your brother? He's seen you and Seth in action against a supernatural beast. How are you going to handle him?"

"Tomorrow's wish," I replied in a matter of a fact style.

Seth grumbled. "You need to stop depending on these wishes.

You're only going to get into more trouble if you keep on thinking you can wish your way out of these situations."

Mary thumped him on the arm. "Shush. I don't want another word out of you. I'm talking with Sarah."

Seth gave Mary a go to hell look and dissipated into the golden mist, which seeped back into the camera through the lens. Mary shrugged. "Well, that solved what to do with him for now."

"Thanks for picking him up."

"I couldn't leave a demon in your brother's care. The guy looked ready to go off the deep end if he was exposed to another paranormal incident. Promise me you'll wish he had dreamed the supernatural stuff, alright?"

"Uh, yeah, sure." My hand caressed the case of the camera. Warm tingles trickled throughout my body, with a steady thrum coming from the camera itself.

The tires on the truck crunched over the gravel which covered the dirt road. We were moments away from headquarters. The colors of pinks, purples, and yellows streaked the morning sky, heralding the rising sun for a brand new day.

Betsy rolled into her spot on the grassy lawn out front, devoid of other vehicles usually parked outside.

Mary cleared her throat. I peeked my eye open to see her left arm hitch over the steering wheel. She gestured at the camera and said, "When's the last time you fully charged your camera?"

Butterflies swirled in my gut. I knew exactly where she was going with this particular question, and I swallowed the bile rising up in the back of my throat. My reply came out more like a whine than an actual edict when I said, "Recently. Please, can we skip the shelter?"

CHAPTER
THIRTY-EIGHT

BETSY WAS BACK out on the road. Mary heading directly to the nearest animal shelter. Mary refused to listen that it was partially charged when I had the fight with the mantises. She was insistent I needed to charge it fully just in case I had another battle. I sat white knuckled in my seat and tried to think of an alternative to getting my camera charged up to full.

Seth was seated back in between us when he heard Mary ask about going to charge up the camera. He mentioned he loved seeing my expressions. To be honest, I wanted him out of the camera for the time being so I could slap him if he needed one.

"Do we have to?" I whined.

Mary adjusted her hands on the steering wheel and replied, "Yeah, we do. You know vermin do not power the camera well and I doubt that mantis gave it enough juice. The camera needs more life force."

"The cockroaches were working quite well." I held up a finger to emphasize my point. "In fact, the camera got so full off of those roaches I did not need to charge the camera for at least a month or two."

"Those weren't roaches," Seth quipped. "Those were gremlins."

"No, those were roaches." I shoved Seth. He fell over, playfully, into Mary's lap, grinning up at her.

She shoved him back upright and growled. "Driving here, idiots."

"Yeah, Sarah. She's driving." Seth plastered on his serious face and tried his best to not smirk.

"Whatever." I sighed. "Can we not go to the shelter? Please?"

Mary turned down the road which led to the shelter, geared down to an acceptable speed, and turned her body slightly, hands still on the steering wheel. "And potentially have the camera fail on you or worse, steal all of your life force as you take down the supernatural creatures roving the malls at night? Nope."

"I hate charging the camera this way," I whined, kicking my feet and thumping them on the floor. "No one should ever be allowed to kill poor innocent kitties or puppies down on their luck."

"You're going, deal with it." Mary pulled into the parking lot and switched off the ignition. Seth sat there with a humongous grin. The rat loved seeing me squirm when the situation called for me to steal the life force of the poor innocent souls at the shelter.

CHAPTER
THIRTY-NINE

LOUD BARKS, growls, and pitiful meows assaulted our ears when the employee up front, who was also a member of Wings of Virtue, led us to the back room. The smell of bleach and water lingered in our nostrils while we walked along the cement walkway to the room of no return.

I shuffled my feet and fell behind on purpose. Mary stopped, hitched her hip to one side, her hand propped on her hip, and said, "Come on Blondie, quit dragging your feet."

"No. I'm refusing to do this..." I shook my head, camera gripped firmly in my hands.

The shelter employee looked between us and asked, "Is there a problem?"

Mary replied, "She's being chicken."

"These animals deserve another chance," I cried. "I'm not going to be the monster who ends their life. You can't make me."

"So, you're all for a dog who tore apart a young toddler to keep on living?" Mary remarked.

My brows creased upwards. I was walking a very fine line here. Yes, there were dogs who had three strikes and probably were not fit for society, but I could not bring myself to be their executor no matter what their crimes were.

I looked down at the floor and could not bring myself to move forward. Tears threatened to fall as they collected in my eyes. The view of the floor became blurry. I sniffed, and the waterworks turned on.

Fast on my feet, I turned and ran out of the shelter before Mary, Seth, or even the employee could pull me back to the room to steal some poor dog's life force away. I'd prefer to go to a bug infested building instead of taking any of these animals' lives.

Cool air rushed over my skin, bright light from the sun shined down, when I burst from the door. The camera still gripped tightly in my hands. Parents, kids, young couples, and more were entering the shelter. Some were leaving with a new family member. A smile touched my lips.

A hand rested on my shoulder, and I turned to see Mary standing beside me. She didn't look at me, but I could see she also cried. Of course, she may have put up a badass front, but inside she was a softy and detested taking an animal's life too. And she hated using this method, and she always ended up crying near the end, but this method of recharging the camera was efficient and served two purposes no matter how sad—one recharge the camera and two remove a beast deemed a danger to society.

I said in a low voice, "Don't make me do this."

Mary wiped at her eyes and replied, "Let's go find some bugs."

CHAPTER FORTY

WE ARRIVED BACK at headquarters after visiting restaurants in dire need of vermin extermination. The last one Seth was sure the roaches were gremlins. Mary and I argued the roaches weren't gremlins. Our debate continued until we pulled into Betsy's parking spot and shut the engine off.

The tension from earlier had melted after the first extermination. Mary and I rolled into our usual team dynamics. She even wore a carefree smile instead of the nasty scowl which took up residence on her lips.

This was the Mary I remembered and liked. She let her guard down while we exterminated the bugs and critters, reliving the good ole times. I did not care for the Mary who had a chip on her shoulder and wanted to do anything to deter me from carrying out my mission.

Ivan was inside the house, at the counter, brewing a new pot of coffee.

I inhaled and exclaimed, "Ah, bliss."

Ivan chuckled, grabbed one of the big thick mugs from the top cupboard, waited on the pot to fill before he snagged the carafe from the burner and filled a cup. He handed the mug to me as I took my seat at the counter. Mary accepted the second mug from Ivan and took her seat right next to me.

Seth hung back, his attitude simmering due to my refusal to steal the life force from the animals at the shelter. He considered all life to be forfeit when it came to keeping the camera powered. I disagreed. No one should kill innocent puppies or kitties for the sake of survival. Especially, to offset the curse of my camera.

Ivan filled himself a mug before asking, "So, you saw mantises, dah?"

I bobbed my head and sipped my coffee. Yes, I liked my coffee dark. Mary tugged on my hand and said, "Easy, Blondie. You don't want another caffeine overload, do you?"

"No, to overdoing caffeine. Yes, about the mantises." I sipped more coffee.

Ivan frowned. "Not good."

"Why?" I asked, setting my mug down on the counter with a clink.

He rubbed the back of his neck and said, "Last time was not good. They're somewhat of a herald."

"Herald?" I quirked an eyebrow upwards. "Herald to what?"

"The sins, gathering, to open Hell's gates."

"Wait, what?"

Seth waltzed over to the counter, stole my mug, and took a long pull from the drink. He placed the mug back down and said, "Ivan is right. These mantises have been seen every time the Sins try to open the gates of Hell."

"Do you know more about them, Seth?"

He shook his head. "No. All I know is based on what I've seen over the years. My information is more or less hearsay instead of actual facts. The mantises might be taking advantage of the cracks in our reality to make the leap between dimensions because the Sins are pulling power to home in on the various keys to unlock Hell."

I looked between Ivan, Mary, and Seth. My head ping-ponged between all of them and asked, "Well, if you ask me, these mantises are bad juju in and of themselves and I'd like to find out how we can defeat them. When I tried to capture two at the same time, the camera was only able to handle one. Not to mention, they could cast spells."

Mary added sugar and powdered creamer to her dark brew and guzzled the delicious drink. She smacked her lips and said, "I'm with Blondie. We need more information on these guys and not risk our lives with only hearsay. No offense Seth."

"None taken." He motioned my stolen mug at Ivan for a refill. Ivan took the pot off the burner and refilled all three mugs. I sat back on the stool since I no longer had a drink to nurse.

"So, does this new place have a library?" I asked.

"Of course." Ivan grinned. "Come, we go now."

Mary and Seth both pointed at their mugs. Ivan rolled his eyes and let out a sigh. "Your drinks may come too, but do not spill or you will have the librarian's wrath upon you."

CHAPTER
FORTY-ONE

OUR RESEARCH WENT WELL into the late hours of the night. Several refills of coffee happened, but I was left out of the caffeine fest and forced to drink only water. Which meant yours truly had to do many bathroom breaks.

What we found was Seth was kind of on the right path with his suspicions regarding the mantises. They were interdimensional beings who took advantage of weakened veils because of power being pulled for other purposes. Though we could not make the connection between the mantises showing up at the same time, the Sins, yes, we were talking about the original Sins, were making a play to open Hell's gates.

None of the translated text, scrolls, or ancient tablets showed the mantises working with the Sins to act as a distraction. They were both working on separate agendas. Mantises to sate their hunger for human delicacy, and the Sins to open the gates of Hell.

In addition, it didn't explain why the mantises were parading as store mannequins. Were they using them as a beacon to enter our world? Were the mannequins a unique doorway?

The records for Wings of Virtue went way back. Almost to the times of the Romans and Greeks. They even had records of Pandora and her box, which released the Sins upon humanity. I buried my head into the story, followed the timeline and the events which happened after she released the Sins and what I found chilled my blood.

Ivan's heavy hand landed on my shoulder. I jumped back in my chair with a yelp. He peered over, looked at the documents, and asked, "Find something?"

"Uh, yeah." I rubbed my face. The thought of a shower rumbled through my mind for a split second. "What do you know of Pandora's box?"

Mary replied, "Her box released the Sins upon humanity."

I bobbed my head. "Yeah. But do you know the history after that?"

"There ain't no history after that." She hovered over the table, sifting through more ancient parchments on the tabletop before her.

"Wrong," Seth and I both answered in unison. I gave Seth a sidelong glance and made a mental note to ask him about what he knew later.

I pointed at the scroll before me and read out loud, "The gods and goddesses are vile for tricking me into unleashing these horrible Sins upon humanity. I vow to find a way to reverse my mistake, even if I must lose my life to make such things happen."

Mary shrugged her shoulders. "So? Pandora made a vow to

undo her mistake. What good did her vow do, since she obviously failed?"

My fingers traced the translated text, and I stabbed at one spot. "No, further down she mentions Michael. Could she be talking about our Michael? The founder of Wings of Virtue? Do you think he might know more about the mantises and maybe Pandora's box?"

"Why does Pandora's box even matter to you, Blondie?" Mary turned her gaze back to the papers in front of her. She took another swig of coffee, but the effects of caffeine were clearly not as potent anymore. The entire team appeared to be waning as time went on.

Except Seth. Demons didn't sleep.

Tapping the camera which hung around my neck, I pondered aloud, "What if my camera is Pandora's box?"

"That's crazy, Blondie." Mary snorted. "Clearly, we all need to stop and get some sleep if you're coming up with ideas like your camera being Pandora's box."

"But what if the camera is?" I argued. "Certainly would explain why the camera can capture supernatural beings."

Mary shook her head. "No, Blondie. There's no way your camera is Pandora's box. For one, the box would be releasing bad stuff instead of capturing evil. And another, the box would only focus on sins, not supernatural critters."

I turned the camera in my hands and looked at the lens. Part of me was sure this camera was indeed Pandora's box, but I needed more proof.

Ivan patted my shoulder, stretched his arms upwards, and gave out a loud yawn. He turned to the group and said, "It's late.

We'll pick up tomorrow. Good sleep will help us all get to the bottom of our problem with the mantises."

Mary straightened her back and stretched her limbs, echoing Ivan's yawn, and replied, "Yeah, Blondie. Let's get some shuteye and hit this tomorrow."

I waved them off. "No, I'm just getting started. Don't worry about me. I'll sleep later."

Ivan frowned and replied, "Sarah, you should sleep too. Not healthy to skip your rest."

"Okay dad," I snarked back. "Seriously, go, I'll sleep later."

Ivan and Mary gave me one last look before they headed up the stairs to the main floor. The library was situated just like the gym, but on the other wing of the massive house. The librarian was a gargoyle who sat at her desk and glowered at those who talked louder than a whisper and brought drinks or food into the library.

After the two left, Seth plunked his butt down in the chair beside me and scooted closer. I leaned on my elbow and asked him, "So, what do you know about Pandora's box?"

CHAPTER
FORTY-TWO

SETH TILTED his head to one side and smirked. He pushed away from the table and wandered to the scrolls section of the library, turned, and crooked his finger for me to follow. I moved my chair across the floor; the scrape emitting a loud sound, enough to make the librarian scowl deeply at me.

I traipsed across the open space where tables offered the opportunities to study the treasures of knowledge in a quiet area. Seth waited, leaning against a column, as I waltzed on up to him.

Once I got to where Seth stood, we journeyed further down the aisle, which held all the scrolls translated from their ancient counterparts. He perused the cubbies, on the hunt for a specific scroll, and I trailed after him, taking note of how many scrolls Wings of Virtue had translated over the years. Seth stopped in front of one cubby, pulled out the scrolls until he found the one he sought.

His fiery golden eyes caught mine and asked, "How much of

Pandora's story do you know? How much of her continued story did you read?"

"I know she was sent as a gift to Epimetheus, and Zeus gave her the box or, in some translations, a jar which contained the sins or various turmoil and diseases to be spread upon humanity. Her curiosity got the best of her, and she opened the box which let out the sins, a pestilence upon humanity."

"Right. And afterwards?" he asked.

"Supposedly vowed to find every last sin and put them back into the box. She supposedly talked to Michael to help change the box and make the box snare sins instead of releasing them."

Seth bobbed his head. "Yes, Michael used 'hope', which was trapped in the box when Pandora released the sins. Hope was used to transform the box's purpose."

I noticed Seth never unraveled the one scroll in his hand. Gesturing at the scroll, I asked, "Does the scroll have more information or more clues as to if my camera is the box?"

"No." He shook his head. "This scroll is more of Pandora's writings… you can call this her diary, for there are far more details here than in the other scroll you found."

"Do you think the camera could be the box?"

"I cannot confirm nor deny your suspicions."

Now, that was suspicious. His nonconfirmation sent warning bells through me, and I involuntarily caressed the camera once more. The reassuring pulse throbbed through me, easing the nerves from the sudden revelation.

"I'm going to guess you know more than what you're telling me, Seth."

He pulled out another scroll, unraveled the paper, and said, "Hmmm. Interesting."

"What? What's interesting?" I peeked over his shoulder to read the same thing.

The scroll contained a mingle of pictures and words describing the events which took place centuries ago. On the paper, the story said, the Sins will continue their search for the seven keys, which combined would unlock the gates of Hell. Solomon and Pandora were the last known individuals who fought against the Sins, thwarting their attempts at unleashing Hell on Earth.

Solomon and Pandora took the keys and strewn them across the Earth, hiding them from the Sins. Pandora continued her quest to trap the Sins no matter how many times they multiplied and split from their original host.

Yet, tragedy struck when Pandora and Solomon were killed in their last stand off with the Sins by a demon who was supposedly under the control—

Seth rolled up the parchment.

"Hey, I was reading—" I tried to snatch the scroll away from him.

Seth shook his head and cleared his throat. He waggled the scroll. "This isn't useful. We're supposed to be looking for a way to defeat the mantises."

"Knowing more about the box seems useful to me." I crossed my arms across my chest.

"Later." He slipped the scroll back into the cubby and stacked the others back into the cubby as well.

I noted where the scroll was and planned on coming back to

read the text when Seth glued himself to the premium movie channels and TV shows again. The last passage seemed important, and I found Seth's behavior rather odd when he sensed I was reading something he didn't want me to read. Especially the piece about a demon who was supposed to be under the control of something. The talk of betrayal struck home, for I remembered what the Valkyrie told me about needing to bind Seth, and he would betray me if I did not bind him.

Seth's voice penetrated my train of thought. "You coming?"

I blinked, shook my head, and asked, "Huh? Sorry, what?"

"Okay, obviously, your hamster is done for the day. Let's head back upstairs and go to bed. You're not going to learn or retain anything new while your brain has gone on vacation."

I harrumphed and stood up, stretched my limbs while yawning. My back popped and instantly told me I was too old to be crouching or pulling all nighters.

Seth walked back, took my hand, and tugged. "Come on. Time for beddy-bye."

I nodded and followed him down the hall, through the open space with all the tables, and absently waved at the gargoyle librarian as we headed upstairs for bed. The entire time during our trek until my head hit the pillow, I could not stop thinking; was Seth the demon who betrayed Solomon and Pandora?

CHAPTER
FORTY-THREE

THE DOOR to my room slammed open and Mary shouted, "Wake up, Blondie!"

I rubbed my eyes because I was woken from my slumber in the wee hours of the morning, the remnants of the dream involving Pandora and Solomon were chased from my mind, including a warning about Seth which faded into the nether, no matter how hard I tried to hold on to it.

"What the hell, Mary?" I grumbled.

"Your brother called." She tossed my discarded clothing and shoes on the floor toward me.

I snatched them out of the air with each toss. "Jake? How'd he have your number?"

"Thought you gave our numbers to him, Blondie."

"No, I did no such thing. Seth?"

Oh yeah. Right. He's still in the camera by the door. He wouldn't be able to respond to my questioning until I touched the camera. Mary was one step ahead when swooped down and handed the camera to me. My fingers grasped the cool plastic casing while she walked out the door. She paused for a second, "Oh and hurry cause your brother is still on the line."

Crap. Simultaneously, I called out to Seth while I rushed to get dressed. His usual golden plume of magic funneled out of the camera to form in front of me. A smirk plastered his lips.

"Good morning." He chirped.

"Did you give my brother Ivan and Mary's number?"

"Yes. Figured he should have them in his contacts for just in case situations."

"Ah." I said while I struggled to put the left shoe on my right foot.

Seth rolled his eyes. "Slow down. You're going to strain yourself this early in the morning."

"Shaddup." I replied and switched the shoe to the correct foot.

My phone buzzed from my back jean pocket. I fumbled and fished it out to see a text from Mary with 'You coming?'

Again, not my fault. The involvement of Wings of Virtue is not my fault. After the call with my brother, Ivan and Mary had the bright idea we should go scope out the mall. Yeah, the place I was told by the police and by Nathan to not step foot in. However, the two were insistent we should all meet up with my brother. Who informed us there were stores where other mannequins had mysteriously vanished the previous night.

The mystery was enough to pique both Mary and Ivan's curiosity to drag me along to use my camera's special abilities to see traces of paranormal activity which may have happened in the area where the mannequins once resided. Details such as ash piles where they once stood were the only traces they left behind. The two gave me one cup of tea, not coffee, to wake me up. Needless to say, the tea was not working.

I sat in the back of the slug bug with Seth seated next to me. Ivan was up front, knees bent up to the steering wheel, and hunched over due to his large frame. Mary sat in the passenger seat, sipping her sweetened sludge she believed to be coffee. If you asked me, coffee was only good black. No creamer or sweeteners. Any other way was ruining the intended taste of the specific bean.

Seth rubbed in the fact I could not have any coffee by slurping his enormous travel mug. The thing looked more like a travel carafe which dispensed coffee and not a vessel from which you drank. Even more, why in the world did he bother? If demons didn't need to sleep, why did they bother eating or drinking? They were immortal, right?

"I see the look, Sarah," he said after another loud slurp. "Yes, demons need to consume sustenance. Whether the nourishment be what humans deem acceptable or not does not matter. All that matters is we demons devour the essence needed to survive. Kind of like your camera."

"Ugh." I sunk deeper into the oversized hoodie given to me by Ivan. "Way too early to care, Seth."

He smirked. "Well, your hamster thought otherwise. I could

see the poor thing working overtime as you mulled over the questions flying over your head."

I stuck my tongue out at him. "How kind of you. Surely my hamster can rest now."

"Ha." He snorted and sipped more coffee. I took another swig of my rapidly cooling tea. The tea wasn't bad, for the brew was a nice breakfast tea which offered some perk and less caustic on my stomach for these early hours. Ivan thinks my sudden allergies toward caffeine might be because of stress. Though, his theory was falling flat because tea also has caffeine. What was certain was the amount I had consumed. Too much was guaranteed to induce migraines, which if not handled with pain meds would devolve into the same sickness I experienced the other night when Seth teased me with his adult form.

Either way, the bottom line was, limit my caffeine consumption and the world would be alright.

I was nursing my drink while the slug bug hobbled through the morning traffic to the mall. I asked, "Why did my brother tell you about these mannequins? Why is he getting involved?"

"You never made your wish to make him forget," Mary replied, turning in her seat to look back at me. "Besides, he wants to clear your name. He believes there's something going on with the store owners and those mannequins."

"Hmm, I recall Mr. Sels getting rather hot around the collar when Seth and I initially tried to check out the mannequins. Especially when Seth said there was something weird about them." I glanced down at the plastic lid on my paper travel cup, sighed and took another long pull, drinking up the dregs of tea leaves from the bottom of the cup.

Mary slapped my knee. "Girl, why didn't you tell us? That's some vital info right there."

I uncrossed my legs, rubbed the assaulted knee, and glared back at Mary.

"Seth and I were suspicious you set us up. Why would we tell you about paranormal activity if we thought you were in cahoots with the owners?"

Her brows creased together; her eyes hidden behind her dark sunglasses. "Oh, hell, no, Blondie. You thought I was working with the baddies? Naw. You both know better."

She shifted in her seat to glance at Seth and said over her shoulder, "Seth, why you disrespecting me like that? After I let you watch all those movies and shows, too. I feel betrayed, man, real dis on me, for sure."

Seth sipped his large mug, fiery golden eyes sparkling. "Demon, remember?"

"Oh, you just lost access to my account until you've made up your dis to me," Mary snapped back at him.

His head snapped up, blinking rapidly; the large mug hung loose in his hands between his legs, and he replied, "What?"

"You heard me. Your access has been revoked. Think of that next time you plan on disrespecting me," Mary said, her teeth bared to drive home the point she was serious.

I shoved him. "See? Told you to not make up wild stories. Demon or not—"

He held up his hand to my face. "Sarah, don't even finish the statement. You cannot change who I am. Demons live to twist the truth and cause havoc. You and Mary happened to be in the crossfire this time around. Maybe you should consider redirecting my demonic abilities and mannerisms toward something which could be of use?"

"Wow, and I was the one who didn't have coffee this morning." I reclined back in my seat. Outside the windows were several parked cars which whipped on by while Ivan searched for the perfect spot.

Mary slapped Ivan on the bicep. "Jus' park. We have legs, we can walk."

Ivan replied, "What if we need to get away fast? Not having the car close works against us."

"Jus' park," she harrumphed, arms crossed and sunk into her bucket seat. "We'll walk."

"Fine. Parking, now." Ivan grimaced. "If we need car in a hurry, remember, I told you so."

CHAPTER
FORTY-FOUR

THERE WE WERE, the four of us, scouting out the various shops in the mall where the mysterious mannequins were last seen. I drew on the cords to the hoodie which covered my stark blonde hair, sinking into the dark blue material, hoping to the gods who were listening that no one recognized me. If my cover was blown, I would be thrown back into the holding cell faster than you could say 'Jack Rabbit'.

My brother waited in the food court, at the same table where I had lunch with Nathan only a few days before. Dark circles present under his eyes. He waved us over; more hot brews waited in paper cups, and my hand reached out to take one when he snatched them away.

"No, remember? Caffeine bad. At least for you." Jake handed the cups out to the rest of the team. Seth snagged one and took a long pull from his, smacking his lips in satisfaction and to get under my skin.

I snarked at Seth. "Aren't you a little too young to be drinking so much coffee?"

"Looks are deceiving," he returned with a wink.

Jake cleared his throat and handed Ivan the manilla folder, which held his carefully crafted notes of the shops where mannequins had gone missing. Ivan flipped through the folder, nodding at each page, eyes scrutinizing the photos printed out and asked, "Were there anymore murders?"

My brother shook his head. "No, strangely, only The Glen suffered murders among their employees. None of the other shops had any deaths, employees or customers."

"Hmmm." Ivan scratched his closely cropped salt and peppered beard. "We will go look. See if Sarah's camera can spot these anomalies."

"I still don't see how a simple camera can spot strange things," Jake replied, his eyes darting to the camera which hung around my neck and back to Ivan.

Ivan tucked the folder under his arm, grabbed his paper cup, sipped, and replied, "Trust. All I ask is for you to trust. Later, I will tell you all you need to know."

"Uh, thanks," Jake said.

"Least I could do," Ivan replied with a shrug. He turned and waved us on. "Come, we have many shops to see. Might not see all if we dawdle too long."

I nodded, gave my brother a half hug, and jogged after Ivan. Seth followed close behind, loudly slurping his coffee, a reminder he had what I was craving and could not have. Twerp.

Mary walked alongside Ivan, arms held behind her back, and asked, "So, which shops had these creepy mannequins?"

"Mostly clothing stores. There are many, but I am confident we'll get through them before dark." Ivan's strides became longer, making all of us double time to keep up.

I huffed and puffed. "Okay, but what is your plan to keep me from being discovered by the police who are still roaming the mall?"

"Your brother has agreed to run interference. He has labeled each store in order and indicated he'll keep the police's attention at the opposite ends of the mall while we investigate."

"And I gather we have a tight schedule to follow?"

"Yes. No more than ten to fifteen minutes per store, so we do not fall behind and risk discovery."

"Ugh. Is this why you're practically making us all run a marathon right now?"

"Yes, now, let's hurry."

When I didn't think Ivan could go faster, the tall Russian man hastened his pace and the rest of us were jogging to keep up. When we finally stopped at the first store, all of us, except Ivan and Seth, were red in the face, sucking in air like the substance was a precious commodity. Okay, fine, Mary was barely winded. I was the only one about to fall over. Without adrenaline to fuel my sudden need to run, my body protested at any ounce of exertion needed.

We entered the store and tried to act inconspicuous. Seth put on his best seven-year-old boy act and pulled Mary and Ivan around, asking for things like any young kid would do in a store. I removed the lid from the lens of the camera and brought the lens up to scan the store. Remnants of supernatural activity whorled close to platforms devoid of any display. I moved in closer.

Bits of blue, purple, and green moved in and out of our dimension; ragged edges fluttered in place like someone or something had ripped a hole and hastily pulled the tear back together. I moved the camera around the area, looking for more clues or more paranormal residue left behind by our insectoid visitors.

Why didn't these other stores suffer horrendous deaths like The Glen did? Unless they had and could cover up the murders better because they were already closed at night. The more I thought about the angle, the more the hypothesis seemed plausible.

I lowered the camera and glanced around the store. Patrons were oblivious to me scanning the empty platforms. The employees, however, were keeping their eyes on me. I caught Mary's attention and jerked my chin at the employees. A slight smile pulled at her lips. She waltzed over to the workers, who were watching me like hawks.

Weaving in and out of the clothing rack, I made my way over to where Mary, Ivan, and Seth were grilling the workers. I caught the tail end of the conversation.

"So, you're saying those booths never had anything on them?" Mary asked, her hand gesturing to the empty platforms close to the store's front windows.

The young man she was questioning shook his head. "No, Ma'am, we've never had anything there. Those booths have always been empty."

"Are you sure?"

"Yeah." He bit out his reply. "I'm not lying if this is what you're thinking."

"Naw, I just want to be sure. Thanks, man," Mary said and turned to me.

Ivan tapped his watch, and we all exited the store. I felt eyes boring into my back. I looked over my shoulder but saw no one glancing my way.

Mary said under her breath, "I wonder if the next store employees will say the same thing about the empty platforms."

Seth added, "Seems to me their memories were tampered."

"I wouldn't doubt it." I agreed with him, rubbing my arms as a chill went through me. "But we need to ask the employees of the other stores to be sure their memories were tampered."

Ivan pointed at the upcoming store, and we entered and followed the same routine. We did this for the next five stores, empty platforms, ash piles suspiciously wiped clear, with the same signatures of torn and sloppy mended holes in the fabric of reality, and employees who swore they never had anything on those platforms.

Each time we exited the stores, a menacing sensation went through me, but I could not see who was behind the hair-raising tingles. My hands clutched the camera tighter, fearful someone had their eyes on my precious. Seth noticed my sudden overprotectiveness of the camera kick in; a slender eyebrow quirked upwards, but said nothing.

In the seventh store, I wandered over to the empty platforms and scanned the area with the camera. The same blue, green, and purple shimmered in and out of the torn and poorly mended hole of our dimension. My hands were adjusting the lens for a cleaner look when a sudden jerk happened, pulling me backwards.

I landed on my butt, hands instinctively going for the camera, only to have the strap which was around my neck be wretched away from me. The one security line was cut, and the camera gone. I shouted, "Seth."

He ducked and dodged around Mary and Ivan and ran after the perp who stole the camera. I tried to roll to my feet, the stabbing pain catching me halfway, and I paused. I wasn't twenty anymore. With the aid of the nearby booth, I pulled myself up and saw Seth running after the thief.

They raced outside the store, and I did my best to send my train of thought to Seth, camera or no. I hoped he heard me. *"Seth, catch the bastard. If this is my only wish for today, I wish you'll catch him so I can beat the living shit out of him."*

For a brief moment, I didn't think it worked because I did not have the camera in hand, and to be honest, I wasn't sure if our connection was that strong outside the camera.

He replied, the tension clear. *"Granted."*

CHAPTER
FORTY-FIVE

SORENESS STABBED my glutes and pulled as I hobbled out of the store, ever so slowly following Ivan and Mary, who ran after Seth. I clenched my teeth, using the wall as my makeshift walking aid. The two were gone from sight, and I couldn't hurry up since my limbs protested at the sheer thought of speeding things up. Leg cramps threatened to stop me in my tracks if I even dared to push myself faster.

After what felt like an agonizing hour, which was probably only five or ten minutes, I found my crew, Ivan distracting the people while Mary was on the ground sitting on top of something, looking like her sitting there was natural and nothing was wrong, and Seth was on the lookout for me. His eyes sought mine out in the crowd of mall goers. Once his eyes locked onto mine, he beckoned with his hands for me to cross the steady, heavy stream of people in the mall walkway.

Sucking in a lungful of air, I prepped myself to push away

from the wall to amble, ever so sloppily, to the other side, where my crew awaited me. A few patrons bumped and sideswiped me on my crossing, sending me into a zigzagging pattern. I ended up on the other side after navigating the sea of people.

Ivan merely lifted an eyebrow when I leaned against the wall and let out a loud sigh. Seth came over, handed me the camera; the soothing vibrations and warmth rushed through me. The sensation was something which never got old. Almost like a drug, a drug in which I didn't know I craved until I was reacquainted with the warm tingles.

Seth jerked his chin to the pile under Mary and said, "The perp is still conscious if you want to go kick the living daylights out of him."

"Him?"

"Yeah. The bonus is you'll be paying the jerk back for last night, too." Seth grinned, his fiery golden eyes flashing brightly.

"Wait." I caught his shoulder before he could walk off. "Are you saying Bones is the one who stole the camera?"

"No, the Easter bunny stole your camera." Seth rolled his eyes. "Of course, Bones was the one who stole your camera. Who else would be stupid enough?"

I flicked his ear with my finger. "Um, you're forgetting Avarice, Vincent, and Mrs. Smith. Either one of them would be delighted to steal my camera, too."

"Yeah, sure, like they would stoop so low to stealing the camera with their own two hands." Seth rolled his eyes again and let out an exasperated sigh.

"You'd be surprised," I replied, frowning when I glanced

down at the bundle of clothes under Mary. I asked her, "Is he conscious?"

Mary smiled, smacked the backside of the hooded figure who was face down on the ground. She said, "Hey dummy, Blondie has some questions to ask you."

"Will you stop hitting me?" He groaned, moved his hand, and rubbed the sore spot on the back of his head. Bones grumbled and wheezed, "Do you mind getting off me? I can't exactly talk with you sitting on top of me."

"And let you get away again? Oh, hell, no."

Ivan cleared his throat and said, "Mary, please get off the young delinquent. There's enough of us here to manage him. He will probably not talk if he is too uncomfortable."

Mary huffed, rolled to her feet, and stood up. Bones rolled over, groaned, and pulled himself to a sitting position, his hand still rubbing the back of his head. He glanced up at Ivan and gave a smirk.

"Thanks, man," Bones said. "I don't know how much longer I could bear her weight."

"Oh, hell, no, did you just call me fat?" Mary rushed at him. Ivan caught her by the shoulders and pulled her back.

Bones backed up, hands held high in a placating manner, and said, "Geez, no. Sorry, man."

Sheesh, better stop him in his tracks before Mary pulverized him, and we didn't get our answers because he was a puddle of sludge. I stepped between the two, hands held up, and said, "Look, let's cut the crap. Answer my questions and we'll let you go."

Bones bobbed his head. "Sounds fair."

I kept a sharp eye on him. Seth and Mary held back, ready to leap into action like a tiger poised to rend its prey if the cornered animal made any sudden movements. I turned to Bones and said, "First, I need to know why you were trying to steal my camera?"

"Money, duh," Bones replied.

"Wrong answer," I said and added, "Mary?"

Mary cracked her knuckles, moved in close to Bones. He jumped back, bumping into the wall, eyes wide, hands held high as he said, "Wait, wait, wait, okay… I needed a new phone, 'kay? And some dude saw me looking, noticed I didn't have the funds to get the phone I wanted. They approached and offered me the money, but in exchange for your camera."

Seth broke into the conversation. "Did you see what this person looked like?"

"Naw, dude. They wore a mask, but I'm pretty sure the person was some guy, but I'm not like a hundred percent sure, because they had a voice distortion device, y'know?"

"Where were you supposed to meet them?" I asked, knowing he probably was en route to hand off his ill-gotten goods.

Bones simply shook his head, gave a slight laugh, and replied, "Man, if you were hoping to meet up with them, you're sorely mistaken. Cause the dude only gave me a drop off location. And this was the location, man. Other than them receiving the camera, I wouldn't get paid until the successful transfer of such assets. So, really, all of you owe me a new phone."

Mary slammed him into the wall in the blink of an eye. Her other hand pulled back ready to launch a mean punch, but she held her fist aloft and said, "We ain't giving you shit. Sarah owes you nothing. Be glad we're not gonna snap away your sorry life force to charge the camera."

Ivan kept moving people on and said we were filming a scene for our college class when people stopped to ask what we were doing. He was rather convincing, so we didn't have to worry about additional mall security popping up to stop our interrogation. My brother's presence helped assure the mall goers this was only an act.

The Adam's apple of Bones' throat visibly bobbed up and down when he swallowed, loudly. Mary kept a firm hold on him, using leverage to offset the weight difference between her and him. She sneered, "And I don't want you to be telling any of your followers about any of this. If I find out you've been saying anything, you better believe I'm gonna come beat your ass. Got it?"

Bones nodded, swallowed again, and replied, "Yeah, man."

The burble of the mall goers filled in the silence between my crew and our captive. After a moment, Mary growled, "And right here was the drop off location?"

Not letting his eyes wander from the threat in front of him, Bones answered, "No, the drop off location is The Glen."

CHAPTER
FORTY-SIX

"YOU CAN'T DO this to me," Bones shouted.

Ivan dumped him like a sack of potatoes onto the empty platform, the same platform the creepy mannequins once occupied, in front of the store. Why the mannequins weren't present again, like they usually were after a night's disappearance, was a mystery.

Mary paid Mitch and Melissa to suddenly become scarce while we commandeered The Glen to set up our trap. Jeremy was nowhere to be found, which was rather odd. During the day shift, his tightly pinched rear end was never too far from hassling Mitch, Melissa, or me about being behind schedule for a merchandise switch. Considering he was always there when things got tense, his absence made my stomach churn. He was bound to show up, eventually.

Shrugging my shoulders to throw off the uneasy feeling, I sidled up to where Ivan stood guard, hands on my camera, scanning the room of patrons slowly leaving the store, and placed the camera down beside Bones.

With one withering look at Ivan, I said, "You better be right."

Everything in my body screamed for me to go back and retrieve my camera before something bad happened. Seth stood with me, well actually in front of me, so I would not rush over and snatch up my camera once more.

Mary and Jake were busy rushing stragglers out of the store. Some customers were being stubborn and claiming they had no right to push people out when there wasn't any emergency. Jake scrubbed a hand down his face and replied to the difficult person, "Look, we've been told there's a gas leak. So, you need to leave."

"What about them?" The person splayed their hands our way. "Why aren't they leaving?"

"I'll get to them," Jake gritted through his teeth. "Now, go."

The customer's eyes shifted from us and the other customers meandering out the front; they licked their lips and asked, "Will I get a discount? You know, for the inconvenience and all?"

"How 'bout a renewal on your life?" Mary chimed in. "Unless you want to cut yours short."

They visibly blanched, color draining from their cheeks, while their mouth gaped open. With a shake of their head, they dropped the merchandise they had in their hands and scrambled out the door and called over their shoulder, "Life's good, I choose life."

Mary nodded her head and chased other customers out of the store with Jake's false story about a gas leak. People left in droves upon hearing the false story. Once the store was empty, we shuttered the front gates and locked them. Then we waited.

A thud sounded behind me. I looked over my shoulder and found Mary wrestling with her duffle bag of goodies on the counter beside the registers. She had taken a moment to grab her bag from the Slug Bug while we prepped Bones and paid off Mitch and Melissa. The zipper on the bag sounded while she drew the toggle back and opened the contents.

Crossbows, ornaments filled with holy water, pikes which needed assembling, and more weapons were placed and arranged upon the countertops. Seth sauntered over to the selection of weapons, fingers brushing along the tops of the various tools of defense, and halted in front of one in particular. He lifted the simple leather item, with a thick flat piece of leather in the middle of the thin strands of leather cord, the corners of his mouth tugging downwards, while he held the thing between two fingers.

He glanced over at Mary and said, "A sling? Really? You're bringing a slingshot to a potentially highly magical fight?"

Mary snatched the slingshot from his hand and growled, "That sling, you know, is the very same one used by David from his fight with Goliath. Don't dis religious relics."

"But still, a sling? Really?" Seth's eyebrow quirked upward.

"Jus' for that, you can't use none of my weapons. You're banned."

Seth's mouth popped open. His eyes flashed before he whirled his back on Mary, arms crossed, and huffed, "Fine. I didn't need any of your lousy weapons, anyway."

Outside in the mall, people continued to stream on by the

store, pausing to stare at Bones, who was all tied up and on display. Noticing the crowd we were collecting out front, I called over to my brother, "Hey, Jake, any way we can shutter these windows? I kind of don't want the police showing up in droves like a midnight special for donuts."

Jake nodded and walked toward the back. "Yeah, I think there are some controls in the back room. Let me go do—"

The door to the back opened and Jeremy waltzed in. A gun in his hand, pointed at my brother, and answered, "No, I'm afraid I cannot let you go anywhere."

"Jeremy?" I said, "What the hell?"

His eyes darted my way. "Shut up, Sarah. You've always been a pain in my ass. Finally, you're gonna be good for something. The boss wanted me to make sure you stay—"

A crossbow bolt embedded itself into the doorjamb close to Jeremy. The loud twang echoed into the room as the bolt shuddered upon impact. He paused, blinked his eyes back at Mary, pressed his finger against the bolt and ducked under it. His gun still trained on Jake.

Jeremy cleared his throat. "Call your bitch off or your brother dies."

"Oh, hell, no, he did not jus' call me a—" Mary swung her crossbow back up, aiming the sights on Jeremy, when Ivan called out.

"Mary, stop. He has a gun. You know he'll shoot Jake before you can even take him down."

With the crossbow held steady in her hands, trained on Jeremy, Mary clenched her teeth, finger near the trigger, the room silent and thick with tension. She swore and lowered the weapon. Jeremy motioned with his gun. "Good girl. Now drop your weapon."

"I ain't no dog," she spat.

Jeremy sneered, "I said, drop the weapon, unless you want to see poor Jake die."

The next moment, his hand aimed low, an explosion of blood splurged out the back of Jake's left knee. My brother yelled out and crumpled to the floor, hands immediately rushing to the sight of the gushing wound, face drained of color. No time to think. I tried to rush to him when Jeremy swung the gun back up and pointed the muzzle at me.

"You asshole," I screamed back at him, held up my hand, and stopped in my tracks. "Can you take the crazy down a notch? I just want to help my brother."

"No." Jeremy's lips lifted away from his teeth in a snarl. "The boss will be here any minute. Get back to the platform. All of you. Tell your guard dog to drop her weapons. Or the next bullet is going into your dear brother's head."

Seth interrupted. "If I were you, I would not let Sarah anywhere close to the camera."

"Yeah, man," Bones added. "Listen to the little dude. Don't let the blonde lady get her hands on the camera if you value your life."

I whipped my head toward Seth and half yelled, "Seth, who's side are you on?"

Seth merely shrugged and replied, "My own."

CHAPTER
FORTY-SEVEN

HOW COULD SETH BETRAY ME? He was bound to me. Such betrayal should be impossible. Even the Valkyrie told me to bind him to me to keep him faithful. What was Seth playing at? Was he even bound?

I stood there, my eyes nearly bugging out of my skull, and was at a loss for words. Even Ivan and Mary were speechless. My brother had other matters to worry about, while he fumbled to staunch the blood flowing freely from the gunshot wound to his knee.

Jeremy narrowed his eyes at Seth, motioned with the gun, and said, "I don't give a shit. Get back to the platform."

"Do you really think your pathetic piece of weaponry could take me down?" Seth glowered.

"Ha." Jeremy barked out a laugh. "You're just a kid. What the fuck are you going to do?"

"Wouldn't you'd like to know?" Seth replied.

In an instant he was on Seth, gun held to his forehead, lowering himself to get face to face. "Little young to be growing a set, eh, little man?"

Molten gold flashed in Seth's eyes. His lips pressed into a firm line. "Don't test me."

"Seth," I cried. "For gawd sakes, back off. Please."

Seth threw me a knowing look and said to Jeremy, "Before you blow my brains all over the floor, how about you enlighten us about what's really going on? Are you the one behind the murders?"

Jeremy sneered, "All I know is your mummy was hired to be the patsy for these murders."

"Wasn't Squeaks supposed to take the fall for them?" Seth asked.

"She was until the dummy went and got herself killed. But my boss already knew she was to be sacrificed." He pressed his lips tight, then said, "That's why he hired your mom, to take her place as the patsy."

"Sarah isn't my mom."

"Whatever. I don't care, you little shit. She'll be behind bars soon, and my boss and I will have everything we've been promised."

"So, you both are not working alone on this? Who are you working for?"

"Enough. I don't have to tell you anymore."

"Ha, probably because your boss didn't tell you all the details."

"Shut up." Jeremy's trigger finger twitched.

I shouted, "Seth, quit poking the damn bear!"

Jeremy smirked, twisted the gun on Seth's forehead. "Listen to your mummy, little man. I have the upper hand here."

"So you say." Seth quirked an eyebrow upwards. His reaction was completely the opposite of what a normal seven-year-old boy would have with a gun pressed against his head. "You severely underestimate me because you see, appearances can be deceiving."

The upper lip on Jeremy curled away; he shoved the gun harder. "You playing with me, punk?"

Bones shouted, "Dude, he's just a kid."

"Shut up." Jeremy sneered, licked his lips, and darted his eyes around the room. His eyes grew wide. He whipped around and pointed at the registers. "Hey, where'd your guard dog go?"

A loud meaty thwack sounded as the long wooden pole connected with the side of Jeremy's head and he crumpled to the floor. The gun clattered out of his hand and thankfully did not fire.

Mary stood over the unconscious form; long wooden clothing pole held in her hands. She inhaled deep and said, "Right here, motherfucker."

"Thanks." Seth grinned, his molten eyes swirling brighter.

She dropped the wooden pole; the wood clunked and rolled away on the tiled floor. Mary toed Jeremy and nodded at Seth. "Couldn't have taken him out without you distracting his ass."

"I aim to please," Seth chirped.

I ran my hand through my hair and swallowed the lump which formed in my throat. A realization hit me hard; maybe he wasn't betraying me. I choked out, "So you weren't betraying me?"

Seth's eyebrows creased together as he frowned. "Uh, I'm bound to you, remember? I couldn't betray you, even if I wanted to. Besides, we needed information."

Ivan cleared his throat and gestured at Jeremy. "This is nice and all. But this still does not explain all the mysteries. Such as who is behind the creatures and who promised them things?"

With the information Jeremy shelled out, part of me knew he wasn't the top dog in this whole mystery, but I still called over to Bones and asked, "Was this the guy?"

Bones shook his head.

I shrugged my shoulders, looked at Mary and asked, "You got anymore rope?"

"Yeah." Mary hurried over to her duffle bag and pulled out more nylon rope. She grabbed a tin box as well. She tossed the box my way as she walked past to tie Jeremy up. "Here, tend to your brother."

I examined the box and saw the big red-cross logo, a medical kit. Immediately, I hustled over to Jake, who was white as a ghost, teeth clenched while he kept his hands compressed on the wound. I shooed his hands away and said, "Let me look."

My brother shook his head. "No, need an ambulance."

"Jake, let me treat your wound," I snapped and popped open the box, pulling out the gauze, sterilizing solution, and bandages. Holding the solution over the knee, I said, "This is going to hurt."

Jake nodded and allowed me to treat him. During the process, the back door opened. We should have locked the damn thing. I glanced over my shoulder to see Mr. Sels cautiously step into the store. His back all hunched while he crept further inside. He called out in a whisper, "Jeremy? Is it done? How much longer do I have to wait out in the hallway?"

My boss, Mr. Sels, scanned the room, saw the unconscious Jeremy, sucked in a breath, and backed away, inching closer to the door he entered.

"That's the dude," Bones shouted. "He's the one who hired me to steal the camera."

Mr. Sels shot up from his hunched position, turned, hurried his chubby legs with fast steps, and rushed toward the door. Mary, quick on her feet, snatched up her crossbow and sent a bolt through the door handle. Mr. Sels jumped back with a squeal.

"Don't shoot me." He held his hands up. "Please don't shoot me."

Ivan moved in and apprehended Mr. Sels while he was distracted by Mary. Another squeal escaped Mr. Sels' lips when Ivan's massive hands landed on his shoulders.

"A word," Ivan said. "We simply want to talk."

Sweat beaded on Mr. Sels' forehead. He removed a cloth from his pant's pocket and mopped his brow. Eyes darted between me and Mary. He winced when Ivan squeezed his shoulder and squeaked, "He'll kill me."

"Who?" I asked.

"The tall, dark and handsome fella, who makes you feel good." Mr. Sels pulled at his necktie and coughed. "The one who makes you feel good, in a sensual nature."

"Vincent?"

"Yes. Him." He trembled, mopping more of the sweat from his brow.

"So, no woman with silver hair and eyes of old faded money?" Ivan asked.

Mr. Sels shook his head. "No, we never met. All meetings were with him and only him."

Ivan rumbled, "Tell us more. Maybe we can help. We have helped others in dire need before."

"No." Mr. Sels shook his head and continued his denial. "No, no, no. He'll kill me."

Mary quipped, "How'd you get to be a boss if you're jus' a whiney lil' bitch?"

Mr. Sels mopped his brow again and glanced at her. "Because I've made deals. Deals I'm not proud of, but deals, nonetheless. That's how."

She spat on the ground. "You make me sick."

Ivan held out his hand. "Enough, Mary."

Mary shifted her weight but kept the crossbow trained on my boss, my former boss. He swallowed hard and turned his attention back to Ivan.

"Tell me," Ivan began. "What deal you make with Vincent?"

"He had me put these mannequins," Mr. Sels gestured at the remaining mannequins in the store, "in all of my stores here in the mall."

"You own more than one store?" I asked.

He puffed his chest out and beamed. "Yes. That's why I'm able to afford to close any shop for a few days."

"But why?" Ivan asked. "What were you getting in return?"

"Vincent promised I would—"

The back door burst open and knocked Ivan and Mr. Sels into the clothing rack before them. Tall, dark, and ick rolled into the room, stopped, straightened his clothing, brushing off imaginary dust. He turned toward Ivan and Mr. Sels, who were sprawled amongst the clothes scattered on top of them.

"If I were you, I'd shut up about now," Vincent said, his lips widening into a predatory grin. "That is, if you value your life."

CHAPTER
FORTY-EIGHT

I STARED BACK at the door while I held pressure on my brother's gunshot wound. Vincent caught me looking past him and asked, "What?"

"Anyone else?" I snarked right at him. "Because you're the third one to come barging in through the back door. Does Avarice have a zombie party scheduled we should be aware of? Is Avarice going to make an appearance?"

Vincent rolled his eyes. "Guh, Sarah. There you go… you killed the drama here."

"Yeah, and? How many more should we expect? I gotta make sure I have enough party favors here."

"Always gotta one up me, don't you?"

"Look, I only want the best for everyone. So how many more?"

"None."

"None?" I said, my brows rising. "Look, since you

interrupted Mr. Sels' monologue, maybe you can clue us in as to what the fuck is going on."

He let out a long laugh, ran his fingers through his dark voluminous hair, and replied with a toothy grin, "You have no idea, do you?"

Seth commented, "When does she ever?"

I gawked at my djinn. "Seth, not helping."

Another chuckle escaped Vincent's lips. "Your djinn is right. You were always the slow one."

"Augh, will you stop with the blond jokes?" I grumbled. "Tell me what the hell is going on."

"I don't think you're in position to be making demands." He smirked.

A crossbow bolt whizzed past him because he stepped back at the last second and the bolt embedded itself into the wall to his far left. He glanced over at Mary.

She sneered, "Oh, hell, no. I think we have all the leverage we need. You have only your claws, demon. What the hell can you do?"

Vincent replied, "This."

He snapped his fingers. Beside him, shining up from the floor, the whirlpool of blue, green, white, and purple lights dazzled into view. The loud chittering sounded, and I saw Mr. Sels flinch with a whimper.

"I knew you were up to something," I spat at Vincent. "Anytime your slimy ass shows up, I can be guaranteed you're doing Avarice's bidding."

"Close but not quite. I'm working my own agenda here. Avarice isn't behind this scheme and has no clue. Soon, with the camera in my possession and my own small army, nothing will stop me," Vincent said and snapped his fingers again.

More whirlpools appeared on the floor. Mr. Sels threw his hands over his head, his scream muffled by the clothes littered on the ground. "They made me talk. I'm innocent. I did what you asked. Please spare me."

Out of the whirling lights, mannequins rose from the floor. Each emitted a high pitch chitter and vibrated. When the portals faded away, the new and existing mannequins increased the vibrations until their exterior shells shattered into a thousand pieces.

The creatures had large multifaceted eyes, saw arms, long slender necks, and triangular heads, and stepped forward from the shattered remains of the mannequins. They stood over the prone store owner. Ivan threw himself over Mr. Sels. The creatures opened and closed their mandibles and turned toward Vincent. A high pitched chitter intermingled their words and hissed, "Where'sss the sacrifice?"

Vincent pointed at the platform. The mantises turned in unison, emitted an earsplitting screech, and moved toward where Bones trembled and tried to get away.

"Wait," Vincent called out. "We had a deal."

The mantises halted in their tracks. Their sawlike arms waved in the air in unison with one another. A hive like mind when they all answered, "Yess. Camera for sacrificesss."

"You must break the spell on the camera." Vincent pointed my way. "Or the deals off."

"Demon, you underessstimate our abilitiesss?" the one closest to Vincent hissed.

Vincent narrowed his eyes and glowered. "As you do mine."

A mantis inched closer to Bones on the platform. Bones shouted, "Let me go, man. I don't want to die."

Bones scooted his butt to the edge of the booth and rolled off. His body thudded onto the ground with a meaty thwack. Mere seconds later, Bones was seen inching his way to the front of the store with his knees and chin. His hands and feet tied firmly in place, making his escape almost impossible.

The mantises tilted their heads in unison and studied their prey while he made slow progress in his escape.

Outside, the people continued to gather and gawk at the show unveiling before their eyes, camera phones recording the whole situation.

"Enough. Our sacrifice isss escaping," they intoned with high pitched hisses. "Catch him."

Monstrous insectoid legs crawled, tapped, and clicked on the tiled floor when the mantises moved as one to recapture Bones who bawled like a newborn babe.

Ivan, Mary, and Seth launched themselves at the mantises and became the buffer between them. Vincent hung back, a smug grin on his face, inspecting his cuticles while his insectoid minions fought for him.

Jake gave me a shove and said under his breath, "Do something. Stop gawking."

Uh, right. Keeping low to the ground, I stalked across the floor, using the booths as cover. I did my best to not pay attention to the screams. The camera called out to me and my entire being sang as I got closer. My hands mere inches from snatching the camera from its perch.

Green energy pulsed from the camera. The intensity increased as my hand closed the distance. Once flesh caressed the dark, hard plastic body, warmth rushed inside of me. A chill which had taken residency in my spine was sent packing. More electric tingles surged downwards.

Finger on the trigger, I hopped up, turned, and flashed a bright, toothy grin at Vincent. "Smile."

The asshole dove down into the heap of clothing where Mr. Sels hid from the mantises. A loud squeak emitted from the pile. One mantis skittering by, halted in its tracks, turned its triangular head, mandibles clacking, and screeched when it leapt at the clothing. Vincent rolled out from the clothes and shouted at the mantis, "Is this how you treat your master?"

"Sacrificesss." The mantis slavered, stepped forward, sawlike arm lifted. "You promisssed."

"Our deal has not been completed. You've stolen plenty prior to delivery. No more sacrifices until you deliver, bug."

The monster threw back its head and screeched again. The others in the room stopped and joined the loud screech. Ugh, I don't think plain o'aspirin was going to handle this massive migraine these fuckers were causing. Camera pointed at the offending bug. I mashed the shutter button. Green light flashed as the creature's life force was drained away.

The empty husk fell to the floor and shattered into dust. Eww, gross.

Seth called out, "Sarah, behind you."

I turned in time to see a mantis hover over me and latched one sawlike arm around my neck. The mantis pulled me back, and I did not fight him. It hissed in my ear, "Give me the camera."

"No," I said. The camera's pulse tempo picked up in time with my own.

"Camera for life," the creature crooned, the sound like a crinkly bag mixed with fingernails scratching down a chalkboard. Goosebumps erupted down my arms, the hairs on my neck rose, and I gritted my teeth.

Mary stepped into my point of view, crossbow at the ready and shouted, "Don't give the bug anything, Sarah!"

"No, Mary, don't," Ivan cried. He hovered over my brother's prone body to keep the mantises from attacking him. "You might hit Sarah."

She ground her teeth and lowered the crossbow. "Dammit."

The mandibles scraped close to my ear. "Camera, yesss?"

Seth inched closer when the mantis tightened its grip around my tender neck. "Ssstay."

We were at a stalemate. The choices were, give up the camera and die, or die, and they still got the camera. Not really a win-win situation if you asked me, but I'm one to hedge my bets toward life. With a well-aimed elbow, I jabbed the creature's abdomen. Pain bloomed, like when you hit your funny bone and the pain wasn't funny, when my elbow smashed into the hard armored underbelly of the mantis.

The creature and the rest let out a series of hissing sounds, almost like they were laughing. If my hairs weren't already raised, they were now because the sound of their laughter sent chills throughout my entire being. And even with the camera keeping me warm.

"Enough," said the one who held me captive with its sawlike arms. A warm trickle trailed down my neck, the sharp appendages making tiny nicks into my flesh.

Everyone stood still, the air thick with tension; no one dared to move. The camera pulsed again, compelling me to mash the shutter button. An itch with a burning intensity increased in the tips of my finger, only to be extinguished when I complied, plunging the metallic button deep down into the plastic housing.

A loud screech filled the store as the mantis who stood to the right of me was engulfed by the bright green light. The creature's life force streamed back into the camera, the light faded, revealing an empty husk, which collapsed to the ground and shattered into dust.

My captor screeched, my ears now pounding with a high-pitched tone, everything else muffled around me. Mary, Ivan, and Seth jumped back into the fight. Vincent stood his ground, a mantis slashing forward with its razor-sharp limbs, but Mr. Sels, who just stood back up, was knocked forward and used as a shield. A large red gash split diagonally across the store owner's chest, his face drained of all color, and his knees buckled under him. He fell to the floor on top of the heap of clothing, blood marring the pristine fabric. His limp form still let out shallow breaths.

I struggled to keep the mantis' arms from slitting my throat. My left forearm moved between the creature's sharp appendage and my neck. While I fumbled with my right hand to angle the camera back at my captor.

Blood gushed down my arm, the saw moving back and forth, slicing into the muscle. I bit down on my cheek to keep from screaming. The blood dripped down onto the camera, making the plastic slick and hard to maneuver. Seth saw my struggle and moved in.

He snatched the camera from my hands, pointed the lens at the mantis and shouted, "Say cheese."

Green flashed, and the creature dissolved into dust. I tripped over Jeremy's prone form, fell onto my butt, and rolled, as another mantis rushed in. Seth took its picture too. A cheeky grin spread across his face when one more mantis launched itself clear across the room and slashed down at Seth's wrists.

The camera clattered to the ground, followed by the meaty thump of Seth's severed hands. His stumps were charcoaled instead of bloodied. Seth's eyes were wide as saucers, but quickly darkened with flares of fiery gold. The creature laughed, swooped down, and snatched the camera from the floor.

"Yesss," the mantis hissed. "The camera isss oursss."

A mantis close to the far wall worked his forearms and slammed a claw against the drywall. Portals opened near the creature; the same whirling bits of light, with blue, green, and purple, swirled into existence. The hive of mantises walked toward the exit.

Vincent shouted, hands splayed out beside him, "No. We had a deal."

"No," they all chittered, mandibles scraping like glass against stone. "Deal isss no more. We have camera now. We hold your fatesss."

Vincent's hands engulfed themselves in fire and rushed at the mantis close to him. The creature bobbed and weaved, escaping his lethal fiery punches. Vincent growled, "Traitors, all of you."

"Yesss. Alwaysss the plan," the mantises said in unison. "Never give camera to Sinsss. We take and control, yesss."

"Da fuck you bug heads talking about? The cursed camera doesn't have the power to control Sins," Mary said, her crossbow held in the crook of her arm, ready to fire once more.

A mantis closest to her hissed, mandibles clacking together, and replied, "Camera takesss and consumesss Sinsss. Sinsss want camera to find keys to open hell and once done to dessstroy camera. We use camera to control Sinsss."

"Vincent ain't no Sin," Mary spat and cocked the crossbow back. "He's jus' some stupid sex demon who got greedy."

"Nooo hess not sinsss. Hesss ssslave." The mantises hissed. I clamped my hands over my ears to salvage what was left of my hearing.

They all hissed, "Foolsss. Avarice isss one."

"That's quite enough," Vincent barked and threw a fiery hand at the mantis in front of him. His hand clamped down tight around the mantis' thin neck and squeezed. The creature slashed at him leaving a red trailing gash on his forearm he used to deflect the attack.

Seth cashed in on the distraction, hurled himself at the mantis with the camera, and tackled the creature to the floor. Even without hands, Seth laid into the creature, pummeling the exoskeleton until the sound of an egg smacking against the pavement sounded. The mantis' keening died out. Seth smeared the bug guts down on his t-shirt, leaned over, hooked the strap with his stumps and hurled the camera over his shoulder my way.

Crossbow bolts were flying, but it didn't stop me from

launching myself into the air to snatch my only weapon against these psycho killer bugs. Just as my hand latched onto the strap, a wayward bolt flew past, mere millimeters from burrowing deep into my hand.

A quick scan of the room showed the crossbow bolts were embedded into several mantises, some creatures dropping dead when the bolts hit between their eyes. Ivan kept vigil over Bones. Unfortunately, there weren't enough of us to protect my brother, Jeremy or Mr. Sels, who was still breathing, shallow, but still breathing. And yet, luck was on their side because the mantises were focused on little ole me.

They wanted the camera, and they wanted it bad. Maybe there was truth to the camera being Pandora's box, but the mystery wouldn't solve itself if we all got devoured by the killer mantises. Seth shouted at me since I couldn't hear anything lower than a yell, and said, "Hold the button down and do a panoramic scan, Sarah."

D'oh, why didn't I think of that? But did the camera have enough film left to do such a scan? Shrugging my shoulders, I tossed my hair back, planted my feet wider than shoulder width, one foot further in front to keep a steady stance.

Mary shouted as she dove for cover, "Oh, hell, no! Ivan, get down!"

Pressing down on the metallic button, the camera pulsed, sending out waves of green light which washed over the remaining creatures while I swept the room from side to side. Everyone, including Vincent, who extinguished his fire, minus the bugs, ducked down and out of range of the camera. Loud screeches erupted from the creatures when the camera latched onto their life force and sucked them dry.

One by one, the mantises turned into hollow shells, cracked, and shattered into dust. The final mantis hissed out a warning while its body leaked the last bit of life essence into the camera. "You can't ssstop the apocalypssse. It hasss begun."

Chills creeped up my spine, but I held fast on the shutter switch to ensure our insectoid menaces were well destroyed and very gone.

The portals on the far wall winked out like a light switch, like they were never there. Piles of bug dust were the sole evidence of the inter-dimensional creature attack we survived. Without the camera, we would have been bloodied torn remains on the white tiled floor.

The room was silent. Only the rushing of blood in my ears overshadowed the calm befalling the destroyed storefront. I released the shutter, along with the breath I held, heartbeat thudding with new oxygen.

Behind me, sudden applause and whistles roared into being. I turned, my heart stuttering, and I tried to swallow the hard lump in my parched throat. Outside the store were people, mall goers, crouched, with their phones in hand, who saw everything.

Crap.

CHAPTER
FORTY-NINE

I DON'T NEED to say exposure to this level was bad. Sure, Seth could handle the exposure when Bones recorded me using the camera, live, to his fellow Tok'ers. Of course, previously I had a wish available to use at my disposal. But not this time around.

What's worse was everyone out in the mall had their phones out and had videoed the entire fight. Crap, crap, crap, crap, crap. Essentially, crap in a hat.

The sound of a bowstring twanging brought my attention back to the room. A crossbow bolt had lodged itself into the edge of Vincent's sleeve and tacked him to the door frame. Mary yelled, "Oh, hell, no! You sit your demon ass right there. We ain't done with you, Vinny."

Ivan marched on over to Vincent and blocked his only exit. Vincent sneered and tried to threaten Ivan with fiery fists. Mary remarked, "Better douse those flames sex fiend or this next bolt will go between your eyes."

Vincent hissed but extinguished his flames.

I cleared my throat and shouted, "Uh, guys. We have a problem here." I gestured at the store's front windows. The ever-growing crowd continued to shoot the footage unveiling before them within the popular store, The Glen.

"Shit," Mary spat, tilting her head at the crowd, and asked, "Seth? Care to crowd control these lookie-loos?"

He shook his head and raised his stumps. "Nope. Sarah already made today's wish. Rules are rules."

"You're a demon. Fuck the rules," Mary retorted. "Or are you that weak?"

Seth growled, fiery eyes flashing the dangerous molten gold. "I'm not weak. And for the record, I have more than enough power and could take care of these people, but like I said, Sarah already spent her wish earlier today on that flesh bag, Bones, who's hiding in the clothes rack. So, you need to figure out another plan for crowd control."

Jake, of all people, spoke up, "Seth, look, I really am confused about your relationship with my sister, and I kind of picked up you were more than a kid, but could you please reconsider your one wish a day rule? Cleaning up these social media videos the normal way will be nigh impossible."

"Huh, a member of the Knight family has a brain. Impressive," Seth snarked.

"Seth," I half-yelled. "Quit being an ass."

The djinn's slender eyebrow quirked upwards; his bottom lip slightly jutted out and replied, "If I were you, I wouldn't be making such demands. What if I decided to not help and go back into the camera? What would you do?"

Another enormous sigh escaped my lips, and I pinched the bridge of my nose. "Look, if you give me two more wishes, I can wish for your hands back."

"I don't need your wishes to reattach my hands." His nose wrinkled.

"Wait, what?" My brows furrowed upwards. "How—"

"Magic, duh," he snapped. "If you'd just listen, you'll know what I want."

I still didn't see how this was going to give him his hands back, but I zipped my lips and threw away an imaginary key. With a nod, I signaled Seth could continue with his terms to grant me more wishes.

"Am I good to talk?" Seth asked in a loud voice. He peered over his shoulders at Ivan, Mary, Jake, and Vincent. None of them made a peep. Mr. Sels writhed on the pile of clothes from the mantis slash. Jeremy was still unconscious, and Bones was hidden in the round clothes rack near the front, which he scrambled to during the mantis fight. The metal gate leading out of the store was locked. No way Bones could escape through the front. His only means of escape was the back door, the same door Ivan was guarding, and kept Vincent from leaving.

Seth bobbed his head and said, "Good."

The djinn turned back to me, looked me up and down with a piercing stare, a firm line defining his lips before he spoke. "If I give you one more wish, I want you to use the wish to allow me magical freedom."

The crew cried their outrage. Vincent barked out evil laughter, and my eyebrows skyrocketed up through my hairline. Did Seth just ask for magical freedom? I might not be the brightest crayon in the bunch, but damn, I'm not that stupid.

My mouth blabbed the next few words without checking in with my brain. "Are you fucking kidding me?"

Seth inspected his charcoaled stumps like one would inspect their cuticles on pristine fingernails. His mouth turned downwards, and he shrugged. "Fine, try and undo the damage on the Internet. Spoiler alert, you can't. You and your motley crew have become so damn dependent on these wishes you continue to have dug yourselves into a rather steep hole. One which only magic can undo. Don't say I didn't warn you."

"Seth, I can't," I groaned. "Giving you magical freedom is like letting another Vincent on the loose."

His nose wrinkled and caught me with a stern glare. "I'm nothing like the depraved thing over there. I have higher standards, you know. Besides, remember, I'm bound to you. I can't do anything unless the outcome benefits me and you."

Ivan spoke, his voice higher because he guessed I was hard of hearing, since I was talking louder than usual. "Sarah, we need Seth to do his thing. Cleaning such internet magical unveiling will take too much time. Even Wings of Virtue would take years."

"Oh, hell, no," Mary added. "Ivan, you of all people, really? Want to give a demon *more* power?"

"We have no choice." Ivan shrugged. "This type of exposure—"

"Bullshit." Mary ground her teeth. "Wings of Virtue has managed coverups way bigger. Da fuck you talkin 'bout?"

Ivan frowned, darting his eyes my way and back. Mary

followed his glance, her mouth opening in realization. "Michael? Since when?"

Things became clear at this moment. Ivan wanted Seth to handle this problem because Ivan and Mary, or basically any members of Wings of Virtue, were not to help with any paranormal nonsense I brought their way. Doing so invalidated my agreement with them and I would be back on the hook with owing the big chunk of money. Luckily, not to Avarice. However, I had no idea how angels dealt with debt and if I was in more dog doo this time around. Mary finally understood the true reason why I left.

"Gawd dammit, Sarah. Why da fuck you didn't tell me? I mean we're friends, right?" She yelled at me and held up her hand in a *'don't say anything'* manner. "No, wait, don't say anything. Michael probably had a gag order as part of your agreement."

Vincent smirked and added in his two cents, "My, my, my, your debt continues to follow you around like a long trail of goldfish poop, doesn't it, Sarah?"

We all shouted at him, "Shut up, Vinny!"

Seth cleared his throat and asked, "So, what will you choose, Sarah? Become enslaved to an angel because of your massive debt? Or grant me magical freedom to bail all of you out of this pile of shit?"

Dammit. The bastard had me. Seth knew more than anyone how much I didn't want to be responsible for the kind of financial woe which would consume the entirety of my paychecks for life. Mainly because the imp could rummage around in my head while he was contained within the camera. So, he knew more than anyone else would about me.

We really did not have a choice. If I chose to not follow through on Seth's request, Michael would learn of Ivan's treachery in bringing me back into the fold when I was supposed to be excommunicated from Wings of Virtue, even though I was a full member when I was tossed out on my rear. And Mary would also partake in the punishment. Even if the organization was supposed to be goodie-goodie, there were rules, and there were consequences.

Ivan had broken the rules, the big lug had a big heart, and Mary went along even though she didn't know the whole situation. But after these last few minutes, she was well aware that her antagonistic attitude toward me was completely unfair. I could hear the slight tremor of my bad-ass friend, who didn't care, shatter into a thousand pieces.

Mary's face told me she wavered in her initial stance of giving Seth magical freedom. Ivan counted on me to cave and grant the djinn's selfish wish. And part of me, a tiny part, doubted our bond would survive the wish if I gave him what he wanted.

"The longer you consider your options, the more doors close, and your opportunities will slip away. If I were you Sarah, I would decide in," Seth said, his slender eyebrow still raised, "five, four, three—"

"Okay, okay," I said and continued pinching the bridge of my nose. "Dammit."

"Better say those words before the cops show up, because you know someone in the audience has already called them."

"What?"

"Oh for the love of Morningstar. Just friggin' say the wish." Seth rolled his eyes and huffed.

My heart fluttered, but I took a deep breath to calm my beating heart. Nerves tinged with the edge of flight or fight response, everything in me begged to not grant him his request. But I had no choice.

Or did I? I didn't have to give him complete free rein. If my time with the Supernatural Underground Mafia taught me anything, you never agreed to something without adding in your own terms. I rolled my shoulders, cracked my neck, and took a deep breath.

"Seth, I wish for you to be able to cast magic with no need of my request in the form of wishes…" I said, holding up one finger and added, "AND your magic can only be cast if the situation benefits you and me, for you are bound to me and must take our lives into consideration per each magical spark which parts from your being."

"Spoilsport." Seth pouted, slammed his charred stumps together and said with a nod, just as the sound of several heavy footsteps clamored outside in the back hallway nearing the door, "Granted."

Many things happened at once. The camera flared to life in my hands, levitating into the air. A golden green glow sparkled, the light flashed outwards. The police barged into the store through the back door, knocking Ivan aside, and on the ends of Seth's charred stumps formed translucent golden hands.

A devilish smirk crept across his face, molten eyes whirling with magic he brought up one golden translucent hand, with the index, middle, and thumb touching. The police continued to funnel into the room but stopped short when they witnessed magic on display before them. Even the audience we had gathered outside the windows kept silent while they recorded the entire paranormal activity on their phones.

"You idiots have no idea," Seth said to the room in general, then snapped his fingers.

CHAPTER FIFTY

THE MAGICAL AFTERMATH of Seth's first no wish spell was interesting. Needless to say, he wiped everything out. All the footage of magic, the battle of mantises, and unfortunately, the confessions too.

The police stood there dumbfounded and blinked their weary eyes while the mallgoers continued with their shopping, oblivious to what happened only moments ago. One officer zeroed in on me, pulled out their cuffs while they ambled over the floor strewn clothing on the floor to my position. Vincent shouted, "Hold on there, officer!"

The officer stopped in their track and turned. "Detective, I didn't see you there."

"Leave the woman alone. She's not the one you want. He is." Vincent pointed down at the pile of clothing which Mr. Sels laid upon. As if on cue, my former boss groaned, then slowly sat up.

"Mr. Sels?" The officer's jaw dropped. "I don't understand."

Mr. Sels whined and pointed at Vincent. "I'm innocent. I'm innocent. Please don't arrest me. He's the one you want. I didn't kill those people. He did."

Vincent cleared his throat and purred in a low thrumming sensation. All the officers swayed on their feet while his influence wrapped them into his web of manipulation. He pointed at Mr. Sels, Bones, and Jeremy and said, "No time to explain. Bag these three and let's go."

"Yes, sir," each of the cops replied in unison.

I tilted my head to one side and mouthed to Vincent, "Why?"

Vincent's smoldering eyes stared back, and he merely grinned. He replied, "Because you'll owe me another favor. You might be the camera's owner, but I know the power of a favor. In due time, I'll come to collect, but for now, I'll keep you out of harm's way. You're more useful to me out of jail."

Ivan held Mary back and covered her mouth. Her eyes cut back to him. She shook him off and said in a quiet voice, "What the hell, Ivan? You jus' gonna let that slimy son-of-a-bitch gain another favor off of Sarah?"

He held his hands up and replied, "We take what we can. Right now, the police will leave Sarah be. If a favor is needed to do so, then favor we'll pay."

"We ain't paying the favor, Sarah is," she replied and jabbed her finger into his chest. Ivan winced.

"You know we'll find a way," Ivan insisted. "Good will always prevail. Even when it is darkest."

"'Bout right now seems like evil is winning here, Ivan."

He shook his head. "Patience. That's all I ask. We'll find solutions. Let the demon have his win for now. For it is only temporary. Good always wins. Besides, I doubt we should continue helping because of Michael."

"He ain't got no right telling us not to help Sarah."

"We'll be kicked out, too. It's a personal matter for her. Until we find a loophole, we cannot help her."

"Whatever." She flipped her hand at him, turned her back, and crossed her arms in a huff.

They stayed close to Jake and kept quiet. None of the officers took notice of them because Vincent had directed their attention to the three goons: Jeremy, Bones, and Mr. Sels.

A wail echoed in the room; the cops pulled on Bones who clung to the round metal clothes rack. "Dudes, I didn't do those murders. Check my 'Tok, I'm innocent."

The officers didn't even bat an eyelash and pulled him from the rack. They read him and Mr. Sels their Miranda Rights while one cop sat with Jeremy's unconscious form. The paramedics showed up and rushed in through the back door to treat the injured.

Debbie had shown up with them and helped stabilize my brother, who had lost tons of blood due to the gunshot wound to his knee. Jake had no memories of how he got injured. Apparently, Seth had wiped his mind too. With Jake no longer in danger, she rushed over to Seth and me and whistled slowly at the damage. She muttered under her breath, "Damn. Poor kid."

Getting down on one knee, she opened her medical bag and prodded Seth's charred stumps. His golden ones were only temporary and disappeared after the wish. Squeezing white cream onto Seth's injuries, she asked, "Did you consider the position?"

"Uh, what position?" I said.

"The open position at my workplace," Debbie said with a lifted eyebrow while she wrapped gauze around Seth's wrists.

Rubbing the back of my neck, I replied, "Um, what was the position, again?"

She glanced around the destroyed storefront, at Mr. Sels and Bones being ushered away by the police, and said, "To be my assistant. Usual tasks are taking pictures and notes. The position pays well."

I tucked a stray strand of hair behind my ear and considered the opportunity when Seth said, "Come on, just take the stupid job. Much better than being a lackey for Wings of Virtue or even a coffee girl. Think of this opportunity as your chance at being normal."

Seth struck a nerve, the nerve of me wanting to be normal. Butterflies jittered in my stomach. I turned to Debbie and asked, "When do I start?"

Debbie chuckled, "Good. I'll take this as verbal agreement. Though I'll have to get the paperwork started and you'll need to come by and fill out some stuff before we can give you an official starting date."

She patted Seth's newly wrapped stumps and asked, "I meant to ask, where are you currently staying?"

Visions of the ancient cat pee infested couch flooded my mind. Seth answered before I could say anything. "We're currently couch surfing. Why?"

The corner of her mouth tugged upwards and said, "I've got a room for rent. Are you interested?"

EPILOGUE

ONE MONTH LATER

DOWN IN THE BASEMENT, turned studio, of my once college roommate but now landlord, Debbie, I was in the middle of enlarging certain photos from the fight with the mantises. No, Seth's magic did not wipe these pictures. I noticed certain things in the small film strip I wanted to get a better look at.

Red light was the only light source with the black curtains pulled tight over the cellar windows to prevent daylight or light from the streetlamp from leaking into the room. I pulled the expansive photo paper from one tray full of chemicals to the next tray with a set of tongs.

Letting myself ponder on the past event, I waited for the necessary time to pass for the image to process.

Seth was settled over on the futon, slash my bed, currently in couch position, his magically reattached original hands clasped around his knees. Debbie had been so worried about him until Seth wiped her mind. When Seth said magic was the answer for his severed limbs, I thought he meant I had to make a wish, but I found out later what he truly meant.

For when he went back into the camera, all leavings of his being, body parts and so forth, also followed him. If he were to get hurt, sick, or mortally wounded, all Seth needed to do was to go back into the camera and upon his next summons, he would be fully healed. Though there was a catch. Upon his retreat, he was unable to exit the camera for a certain amount of time depending on the injury. If he were to receive a simple cut, then he could be summoned within an hour or less, but if he were mortally wounded, Seth would be unable to be called out of the camera for a month or more.

Yes, Seth would still be able to help from within the camera, though he would not be able to enact his new magical ability until he was outside the camera. Instead, those abilities would have to be channeled through me, which I was not one hundred percent comfortable in experiencing.

"Hey, Sarah?" A knock from the top of the stairs sounded, as Debbie called.

I blinked, shook my head, coming back to the here and now, dunking the tongs into the chemicals and pulling the sheet into the final tray. I replied over my shoulder, "Yeah?"

"I'm going to order pizza. Do you and Seth want some?" she asked through the closed door. Debbie didn't dare open the door due to the sign I left on the doorknob indicating I was in the middle of developing the film from recent escapades.

Seth sat forward on the futon. He flashed a grin at me and

replied before I could. "Pizza? Ohh, can we get barbecue chicken and pineapple?"

I wrinkled my nose at him and said with my tongue out, "You beast. Who eats pineapple on their pizza? Bleh."

Debbie, who had heard our exchange, laughed. She replied through the wooden door, "Okay, one gross pizza and one pepperoni. Gotcha."

"Thanks, Debs," I called back up to her, taking the photo from the last tray and hanging the picture up to dry. The chemicals dripped from the paper onto the plastic which covered the cement floor. Looking around, I made sure everything was clean before turning on the normal lights. My eyes blinked and teared with the harsh brightness.

I stepped over to the picture with a magnifying glass to take a closer look. A dark figure loomed beyond the portals when the door upstairs banged once more.

Debbie yelled, "Sarah, grab your cameras. The chief called and we're wanted on scene."

I tapped on my cursed camera and jerked my chin at Seth. He gave a slight nod and dissipated into the golden mist which seeped in through the camera lens. I yelled back up the stairs, "Details, Deb. What's going on?"

My feet pounded up the wooden steps, the fifth one from the top creaked underfoot, and I wrenched open the door. Debbie stood there, wringing her hands together, her eyes moist and red.

"Good gawds, the situation is bad if you're already tearing up, Debs," I said and moved into the kitchen, closing the door behind me.

Her glistening eyes peered back at me, and she said, "Kids. Kids were involved this time."

An unsettling churn swirled in my intestines. The last scene was last night but did not involve kids. I snatched the keys from the key ring next to the door and said, "I'll drive."

We both hustled out the door and into the minivan, which brought us to the gruesome scene with a lone father and his daughter outside in the cold night. Police were already on the scene, along with the crew from the morgue, as we pulled up in the minivan. Debbie snatched her bag from the back, and we hustled up to the person in charge to get the skivvy on what they'd found.

A mother and her teen son were apparently brutally murdered with a broken wine bottle while father and young daughter were asleep upstairs. Debbie had already donned her surgical gear and was led into the crime scene, followed by the crew from the morgue, who were waiting for her arrival.

While I waited, I happened to glance at the little girl, clad in pink pajamas, crying her eyes out. Though, a twinge of unease shifted up my back, setting the hairs on end. The little girl, who was nestled in her father's arms, snuck a glance my way when no one was looking, and a devious smirk replaced the frown as her eyes flashed black.

Crap.

My hand at once rushed to my camera, informing Seth of our current situation, and the other to the cellphone in my rear pocket. I mashed the speed dial for Mary. She answered with a grumble, "This better be important, or I will put a bolt in your sorry ass for interrupting my beauty sleep."

"We've got demon kids," I whispered, a slight shake in my voice because of the adrenaline rush.

Mary sobered; sleep absent from her voice. "Oh, hell, like demonic billy goats?"

"No, worse."

"Oh, hell, no."

"Oh, hell, yeah, we've got demonic children on our hands. Grab Ivan."

She replied with an undignified grunt and added, "Can't. Remember? We can't help you anymore, else Ivan and I will be kicked out of the organization. Michael let us off with a warning the last time and warned us if we even lifted a single finger to help you again, he'd expel us himself. Sorry, but you're on your own, Sarah."

"Dammit," I growled. "What the hell am I supposed to do? Your organization is supposed to handle this shit, not me."

"Use the camera," she grumbled. "Should grab the nasty hell spawn easily."

And so she hung up on me. I stared in disbelief at the phone and swallowed the hard lump in my throat. The demon child kept its eerie glare on me. Without Wings of Virtue's help, things had just gotten a lot harder.

The story continues in book 3 - Hunt for Wrath
Grab your copy now
https://www.aliciascarborough.com/books/shadow-bound-chronicles/book3/

AUTHOR NOTES
AUGUST 16, 2024

A moment of your time, it will only take a minute, I promise.

If you could leave a review that would fabulous. A simple "I loved it because Seth was a total twerp who kept me in laughing fits until the very end," would be good.

You can use go to my website https://www.aliciascarborough.com/review-books/shadow-bound-chronicles/book2/ to choose YOUR preferred platform to leave a review

With all the awesomeness you've just read, I bet you're dying to read book three of the series. So, to keep you entertained, I've inserted the blurb for the 3rd book of this series at the end of these notes.

AN UPDATE...

I'm currently in the deep dark depths of writing... writing furiously to get the top secret pirate romance written so I can get back to working on the Shadow Bound Chronicles.

Those of you who are subscribed to my newsletter know all about the procrastination, writer's block and more. However, things could go faster, if I could spend ALL my time writing instead of dealing with pesky things like exercise, house chores, my day job... y'know the usual things that normal people deal with on a daily basis.

Oh, yeah, I've been sticking to my New Year's resolution which was to get into better shape. Yeah, halfway through the year and I'm still sticking to it. Cardio AND weight training with dumbbells. Because with hypothyroidism I have to work extra to keep those unwanted pounds off of me. We're averaging about an hour to an hour and a half every day for exercise. So, you see how this is eating into my writing :P ... blame the damn candy bars (mmm, I love me some Butterfingers) or my sugar addiction. I have a terrible sugar addiction... I think? Maybe? Hum, I probably do, TBH. Most people in the U.S. have a bad sugar addiction, not all, but most.

Anywho... that's all I've got for now. Back to exercising and writing. I need to give dictation another try... then maybe I can be writing while I'm exercising, yeah? Think that'll be possible? Don't know until I give it another whirl.

HEARTY THANK YOU'S

Thank you Nola and Dorcia for your ever insightful commentary and keeping my unwieldy writing in line.

Onward to book 3 y'all!!

~A.L. Scarborough

Btw, if you want to keep up to date to know the latest shenanigans of the books in progress, potentially score some goodies and all, then sign up for my newsletter... https://www.aliciascarborough.com/sign-up.html

---

SHADOW BOUND CHRONICLES

Hunt for Wrath - Book 3

Demonic forces claim children and death stalks the streets, can she save her town from a hellish fate?

Sarah Knight is bitter. The last fiasco left her drained, but now the late-thirties snarky woman faces a fresh hell—this time alone. But, when she uncovers the sinister truth behind the children's illness, she fears the town will be overrun by demons.

Reuniting with her rag-tag team—the snarky djinn, her cursed camera, and her weary, mid-life self—Sarah battles to push back the darkness engulfing her town. But, when the plague reaches its peak and every child turns demonic, Sarah realizes her chances of survival are grim to none.

Can Sarah stop the demonic outbreak? Or will her small town be swallowed by the all-consuming darkness?

Hunt for Wrath, the third book in the *Shadow Bound Chronicles*, brings you a heart-pounding women's fiction fantasy adventure. With a fearless female lead, a horde of demons, and a sharp sense of humor, A.L. Scarborough's story promises to keep you hooked from start to finish.

The battle against the demonic forces is just beginning. Buy *Hunt for Wrath* now and join Sarah in her epic fight to save the children!

Be the first to grab your copy here:
https://www.aliciascarborough.com/books/shadow-bound-chronicles/book3/

DON'T MISS MY NEW RELEASES

Join the A.L. Scarborough Chronicles email list to get exclusive access to updates on my latest works in progress, new characters, character profile art, behind-the-scenes peeks, and new releases.

https://www.aliciascarborough.com/sign-up.html

ALSO BY A.L. SCARBOROUGH

https://www.aliciascarborough.com/al-scarborough/series

..:: Shadow Bound Chronicles ::..

Shadow Bound

Night Shift

Hunt for Wrath

UNDER THE NAME OF ALICIA SCARBOROUGH

https://www.aliciascarborough.com/alicia-scarborough/series

..:: Mystical Mishaps Series ::..

Potion of the Hound (Book One)

Rise of the Vampire Brethren (Book Two)

Making the Mark (Short Story)

Becky the Pantry Ghost (Short Story)

The Volkrog Princess (Short Story)

..:: Children of Chaos Series ::..

Play with Me

CONNECT WITH THE AUTHOR

Facebook: https://www.facebook.com/aliciascarboroughauthor

Instagram: https://www.instagram.com/ally.scarborough/

Threads: https://www.threads.net/@ally.scarborough

X: https://twitter.com/foxglove1028

Pinterest: https://www.pinterest.com/foxglove1028/

TikTok: https://www.tiktok.com/@foxglove1028?lang=en

Newsletter: https://www.aliciascarborough.com/sign-up.html

Website: https://www.aliciascarborough.com